KAT CATESBY

Her Cowboy

FLIRTY, DIRTY ROMANCE

Contents

Acknowledgments   iv

Her Cowboy   v

Chapter One   1

Chapter Two   11

Chapter Three   24

Chapter Four   33

Chapter Five   41

Chapter Six   56

Chapter Seven   77

Chapter Eight   90

Chapter Nine   102

Chapter Ten   121

Chapter Eleven   131

Chapter Twelve   142

Chapter Thirteen   151

Chapter Fourteen   159

Chapter Fifteen   183

Chapter Sixteen   195

Chapter Seventeen   212

Chapter Eighteen   228

Epilogue   245

Subscribe to my newsletter for an exclusive free book!   264

Her Boss Preview   267

About the Author   270

Acknowledgments

It took a lot of people to help get this book into existence and words alone cannot convey my gratitude to the amazing people who helped me to turn my dream into a reality.

Firstly, to Mr. Catesby and our Mini Catesby's; thank you for your love, patience, and support. I spent a lot of time locked behind a laptop instead of playing with the Mini's, yet your belief and enthusiasm in my dream pushed me to reach my goals. Love you all more than you know.

To my family, who didn't bat an eye when I told them the risqué content my books would have; thank you for being so cool and unembarrassed by my dirty-mindedness. You've taught me the valuable lessons of love and support and striving for your dreams. Without you, I wouldn't be who I am…and I quite like that person, so thank you.

A massive thank you to my amazing beta readers, Sandi and Mandy; your feedback and love for my characters gave me the courage to carry on and put my books out into the world. In my moments of doubt, your kind words and sharp eyes for my typos made me feel that my dream was achievable.

Lastly, to you. Yes, you! The amazing reader who took a chance on my words. I sincerely hope you stay with me on this crazy author journey because I have so many amazing heroines and sexy heroes that I want to share with you.

Much Love, Kat

Her Cowboy

**New town, new job, new boss.
An insanely hot boss I just witnessed getting down and
all kinds of dirty...**

Smoldering cowboy and ranch owner, Asher Scott, likes it
rough in the bedroom. He'll give you the ride of your
life...but you'll be tied up for it. Just the way he likes it.

New girl Katie Morgan is starting over after surviving a
brutal ex. The last thing she wants is to fall for another
dominant male.

Ash and Katie have different needs when it comes to love, but
they can't deny their attraction and when they collide, it's
fireworks. Can they build a relationship that doesn't send
Katie running for the hills? Or is Ash too much for her to
handle?

Chapter One

Katie

I'm early.

Really early.

Pulling up to the ranch driveway, the heavy timber log sign looming over me, I realize I've made seriously – and uncharacteristically – good time.

It's a revelation actually; I'm the 'late' girl. The one you tell to meet half an hour before an event starts to allow for my lateness. Being early is unheard of for me, which is hilarious because the job that I'm arriving early for requires me to be super organized and punctual.

I, Katie Morgan, am the new Diamond Peak Ranch administrator. While I am hard-working, enthusiastic and organized, punctuality is a bit of a weakness of mine. Maybe the whole 'new town, new job, new me' thing is actually working out? Don't get me wrong, my timekeeping is reasonably good in the working world, but it's like there's a daily quota of punctuality and if I use it all at work, there's nothing left for me in my personal life.

Either way, I'm super early for my new job – so early they're not expecting me – but I have a good feeling that this super punctuality is sure to impress my new boss, ranch owner, Asher Scott.

I'd given him my usual list of positive life and work skills during my Skype interview (no lies needed; I really am an organized administrator who just wants a change of scenery). No need to mention my nervous, insecure streak and that my confidence is mostly just for show and that I'm running away from Colorado Springs because of an abusive ex.

No need to share that.

None. At. All.

We also won't be mentioning that my new boss is an impressive hunk of alpha male sexiness…and that's just his face and shoulders that I glimpsed over Skype.

Diamond Peak Ranch is a half-hour drive from Aspen and has diversified into one of those destination vacation ranches. Super luxurious, spectacular scenery and still a few cowboys left to maintain the small part of the business that's a working ranch.

During my interview, Asher made it clear that he splits his time between dealing with his fancy lodge and its fancier guests, and being a true cowboy and getting his hands dirty with the working element of the ranch. My role is to deal with the paperwork for both elements; there is a ranch manager and a lodge manager and I will basically tidy up after them and do all the jobs they just don't want. That's normally how administration jobs go – your job description keeps changing to cover any and everything your immediate boss can't be fucked to do themselves. Add to that any admin that Asher himself has and I basically have three people handing me work. But I am up to the challenge and the gig comes with food and board – a tiny but incredibly cute looking cottage – which will definitely help me save money for more interesting things. Heck, I'm to be living a stone's throw from Aspen and I love to ski…might have to wait a while for that though, considering it's the end of April and I've missed the season and the lodge is gearing up for its summer clientele.

As soon as I get myself settled in the cottage, I'm going to drive back into Aspen to catch up with my ultimate BFF, Maddie. She was one of the main reasons I chose Aspen when I was figuring out where to run so that I could escape David-the-Devil. My ex from hell.

Maddie and I met my freshman year at the University of Colorado, Colorado Springs, where we both suffered through business degrees. Sure, they were useful but neither of us felt a passion for it. I'd yet to find my passion but Maddie had found hers.

In the three years since our graduation where I had been working administration jobs and dating David, Maddie had taken instructor courses in pole fitness, aerial hoop and yoga and was desperate to open her own gym running these classes. But for that you need clients with money and when you combine that with her love of the mountains and all things outdoors, you find Maddie making the decision to move to Aspen. She wasn't a fool and knew full well that it was going to take time to establish her business and, in the meantime, she would need to do paid work of some sort but Aspen was where she wanted to be.

It didn't take much arm-twisting on her part to get me to join her; I was desperate to put some distance between me and David so that he wouldn't track me down and tie me up.

Literally.

That was his thing. He thought he was a Dominant and that

I was his perfect little Submissive, but he was just a bully who wanted his own way and never listened if you safe-worded. Sex stopped being fun and fulfilling and the power play became a permanent power deficit on my part. Our relationship drifted across the line from kink to abuse but he couldn't see the difference and that was the big-ass fucking problem with him.

He also didn't take too kindly to me dumping him as in his mind there was nothing wrong with our relationship. The police were even involved after one particularly brutal encounter but a combination of a great lawyer and video evidence from our early relationship showing me thoroughly enjoying the kinky sex sessions, saw him walking away with no charges brought against him. The lawyer had successfully argued that because I had been into kink it was impossible to say that I wasn't getting off on the punishments and that I was probably just trying to tarnish the reputation of his stand-up client after *he* ended the relationship.

What. The. Actual. Fuck.

That bullshit had required some major therapy to come to terms with and my confidence and faith in the people who are supposed to protect you is completely fucking shot. I gave my complete trust to David; I gave him total power over my body and my heart and he broke both, badly. I'd then trusted the police and the judiciary system only to find myself labeled as the scorned deviant hussy out for attention or vengeance.

Fucking lawyers.

Two hours after walking out of the police station with a smug smile on his face he was attempting to access my hospital room (yes, he actually hospitalized me), demanding that I go back to his place where he could dispense my punishment for wasting his time at the station. But if I were a good girl and *pleased* him then I would be rewarded after.

The deluded prick really had no concept that he'd been dumped and that's when I knew it was time to leave, time for a fresh start.

I act pretty blasé about the whole thing but the truth is it left me reeling and empty. I want to be in love with someone but I'd have to figure out how the hell to trust someone enough to let them in in the first place.

Fuck if I know how to do that?

So, dating and trust are issues I've been left with. In the year since I left the hospital and therefore David (yeah, it took that long for us to save enough to move to Aspen…it's a pricey place after all), I've put myself out there precisely once. And I'm not in a rush to do it again. In that year, David hung around enough that Maddie and I could never truly relax and get to a place where we knew his bullshit was over. It kept us on edge; me because I worried that he was lurking around every dark corner, Maddie because she was terrified for me, though she tried to hide it, and because David had sort of made her his rage-fuelled scapegoat. He blamed her for 'twisting the truth' and 'turning me against him'. Yeah, he really is a fucking idiot. One I'm glad to *finally* be rid of.

His abuse and psychological bullying also left me with night-mares about the things he did to me and sexually? I honestly don't think I can cope with anything more adventurous than the missionary position in the bedroom now – and even that's a push because it means I'm pinned underneath the weight of a man. Maybe riding a dick cowgirl style is as good as it's going to get for me?

In the time between the incident and being able to move to Aspen, I moved in with Maddie so that we could save the serious money required to move but also because I wasn't faring too well and living on my own wasn't going to help that. Between the doctors who cared for me and Maddie, I never actually made it back to my own apartment as everyone was pretty anxious about David coming by unannounced and trying to beat my door down and drag me back to his like he tried to do when I was admitted to hospital.

It was my fear too if I were being completely honest.

Once I was well enough to be discharged, I was secretly bundled into a shiny SUV belonging to a doctor and he basically smuggled me to Maddie's and then got his friends to pack up my place and move my stuff. I was never more grateful to a bunch of strangers than I was that day. It went a long way to restoring some of my faith in people.

I also underwent some intensive therapy with a therapist who specialized in victims of domestic abuse and she was able to deal with a fair number of my issues, like the frequency of my nightmares and my nervousness with nearly every aspect of my life. I was determined not to let fuck-head David rule the rest of my life through fear and with her help, my progress was surprisingly swift.

She got me to a good place, where although I still have some big trust issues with new people, my confidence is slowly coming back – and I can front the confidence I lack in most situations. I'm slowly starting to feel like the fun-loving, happy girl I was when I was in college. She helped me find the confidence I needed to put myself out there and to go on that one date and have sex – very safe, very vanilla sex – and I'd conquered the mountain of my first sexual experience since David-the-Deranged.

Once Maddie and I had lined up jobs and she secured a

small apartment, we packed up and hauled our ass's outta there. It was going to be strange to not be living with her but life had to get back to normal so in a way it was a good thing that the cottage came with my job as it forced me to live independently again; the cottage is too far a commute for Maddie, who would be working in the center of town while plugging away at building her business.

Maddie had driven out to Aspen a few days before me to get her apartment set up, but in a bid to save as much money for her business as possible, it was a studio apartment with not enough space for both us to stay in so I had no choice but to wait the last few days out in Colorado Springs without her until the Diamond Peak Ranch and my little cottage were ready for me.

I was more anxious than I cared to admit, being on my own in Colorado Springs for the past few days, but it was good for me to pull my big girl pants up and get on with it.

Before making the final turn into the ranch drive, I pull over onto the shoulder and text Maddie.

Katie: I'm here! Well almost.

Maddie: S'up sexy lady. How far is 'almost'?

Katie: About to turn down their drive but I'm early.

Maddie: I'll say. Abide by the speed limit much?!

Katie: HA. Traffic was light. How's the apartment?

Maddie: Small. But I am the queen of apartment Tetris and managed to make everything fit. Txt me when you get settled. Love u xx

Katie: Will do, love u too xx

I put the car into drive and make my way down the last few miles that makes up the driveway to Diamond Peak Ranch, although driveway isn't a particularly adequate word as it

7

is in fact, a private road meandering through expanses of hilly grassland and trees, making its way gently uphill to the impressive chalet-style lodge with an intimidating backdrop of hulking great mountains. The midday sun shines brightly over the breath-taking scenery, the fresh mountain air fills my car through the open window and I feel peaceful.

Yes. This is definitely the place for me while I rebuild myself.

As I near the lodge I spot the little sign saying 'Residences' that indicates a small road that forks to the left and leads to the accommodation for the ranch staff and Asher Scott's ranch house. That is where I'm supposed to report so that he can give me a run down and tour of the ranch, and help me unload my worldly possessions into the little cottage I can't wait to call home.

I can spot a little cluster of cottages as I pull up to the main ranch house – although 'house' is a bit of an insult to the beautiful mini-mansion sprawling before me. Business must be good for a house as stunning as that. A beautiful log style house with giant glass windows overlooking the expanse of nature; a perfect blend of modern and rustic charm and somehow more beautiful than the stunning charm of the lodge. There is definitely a rich wooden and rustic theme to this place.

Climbing out of my car, I stretch all of my achy muscles that were cramped into my overloaded car during the three-hour drive. I squint in the bright sunlight and strain my eyes to see if I can determine which little cottage is mine, half expecting Asher Scott to come out and greet me. After a few moments I realize that isn't happening and go knock on his front door.

No answer.

Not surprising really, the place is massive and I doubt my knock carried that far. I spot what I assume is his truck parked to one side, but that doesn't mean anything as he could be anywhere on his acreage if he's on horseback. I try the door and find it unlocked so tentatively make my way inside. The inside is just as impressive as the outside – the entryway is double-height, flooded with light from the full height windows and just vast, but somehow still homey. I don't want to snoop around too much but Asher isn't anywhere that I can spot from my current vantage point.

I hear a thump from a hallway that leads away from the large living area to the left. I call out as I make my way towards the noise but still get no response. The banging rings out again and as I peer into an open doorway the moaning starts with a vengeance.

There before me is the impressive form of Asher Scott grunting and gasping as he fucks some lucky girl like a beast. The woman in question is spread-eagled on a bed as Asher's huge cock drills its way into her with such force that her beautiful full breasts jiggle seductively. And her moaning…fuck me, the girl has a good sex voice and thankfully she is *blissfully* unaware of my uninvited presence.

But their raw hunger and carnal fucking have me pinned to the spot like some startled voyeur; shocked at the unexpectedly sexy display before me but mesmerized by the exquisite muscles of Asher's back, ass and thighs as he works her body expertly with his skillful thrusts.

The sight before me is so fucking hot.

So hot that arousal begins to pool deep in my core and slick wetness seeps out of me and soaks my panties. If I were still the confident girl who liked life on the kinky edge, I'd go and join them – I'm self-assured enough with my looks and body that I wouldn't be kicked out of bed – were it not for the fact that the sex god is my boss and that I've just noticed that the beautiful girl with the erotic voice moaning my boss's name, is bound to the bed.

Wrists and ankles.

Splayed out for his and her pleasure.

And I try to fight a mini freak out and swallow the bile down to keep it in my stomach and not flying out of my mouth.

She's at the mercy of Asher's massive cock and she loves every second of it but all I can see is the horrific memory playing before my eyes. The memory of being completely bound while David beats me around the head with a wooden paddle until he knocks me unconscious.

Bruised.

Bleeding.

Helpless.

I turn to make myself scarce while the couple finishes their business but bump into the door frame, hitting my head. I curse instinctively at the sharp pain but stumble forward – my goal to reach the front door – despite the shriek from the woman and Asher's distinctive "Oh fuck" growl.

And not an *I'm-coming* 'Oh fuck', a *shit-I've-been-caught-fucking-by-the-new-girl* 'Oh fuck'.

The sound of them fumbling to dress and make themselves presentable fades into the background as I make it to and through the front door and out into the fresh air, which does little to clear the fuzz from where I hit my head.

It seriously fucking hurts.

Chapter Two

Asher

"Oh Fuck".

That doesn't even cover it. Carly didn't come, neither did I and nor will we but never mind. My main priority right this second is the startled new administrator who just saw me fucking like an animal.

Great first impression dick head. Just what the poor girl needs to see from her boss.

Yeah, she's early but I should've considered that possibility before I tied Carly to the guest bed we use when we have an itch that needs scratching.

"We could finish, Asher, I'm so close," groans Carly.

As true as that is, I can see the splodge of blood on the door frame.

Katie Morgan hit her head hard.

"Get dressed sugar. I'm gonna need you to get an ice pack and Jack."

"Why? What happened?" But I'm already out the door doing up my fly and pulling my t-shirt over my head as I go.

I find Katie sitting on the front stoop with her head in her hands, her small form hunched over.

11

"Katie?" She flies to her feet to face me, looking mighty unsteady.

"I'm so sorry, Mr. Scott, I didn't mean to walk in on you and your girlfriend, the door was open and I was trying to find you. But you'll understand why I don't shake your hand at the moment," she babbles, her eyes unfocused.

I take a step towards her, violating her personal space but I can see what's going to happen; blood is dripping slowly down her face, past her dilated eyes. She sways on her feet but manages to flinch away from my hands.

"You smell," her voice is a little slurred and she wrinkles her cute little nose in disgust. She's not wrong, I do smell. I went to town on Carly's pussy and now I smell of sex and cunt. I find the smell pretty arousing but as Katie wasn't the lady I made the erotic scent with, I can see why she's grossed out.

But I can also see her eyes rolling into the back of her head and her pocket rocket body beginning to slump; if I don't grab her with my sex covered hands then she'll fall and hit her head some more. So, I lunge forward and wrap my arms around her petite, curvy frame, scooping her up as she drifts unconscious.

As I carry her inside Carly meets me with the ice pack and follows us to another guest bedroom on the ground floor.

"Well that was dramatic," she says dryly as I lay Katie down on the bed, her wavy blond hair flowing around her shoulders. Carly has thought ahead and brought the small medical kit I keep in the kitchen with her, so I wipe and clean the small wound before placing the ice pack on her forehead above her right eye.

"Did you call Jack?"

"Yeah, should be here in a few minutes. Just a bump though, right? You really think she needs Jack?"

"Most people only faint for a few moments. She's still out; I'm worried she has a concussion." I really was. I could see her breathing deeply and evenly but she wasn't waking up.

"She hit her own head hard enough to concuss herself?" Carly snorts incredulously. She's not a mean girl but I imagine she's pissed we were disturbed before she climaxed.

I can't help the pang of guilt I feel towards both the women in this room. Poor Katie is having a shitty first day and would have the headache to prove it and Carly is most likely frustrated at my lack of interest in finishing the job, which is probably insulting her ego.

Carly is lovely and should be treated better than that and then I feel guilty all over again as I should never have allowed our arrangement, as casual as it is, to flourish. I'm her boss and it can only end one way...badly.

Carly likes it hot and hard, rough and kinky – my kind of kinky. There isn't an abundance of women who like it that way; more than you think but still not enough for me to turn down a fumble with Carly when she propositions me. But as her boss, I shouldn't be thinking about her with my dick but apparently, I'm weak-willed when all my blood rushes south to my pants, leaving my brain starved and out of the decision-making process.

It gets worse; I think Carly is starting to develop deeper feelings for me so I'm really going to have to put the brakes on. I don't want to hurt her. She's a sweet girl and a hard worker and I would hate to think of her feeling hurt and awkward and deciding to quit because of my non-existent self-control.

Just then Jack walks into the house and calls out. I shout our location to him and seconds later he rounds the door into the bedroom and begins to assess Katie's condition.

13

I turn to face Carly. "Thank you but I think its best you head on back to work now. The new girl doesn't need an audience when she wakes up". Hurt flashes briefly in her eyes but she does as she's told with no argument.

Yeah. I'm going to need to have that awkward conversation with her sooner rather than later.

"What happened?" Jack, the ranch doctor asks.

"She hit her head on the door frame," Jack quirks an eyebrow at me in an are-you-serious manner.

"Guessin' she got quite the fright to hit herself that hard; you and Carly at it again?"

My eyes visibly bulge. I had no idea that Carly and I casually fucking was public knowledge.

Shit.

"Dunno what you're talkin' about," I lie and it doesn't sound convincing, even to me.

"Don't panic. No one else knows. But I'm not some dumb shit you can lie to Ash, so don't try."

Jack and I have known each other a long time and it makes me feel like a grade-A shit that I just tried to be dishonest with him.

"Okay," I sigh, "Carly and I occasionally hook up but it's nothin' serious. Sometimes it gets a little…interesting, and that's what Katie walked in on."

"Take it she's the new administrator – providing she doesn't turn tail and quit on your horny ass." He smirks.

"That would be her and I sincerely hope I haven't scared her away. What's the damage?"

"There doesn't look to be a concussion but I'm a little concerned that she's not woken up yet. Her vitals are fine but if she doesn't come around soon, she's gonna need a hospital."

"Fuck! Give me a couple of minutes to shower and then I'll be ready to drive her if that's what she needs." He nods as I bolt out the room and head to my master suite upstairs…the room I don't bring women home to. It's my personal sanctuary and I don't want it being sullied by some one-night stand who can't take the hint in the morning. That's why I basically have a sex bedroom downstairs.

I take the quickest shower known to man, change my clothes and am racing back downstairs within five minutes. When I look at Katie's peaceful, pretty face, I notice her eyelids begin to flutter.

"Looks like she's gonna wake up," Jack confirms. All I can do is nod in anticipation and hold my breath, wondering what kind of shit storm I've just made for myself.

Slowly, she opens her eyes, those striking baby blues looking right at me as they focus.

"Hey there, my name is Jack. I'm the Doc here at Diamond Peak. You hit your head pretty hard, can you tell me your name?"

Katie reluctantly drags her impenetrable gaze from me to Jack, rolls her eyes and somewhat dryly replies, "I know who I am. My name is Katie Morgan. I'm the new administrator. That is if I still have a job?" She looks quite unsure of herself as she asks that.

"Why would you not still have the job?" I ask, equally confused as to why she would think that.

"Wasn't exactly a great first impression I made – dramatic sure, impressive? No. Please pass my apologies to your girlfriend for interrupting you both."

"Carly isn't my girlfriend," not sure why that's the first thing I need to assure her of. "I didn't exactly give you the best first impression of myself either. Of course, you still have a job here with us. I'm just sorry that you hurt yourself on my account. How are you feelin'?"

"Like I have a headache."

"I bet," injects Jack. "I'm still a little concerned about the length of time it took you to come around though. I was sayin' to Asher earlier that I couldn't see a concussion but that doesn't account for how long you were out cold for."

Katie looks incredibly uncomfortable and starts twisting her fingers subconsciously. After drawing a deep breath, she answers.

"I have a pre-existing head injury that makes me prone to passing out for longer."

I can't help but feel she chose her words very carefully and selectively and deliberately left a huge part of the story out.

"What happened?" Jack plows on oblivious.

"It's in my medical records if you should, for some reason, need to get hold of them but outside of that, I don't want to talk about it." And just like that, she shuts the conversation down.

"Well the way I see it, you've got two choices; you can tell me what happened to your head so that I can figure out if I need to be concerned about this new injury or you can keep your secrets and we'll have to take you to the hospital for further tests to make sure there's nothin' serious going on. You're choice. What'll it be?"

I like Jack's reasoning…

Katie clearly doesn't.

She looks torn – although I'm pretty sure her eyes bugged out of her head more at the thought of going to the hospital – and more than a little frightened. She tries to hide it well and most people probably wouldn't notice, but I'm quite skilled at reading people. Whatever happened to Katie's head previously is a painful story…in more ways than one.

Katie takes a deep, calming breath and I prepare myself for either a story that I probably don't want to hear or a long drive to the ER.

"My ex hit me across the head with a paddle. And I don't mean the rowboat variety."

Holy shit. I have a sick feeling in my gut that I know where this is going. "You mean the BDSM kind?" Why else would she have panicked enough to knock herself out in her rush to escape the sight of me dominating Carly?

Katie continues, her voice small but firm. "Yes. He had my wrists and ankles bound and when I saw that he was going to gag me I safe worded; I've always hated the feeling of being gagged. As he moved closer, I kept repeating my safe word but he kept ignoring me and put the ball gag in my mouth all the same. And as punishment for trying to stop his pleasure, he started hitting me with the paddle, deranged arousal lighting his eyes. It started on my torso and even though he cracked a rib or two it wasn't satisfying enough. So, he moved to my head. I passed out on the seventh blow. I'm not sure if he carried on hitting me or if he moved straight on to fucking me at that point but fuck my unconscious, un-consenting body he did. I sure wasn't aroused and judging from the pain I felt when I woke up, he didn't lube up before entering. The pain down below was almost as bad as the pain in my head."

I feel the tension in my fists; my skin stretched tight and white across my knuckles. How could her own boyfriend rape and beat her? I don't understand rape full stop but looking down at the sweet, petite blond with her big innocent eyes I really don't get how any man could stomach treating her that way. The strangest urge to protect her and exact revenge on her behalf grips me. It makes my chest feel hollow and my throat thickens; I can't speak at that moment so I just listen grimly to her story – her eyes glazed and focused on some point in the distance.

"When I came around, he was in the shower and I was untied. I crawled to the second bathroom with my cell phone, locked the door and dialed 911. The operator stayed on the line with me while she dispatched the cops and an ambulance. When they arrived, David told them there was no one in the apartment but him. The operator was communicating with the cops and told them it was bullshit and that I could hear them from the bathroom. I started screaming at that point – it hurt my chest and my lungs but I was just so desperate for them to hear me and help me. The cops handcuffed David then and there for obstruction while the paramedics took me away. I had some cracked ribs and a small fracture to my skull. They told me that one more hit probably would've split my head right open and he'd have killed me. They did a pelvic exam and confirmed rape. I was lucky to be alive and David was arrested."

"Katie, I don't know what to say. I'm so sorry he put you through that. The only silver lining is that he's locked up now and can't hurt you or any other woman ever again." My blood is boiling at the thought of her psychotic ex abusing her trust like that. He's lucky he's behind bars or I'd show him what a real beating feels like.

"You'd think so, wouldn't you? The horrific truth is that he lawyered up with a bulldog and together they presented private videos of our sexual exploits in the early part of our relationship. From the time when the kink was still fun and not abusive. It showed me enjoying myself and they argued that I liked it rough. Despite the medical reports showing how badly injured I was and that the sex was unlikely to have been consensual, his lawyer successfully argued that I was a sexual deviant who got off from exceptionally hard sex. They also spun the lie that David had dumped me and that I had begged him for rough break-up sex and following that I made the abuse accusations as a woman scorned trying to get revenge after being slighted by her lover."

I can't believe what the fuck I'm hearing and yet Katie is still spilling her secret; this tale of horror still isn't over. With a bitter sadness and weary resignation, she continues.

"The detective working my case and the assistant district attorney both believed my account but David's lawyer was too good. The videos of me enjoying it rough made all the evidence ambiguous at best. The DA didn't press charges because it wasn't likely to result in a conviction and they weren't about to waste taxpayer money on an unwinnable case."

Katie's shoulders visibly sag under the weight of knowing that even in this day and age, our judiciary system failed her – and that failure isn't an anomaly. How many women have watched on in horror as their tormentors escape punishment while they are trapped with it for the rest of their lives?

Too many is the sad fucking answer.

"After he was released from custody," she continues, "he came straight to the hospital where he tried to force his way into my room but was removed by security. He stalked the hospital frequently to the point where my doctor didn't discharge me until the end of his shift so that he could hide me in the back seat of his SUV and drive me to my friend

19

Maddie's place without David knowing. Dr. Greg refused to leave me alone and said it wasn't safe to go back to my apartment, Maddie agreed. Dr. Greg gave Maddie his number in case of an emergency and left to meet his friends at my place to pack up my belongings for me. Not two hours into packing up my apartment, David was trying to kick down my front door, demanding that I go home with him for my punishment for all the shit and embarrassment I'd caused. Turns out Dr. Greg and his friends were all ice hockey players and en masse, scared the living shit out of David. The next day the whole team turned up again to help move the last of my possessions across town into Maddie's place – her building had better security than mine. It didn't take David long to figure out that I'd gone to Maddie's but he couldn't get into her building and he thought I had an entire ice hockey team acting as bodyguards, which I did for a while.

"Dr. Greg was a really decent guy – he was there the night I was admitted and I think it shook him up to see the state I was in and that it was at the hands of someone I was supposed to be able to trust. It's truly shocking how many people get away with abusing their spouses until it's too late. Dr. Greg is a young idealist and I think he was terrified that I would be one of those 'too late' statistics if David got his hands on me again. He's probably right.

"I went through some pretty intensive therapy in the months that followed and life sort of got back to normal. We planned our move here, Maddie had to move a few days before me and although we were worried about me being alone, we couldn't avoid it. I called Dr. Greg, the assistant DA and the Detective who worked my case so that they knew I was moving away – I was aware that they were sort of keeping tabs on me to make sure I was safe and I didn't want to just vanish and have them worry. That night Dr. Greg and a few of his teammates showed up so that I wouldn't be alone. Someone was always with me until the day I drove here. Greg said that it was probably overkill but he wasn't going to risk my safety just as I was about to start a new life and be free. I appreciated the gesture but knew it wasn't necessary; I'd heard that David has a new girlfriend, so I wasn't on his radar anymore.

"I called his place on my last day in Colorado Springs, at a time I knew he'd be in work, and his new girl answered. I tried to warn her as best I could – she thought I was just some crazy ex ranting bullshit about her man. I begged her to stay safe and she hung up on me. I tried. But maybe he'll treat her better?"

Fucking unlikely but she doesn't need me to affirm that. Her ex is a piece of work but at least she's now several hours away from his clutches and she has me and every cowboy on this ranch to protect her if David-the-asshole dares show his ugly face here.

"So that's why my head is pre-disposed to passing out for longer periods of time," she finishes and looks exhausted.

I nod at Jack to make himself scarce and he does so, having satisfied himself that Katie is in no further danger.

Once he's out of earshot, I sit on Katie's bed but still far enough away not to be intimidating.

"I want you to know that not all men are like that Katie. I'm hoping you saw that from your Dr. Greg and his friends? But I also want to apologize for what you saw earlier – I can understand that it probably brought up some troublin' memories for you. I also need you to know that Carly one hundred percent consented to what happened in that guest

21

bed. If you want to ask her about it then please feel free to do so."

"Why are you telling me this?"

"Because I want you to be comfortable here on the ranch and around me. I don't want you to be afraid, especially not of me or of any of the things I've done. This ranch is a family and we'd like you to be a part of that. That means we'll all have your back if you give us a chance."

"Thank you," she whispers.

"You're very welcome. There's one more thing," I hesitate for a moment, wondering how she'll take this next piece of information and praying it doesn't freak her out. "There was a massive leak in your cottage in the upstairs bathroom. There's a lot of water damage as it flooded the downstairs. Long story short, the cottage isn't ready and it won't be for a few weeks. The lodge is fully booked so I can't put you in there –"

"I can commute from a B&B in town," she cuts in.

"Don't be daft, that's an hour a day just driving to and fro. There's plenty of space here in the ranch house. There are so many bedrooms and you can choose whichever one you want, as far away from me as you need. Whatever makes you comfortable."

"Is there a room near you? That sounds like some awful proposition but I don't really want to be down here with the sex room and spilling my guts as I did has left me feeling a bit raw. I don't want to be alone in a place I don't know."

She's taking this much better than anticipated and I have to actively try not to look surprised at her request to be near me…although I guess it makes sense that she doesn't want to be alone after the hour she's just lived through.

"The bedrooms upstairs are suites so you can take the one

next to mine. It's probably a good idea for you to take one of the bigger bedrooms instead of the smaller guest rooms downstairs anyway as you're going to be here for a few weeks. Means you can unpack a bit without feelin' too cramped."

"Thank you."

"How about we call your friend Maddie and have her come up here and stay overnight? That way you have your friend to make you feel better and she can keep you company tomorrow."

"Tomorrow? I thought I'd be working tomorrow?" Her face is slightly adorable when it's scrunched up in confusion.

"You aren't working until that head of yours is healed. Now, wait here a moment while I fetch you some pain relief for that headache you're bound to have."

Chapter Three

Katie

Half an hour later I'm dosed up on pain medication, been relocated to the suite next to Asher's and Maddie is on her way having been called by the man himself.

The thumping in my head has mercifully been controlled to just a dull ache above my eye; I haven't dared to look in the mirror yet to see if I have a lump swelling to the size on an egg on my forehead. Even if I do look that horrendous it won't change anything; my insanely gorgeous and frighteningly kinky cowboy boss has already seen me at rock bottom…at least I fucking hope this is rock bottom.

I can't see how the past few hours could've been much worse, short of being carted off to the ER, and as far as first impressions go, it couldn't have gone any more sideways. I hum 'The only way is up' dryly to myself and decide to take a closer look at my surroundings before I psycho-analyze myself and my situation any further.

My room is gorgeous with an intricately carved wooden screen separating the sleeping area from the door and the sitting area with the most fantastic views of the mountains through floor to ceiling windows. The sun shining in illuminates every detail of the warm timber walls and floor covered with the softest faux fur rug. A gigantic bed dominates the wall opposite the windows so that the occupants can enjoy the stunning vistas in absolute comfort; seriously, it's *the* most comfortable bed I have ever had the pleasure of being in. Add to that the fact that I was carried here by the most gorgeous man I've ever seen and it's fast becoming my favorite place.

Despite the overwhelming sexiness that is Asher Scott, I am wary of him and the intensity with which my body is attracted to him. I want to pass it off as purely a chemical response to the ultra-alpha-ness of his presence and physicality, but a warning voice is telling me there may be more to it than that.

And that can't happen.

He's my boss.

I can't afford to not have this job because I made a move and the relationship went sideways, or worse, be nothing more than a one-night stand. I know I did the casual sex thing to get over my fear of sex post-David but I'm not the fling sort of girl and if I let Asher Scott into my panties, he's going to work his way into my heart. I just know it. And no matter how small a piece of my heart he breaks, it's a piece too far in my current state of recovery.

I'm also not even touching the fact that he likes it rough – how rough and how much of a dominant he is, I don't know but even a little bit is too much for me.

I get the impression that he likes control from what I saw of him and Carly earlier and I don't have it in me to give up my control to anyone, least of all to a man in the bedroom.

To the right of my temporary bedroom is a glorious bathroom with a slate flagstone floor, black marble countertops and with matching tiles in the huge walk-in waterfall shower, and a seriously inviting jacuzzi tub set into deep red timber, again positioned to maximize the view of the mountains. There are no other properties at the back of this ranch house so there is no fear of anyone catching a glimpse of nakedness while indulging in this tub.

I run the water and strip off so that I can soak away the crap of the last few hours; washing away all thoughts of Asher and his sex god body.

I need to get the man out of my system and fast.

"Katie?" his low voice calls out.

Shit.

"I'm naked!" I throw my palm to my face, why the fuck is that the first thing I shout out to him? Like its some goddam invitation? "I mean I'm in the bath! Don't come in!"

"I have fresh towels for you. There are none in there. I was hoping to get them to you before you decided to clean up. Sorry."

He could just dump them on the bed but making a wet, naked mad dash doesn't appeal to me. The water is hot so by comparison, the room will feel freezing on my damp body. Not to mention the mess I'll make dripping water everywhere whilst running for the towels.

I slump lower in the bath, making sure my breasts are well and truly not visible, leaving only my head above the surface.

"Um…okay…you can bring them in but don't look at me."

I peer over my shoulder as the door opens and Asher walks in, keeping his eyes to himself and placing one fluffy looking towel on a heated rail within reach of the bath and then storing the rest in a built-in cupboard near the sink.

The small gesture of leaving a towel to warm for me chips away at my resolve. I try not to focus on the way his jeans

26

stretch tight around his perfect looking ass and muscular thighs as he bends over.

I don't fail at many things but I fail in that. I stare…like some sex-starved stalker, I stare at my boss' astonishing ass and remember what he looked like naked, the raw power of those muscles. Then a strange sensation of jealousy strangles me; why couldn't it have been me on the receiving end, taking everything that powerful body had to give?

I've never had such a visceral reaction to someone I barely know and it's more than just his looks, although I can't rightly pinpoint exactly what else it is. No one, not even Maddie, compels me to open up the way I did to him. I could simply have told him that David hit my head repeatedly and left it at that but instead, I told him every sordid detail. As if Jack the doc wasn't in the room and it was just me and Asher. Anything short of the absolute truth felt impossible. He demanded that level of honesty from me and I'm not even sure how he did it but he provokes something in me. Something responds to him against my better judgment; something that fires off my emotions in every extreme direction imaginable.

Seeing him with Carly ripped painful memories out of me and stoked my green-eyed monster at the same time. Watching him listen to my confession and seeing the rage for David in his molten brown eyes and the small acts of kindness he's displayed in taking care of me inspire an intense, primitive and carnal desire for him. So powerful it frightens and confuses me.

Perhaps I've just hit my head really hard and this is all just in my banged-up mind?

Either way, the emotional extremes I'm being pulled in are exhausting me…not enough to dampen my wild thoughts of

Asher though.

Currently, I'm imagining what would happen if I just stood up, glistening wet and naked and invited him to join me in this oversized bath so that he could scratch whatever insane Asher itch I'm hung up on.

I want this man's mouth on me…his cock in me…his hands teasing me…I want to take it all and come screaming his name. And again, I'm thrown for another mental loop; how could I physically and emotionally want a man so fucking badly after reliving my nightmare only an hour ago?

My body is a traitor to my brain.

I audibly swallow past the thick, raw desire in my throat and Asher chooses that moment to turn and look at me – I know that my cheeks are heated from thoughts of him, my eyes are probably dilated with lust and I'm most certainly just staring at him…and now he's seeing all of it.

"You said you wouldn't look at me," I croak out, my mouth dry.

"Fair's fair," he had me there, "plus you only *asked* that I not look at you, I never actually agreed to those terms." He winks at me mischievously and I instantly melt, blush hard and smile back.

"Like what you see?"

What the fuck are you doing? My mind screams at me. I should not be flirting with my boss…before I've even done a day's work no less!

Hunger flashes in those swirling eyes of his, making me squeeze my thighs together in response.

"I can't actually see anything from where I'm standing, that's why I looked over at you from this vantage point to make sure you're okay. I'm not a total perv, especially as you did ask me

28

not to look," the flirtatious glint in his eyes dulls and he looks at me more tenderly. He was trying to be a decent guy and just wanted to make sure I was okay and that makes me want him more.

"Step closer then and maybe I'll give you permission to be a perv."

Shut up, shut up, shut up...stop propositioning your boss!

To my total and complete amazement, he takes several steps closer and looks down at me with those heated, hungry eyes and I know he can see my naked body now.

He crouches down and whispers in my ear, "I wouldn't want to take advantage of a beautiful woman with a head injury."

I blush crimson because he's right. I've no right throwing myself at him when I can't think straight. And how many flings with his employees should I really be encouraging. He was already balls deep in Carly earlier, I should not be fantasizing about him doing that to me in the *same* fucking day!

"Yeah...sorry...not thinking clearly," I mumble through embarrassment. At least in the morning, I will be able to feign innocence and pretend that it was all my head injury and that I don't remember a thing.

Just as that thought begins to comfort me, he whispers, "Of course. But if you are thinking clearly and feel the need to...ah...see to your needs, then make sure you're thinkin' of me." His lips lightly graze my ear and I tilt my head involuntarily so that his lips move to the sweet spot where my ear meets my neck and gasp at the feather-light touch. "Maddie will be here soon, so you'll need to be quick," he whispers against my skin, setting me on fire as he stands and leaves the room.

What a goddam tease but I suppose he does need to mind his

boundaries; how many girls can he take in a single day before he becomes a sexual lothario?

Even so, my fingers drift south to my clit; maybe if I just think of him this once while I climax it will be enough to get him out of my system?

I slip my middle finger inside myself, while my thumb continues to massage my clit, and curl it to rub against my front wall and the tight bundle of nerve endings making up my g-spot. My hips buck and I ride my hand harder and faster, the other hand teasing my nipples, imagining Asher's fingers fucking my soaked pussy and his mouth on my breasts as his teeth graze and pinch my nipples. In less than a minute, I'm coming. Pleasure splinters through me, my body trembles, my cunt constricts around my finger as it gushes and I gasp Asher's name.

Asher

Holy. Fucking. Shit.

That's my name she's gasping.

She actually did it…while thinking of me.

And now I'm hard.

Seriously hard.

But while my sexual morals are apparently quite loose, I am a man of my word; I will not take advantage of a beautiful woman. Period.

I shouldn't have suggested what I did or brushed my lips against the silken heat of her neck given that I'm already in a bit of a mess because I screwed around with an employee. I'm walking a very fine line here but something about Katie is drawing me in like a moth to a flame; it's hot and dangerous but I can't seem to stop.

Her honesty, her big, innocent and open blue eyes and that pocket rocket body that fires my thoughts to the stratosphere. I can't stop drinking in the curves of her petite body and the swell of those delicious, voluptuous breasts; the bathwater did little to obscure her insanely beautiful body and I had to crouch down to hide the semi that was starting to strain against my jeans.

Now here I stand in her bedroom, like some voyeuristic stalker, listening to her come while gasping my name. It didn't take her long to climax either and I can't help the ego boost I get from knowing thoughts of me got her there that quickly. Given what she told me about her ex an hour ago, I can't believe she'd be in the mood at all. Again, the thought that I got her that aroused has me feeling smug and…possessive.

I want her pleasure.

All of it.

That's the sort of dominant I am; I want ownership of her orgasms, to be the one in control of her releases. That's why I'm fond of bondage – there's little a woman can do but take the pleasure I give when she's bound. I get off from the knowledge that I control the woman's climax, not her. The act of coming is to lose control but to not even have the power over when that loss of control happens?

Pure sexual dynamite.

Watching a woman come undone around me while at the mercy of my body is so fucking erotic that was I a lesser man, I'd shoot my load early. That's how hot it gets me. Knowing that I gave a woman that much pleasure is my bliss…I just have interesting ways of getting her there.

And I want to get Katie there.

I may not have had control over the orgasm she just had but I did tell her to think of me…and she obeyed.

Chapter Four

Katie

As my body sags back into the warm bath water, my post-orgasmic glow is cut short when I hear Maddie's voice calling out from downstairs.

Quickly I dry myself and dress in pajama shorts and a vest top. Asher has also left a sumptuous robe and blanket on the bed for me (more thoughtfulness that melts my heart) – I slip on the robe and sit on the bed with the blanket covering my feet as Maddie walks in.

She eye's my surroundings, "Nice place you got," she smirks and raises an elegant eyebrow.

"I bought it with my pocket money," I laugh.

"Your boss is hot by the way."

"Like I hadn't noticed," I reply dryly.

"Just checking the knock to your head didn't mess with your eyesight," her eyes dance with mischief.

Maddie brings her elegant, lithe body towards the bed and sits gracefully next to me. I've always admired that about my friend; her grace and elegance but it's her wicked sense of humor that is a stark contrast to her demure, ladylike appearance that I love the most. She has the body and sensuality that reflects the amazing dancer she is, except her dance of choice is to throw herself acrobatically around a pole in a vision of empowered female sexiness. Maddie is a perfect conundrum, the ultimate 'lady on the street but a freak in the bed'.

Physically we are quite opposite; her deep chestnut hair to my golden blond, her dark stormy eyes to my sky blue, her tall, lithe body to my petite curviness.

I'm not *really* petite, just everyone else around me is a giant. Asher is huge, Maddie is above average height and I'm just a bit *below* average height.

But opposites attract and Maddie and I have been inseparable since we met in college. She's my rock, my strength and my partner in crime. We'd do anything for each other so, it's no surprise that she made it here in record time in my moment of pain, need and acute embarrassment.

Even at the expense of me prolonging my orgasmic mood.

She shoots me a penetrating look. "So, what happened? Why the hell do you have a welt the size of an egg on your forehead? And don't spare me the details."

I breathe out deeply through my nose…here goes nothing. "Well, I guess I was really early, considering I walked in on my new boss hardcore fucking a woman on one of the beds downstairs."

"Nooo," she gasps. "Your boss? As in, the insanely hot, muscled cowboy currently downstairs somewhere?"

"Yep. That one."

"Bet that was a sight to behold?" She can't keep the amusement out of her voice, or her curiosity.

"You have no idea; he was…impressive. All hard muscles and mouth-watering skills. Seriously, I had to consciously

34

stop myself from drooling…and staring. They were hot. Until I noticed that she was tied to the bed…"

"Oh." Her voice falls immediately as comprehension clouds her stormy eyes.

"Yeah. In my haste to escape and get my mini freak out under control, I walked flat out into the doorframe. I made it to the front porch and then passed out just as he came out to find me. I can fill in the blanks enough to know he caught me before I face planted the porch and then he carried me back inside."

"Wait wait wait. He stopped mid-fuck to chase after you?" She lets out a low whistle, "Wow."

"I guess I didn't think about it that way. Why would he do that?"

"I guess to make sure he hadn't scared off his new administrator. Although it must have been *hard* to stop mid-flow," she muses.

That might explain his flirtatious behavior in the bathroom; he didn't get to finish earlier so he was probably still pumped full of sexual tension. Maybe I was just the nearest outlet for his hornyness. And I've no doubt the man has quite the sexual appetite – any man who fucks as hard as he was and then still has the energy to flirt with a different woman on the same day has a serious sex drive.

I can't help but wonder what life would be like with a man as *driven* as that? All insatiable lust and rock-hard body parts. The notion sends a shiver to my still sensitive clit. My body definitely wants a man like that; I've never had my arousal sparked to such a burning degree by just the sight of a man before. It's new. It's exciting. It's something I want to encourage.

I want his smooth, muscular body on me...in me...doing wicked things to me until I can't even scream my own name.

And then I remember how goddam insane that notion is.

"Earth to Katie?" Maddie's voice filters through my X-rated daydream.

"Mmhmm?"

"I never realized the word 'hard' would make you so distracted, you dirty girl. He's definitely left an impression on you, hasn't he?"

There's no point lying to Maddie; according to her, I suck at it anyway. "I think it's fair to call that an understatement. I don't get why or how, but the man is burning up my thoughts to a perilous degree – my sanity is in danger here."

"What sanity?" she teases.

"Madds! Seriously though. What should I do?"

"What do you want to do?" Every explicit thing I want Asher and his cock to do to me flashes across my mind and my face in the form of the fiercest blush I've ever experienced. "That look tells me everything lady. I vote in favor of you fucking him," she laughs.

"Seriously? The man's my boss. How awkward would that be when it inevitably went sideways because I develop feelings for him and he doesn't reciprocate? Besides, he already seems to have a standing arrangement with another employee." I can almost taste the regret, my voice thick with it. It's sharp and bitter and I don't like it.

Logic dictates that I don't go opening my legs to my boss, assuming, of course, he'd even wanted me to. It's a bad call, and I've had too many of those already this past year.

Maddie looks at me seriously for a moment. "You're a smart woman, Katie. *Trust* yourself."

And that right there is why Maddie is my girl. She can cut through my bullshit and see what's really simmering below the surface.

Trust.

I don't trust myself anymore.

I don't trust what my body and mind are telling me.

After the fuck up of epic proportions that was my relationship with David, how could I? I knew something wasn't right but I sure as hell didn't see that level of hurt, betrayal and actual bodily harm coming.

I didn't trust my instincts when I should have and pushed forward with blind faith that everything would be okay when I shouldn't have. My interpretation of everything was upside down and ass-about-face.

Has that changed?

I honestly don't know and that brings me to the crux of my problem…how can I trust myself?

Before that sobering thought well and truly depresses me, Maddie moves the conversation onto blessedly safer territory.

Turns out the job that she had lined up before we moved fell through. Something to do with the original post holder coming back to work following maternity leave after all. She looks mildly deflated but nothing can keep Maddie down for long.

"My savings will see me through for a while but I'm hoping something works out sooner rather than later so that I don't have to blow through too much of it. That money is my studio start-up fund."

"Maybe there's something here on the ranch?"

"Could be worth asking *your* cowboy," she arches that teasing eyebrow at me.

"He's not *my*…" I begin to protest but right on cue the cowboy in question knocks on the door and enters.

Asher Scott enters…all the oxygen in the room exits.

I try not to gasp at the glorious sight of him, so huge he's literally filling the doorframe with his height and broad-shouldered, muscular physique.

"Evenin' ladies. How are we doin'? I hope the patient is okay?" The smooth drawl of his accent haywires my brain leaving me speechless and Maddie answering for me.

"The patients' own stupidity won't kill her today," she mocks.

Asher laughs, warm and gentle while I punch my ex-friend on the arm, shooting her with a look that could kill.

"My head is fine, thank you," I force out a little indignantly.

"In that case, I made some dinner if you ladies wanna join me? Nothing special so don't go gettin' excited, but I'm not totally incompetent in the kitchen."

* * *

Asher Scott, the rugged cowboy of my rapidly developing fantasies, is as far from incompetent in the kitchen as the Moon is from Earth.

The man can cook. And I'll be damned if watching him confidently command his way around the kitchen doesn't turn up the heat of my desire. Much like the ragingly hot oven he just pulled his homemade lasagne out of.

My panties have melted into a puddle at my feet.

Shit.

The creamy smell of the lasagne and warm garlic bread further scatter my senses.

Asher places a plate of the delicious smelling food in front of me and looks at me knowingly. "Enjoy." There's a hint of something in his smooth voice and a suggestive glint to his chocolate brown eyes flecked with caramel. My cheeks burn crimson under his seductive perusal.

Oh. God. He. Knows.

I don't know how, but he does.

Think of me

He told me to, I did…and somehow, he knows. I'm certain of it.

He hands Maddie a plate of food before turning back to me and subtly running his tongue along his kissable, full bottom lip, the sexual innuendo clear and doing strange things to my body south of my belly button.

He. Definitely. Knows.

But how?

I suppose when I think on it, I didn't leave a particularly gracious amount of time between him leaving and me getting buck wild with my own fingers, which raises the tantalizing yet troubling thought that he was outside the whole time.

Listening to me gasp his name.

Oh. My…

Fuck it. I'm gonna pull on my big girl panties and own that shit. If he heard me masturbating to thoughts of him then I hope he enjoyed the show. I'm not ashamed; it was a kick-ass fucking orgasm and I'll probably give myself another one tonight. Because I want to and because I can.

I flash him my sweetest smile and turn my attention to the food before me.

"This is seriously tasty Asher," mumbles Maddie between mouthfuls.

"Thank you, ma'am," he smiles, looking a little too pleased

with himself.

I take a bite of the creamy and perfectly seasoned lasagne, fighting back a groan of pleasure. It tastes so much better than it smells and that's no mean feat.

"Is it okay, Katie?" the genuine sound of his voice catching me off-guard.

Swallowing, I nod. "Delicious."

His responding smile is breathtaking; like my approval is worth having and my compliment made his night. I can't help but return such an earnest and heart-stopping smile.

And then I have to drag my attention away from his beautiful, full lips before my mind unleashes a thousand fantasies of what that sexy mouth could do to me...

My desire is like an unruly child, give it an inch and it will take a mile. I don't need any more fuel to stoke my fire; I'm already ablaze.

Mercifully Maddie takes control of the conversation and makes pleasant small talk with Asher while I finish my meal and then excuse myself. It's still early but the day's events are catching up with me and I'm exhausted. The kind of bone-tired where you don't even feel like you can lift a limb.

Definitely time for sleep.

Chapter Five

Asher

A little while after the women excuse themselves, the sound of footsteps rouse me from the book I've been attempting to read next to the roaring fire in the lounge. It might be spring but the nights are still cold and nothing beats the flicker of real flames and warmth while reading a good book.

Secretly I hope the footsteps growing louder belong to Katie; something about her is drawing me in and I want to spend some one on one time with her. The smiles she was flashing me over dinner had me sporting a semi the entire time – for my dick's sanity, it's a good thing that the footsteps belong to Maddie and not the beautiful woman I'm rapidly becoming fascinated with.

Just because my dick can finally have a much-needed breather doesn't mean I'm not disappointed.

"Everythin' okay?" I give Maddie my full attention. She's a very beautiful woman and objectively I can appreciate her appealing attributes. But not even the graceful sway of her hips can entice a glimmer of my interest. Seriously, my dick doesn't flicker the tiniest twitch and that bad boy has been active all fucking afternoon – ever since Katie walked in on me in all my naked glory. I register a small amount of alarm that not even the sight of a woman as sexy as Maddie can divert some of my blood south to the contents of my pants.

"She's okay but she's crashed for the night. All of today's excitement will keep her knocked out until morning."

This area of the downstairs is open concept but Maddie hovers around the periphery of the living area, unsure of what to do with herself and obviously not wanting to intrude on my reading time. Honestly, though, I couldn't even tell you what book is in my hands; I literally picked it up to try to shove all thoughts of Katie from my mind for the evening. I shouldn't be this preoccupied with a woman I barely know and an employee no less.

I nod my head towards the large sectional sofa, indicating that Maddie should join me. She was full of pleasant conversation at dinner and it would be nice to get to know her a little and glean more information about Katie Morgan in the process.

Maddie sits gracefully and looks at me with piercing storm grey eyes; they tell me everything I need to know – Maddie is a lady, but not one you cross…not unless you've made peace with parting with your balls.

"Tell me about you and Katie? How long have you known each other?"

"We met the first day of college and I've been following that whirlwind of blond hair around ever since," she smiles genuine, true affection for her friend.

One of the things I value in people is loyalty; Maddie is clearly loyal to her friend and that is a damn admirable quality in my book. "Sounds like you're lucky to have each other."

"Katie is one of those rare souls; the type that lights up a room without trying or noticing they're doing it. She knows she's smart and classifies herself as somewhat pretty but she's totally oblivious to her true presence. Katie is unassumingly beautiful, fiercely intelligent and has such warmth and care for others that you want to snap the neck of anyone who would dare to hurt her. I will kill that ex of hers if he's ever stupid enough to be in a room alone with me. Fucking asshole."

I notice how she says she 'will' kill him and something about her tone makes me doubt her threat is empty. Maddie can join the murdering-David queue.

"I want you to know that Katie will be safe here. That *man*" – I spit the word – "is not welcome here and in your absence, I'll gladly kill him myself. No person should ever be allowed to abuse their power over someone like that and get away with it."

"Thank you. Not that it will come to that – he shouldn't be able to find her even if he *were* looking. He has a new plaything to torture now…Lord help the poor woman."

"You don't ever have to thank me for keeping her safe. We're like family on this ranch; we protect our own. That extends to you too, Maddie, anythin' you need, you can turn to us."

She smiles her appreciation at me. "I may need to take you up on that offer but I have something I need to get off my chest first and I hope it doesn't make you rethink your generous offer of including me in your ranch family…" She lets out a deep breath and her posture goes a little rigid. I'm not sure I'm going to like what she has to say but I keep my features open and neutral to invite her honesty.

"…I saw the way you were both looking at each other over dinner. I'd love to say it's none of my business but Katie and her welfare *are* my business. There's nothing wrong with

43

either of you being into the other so please don't misinterpret what I'm getting at as I mean no disrespect to you or her or your intentions towards each other. You're adults after all. But Katie has a big heart of gold and it got battered. It's not just her body that took a bashing; it was her confidence and faith in people and herself too. She has a good handle on most of the demons David unleashed but her confidence and trust in herself are still lacking. She won't trust her feelings towards you so if you want them, you're going to have to work for them. Be warned though, if you work for them and you make her fall for you, she will fall hard. She is still very capable of deep and lasting love so if you pursue her and she decides to let you in, it will be intense and epic and all kinds of amazing so be sure that you want that. Don't be the asshole that made her feel again, only to let her down and obliterate her heart."

"I hear you. Consider the consequences of my actions *before* I make a move, not after. I appreciate your candor, Maddie; you're a good friend and I would never make an ill judgment against someone for protecting their friend. You don't know me so you're right to caution me but I promised you that Katie would be safe here, that includes from me. I can't promise that I won't act on any feelings I develop for her but you have my word that if I do, it will be an informed decision from a man who wants to commit to her."

This is a pretty heavy conversation and I'm not known for wanting to commit to one woman but, given Katie's history, it seems appropriate. I pride myself on being every bit as honest and forthcoming as Maddie is so I'm not lying when I say I will think seriously before pursuing Katie.

Not that I've even actively thought about having Katie that way – it's still just a flirtation but our desire has legs, I can feel it, and those legs will run away with us if left unchecked.

"So, what was the other thing you wanted to ask me, Maddie?"

"The job I originally had lined up has fallen through. Do you know of anywhere that's hiring?"

"What's your skill set?" I don't have anything for her on the ranch but depending on her skills, I might be able to point her in the right direction in town.

"Dance and fitness instructor. My end goal is to open my own studio teaching yoga classes and pole and aerial hoop fitness but while I'm saving for that I can turn my hand to anything. I've done bar work, office work, you name it – I'm versatile."

"Pole? As in dancing on a pole?" An idea has struck me and she's just Dix's type but I need to be cautious with what I say next.

"Not like *dancing-in-a-gentleman's-club* pole dancing, teaching acrobatic skills on a pole; like gymnastics but instead of a horse or beam, there's a pole. There is an element of floor dance in heels if my students want to learn that but it's not for the pleasure of men in a dark and seedy club. It's a recognized form of dance and fitness." She doesn't sound insulted by my faux pas, more like she's had to explain the difference a thousand times in her life already.

"Apologies, Maddie, I wasn't tryin' to insinuate anything by my ignorance."

"Nothing to apologize for. If I can avoid the assumption that I'm a stripper then I'm happy to explain the difference."

"Not sure you'll go for a vacancy I know about then," I say, leaving it open just enough to pique her curiosity.

"There's a stripper job in town?" She gives me a very

uncertain glance as she mulls this over.

"Not 'stripper' and not a strip club. Dancing on a pole, yes, in a seedy gentlemen's club, no. You wouldn't be naked or taking any clothes off; you'd be scantily clad for sure but you wouldn't be revealing any more of yourself during your routine. People are not allowed to touch you either or pay for private performances." I'm being vague but I don't really know how to approach this.

"You sound a little secretive for a job that's just supposed to be dancing." It's not a question.

I sigh, not really seeing much of a way around it. "The club is an exclusive members club – I can't really tell you much about it in case you don't want the job and talk about it where you shouldn't but equally if I don't tell you about the club, you won't think the job is on the level."

"I can keep a secret. Even if the job isn't for me, I'm no blab." She looks sincere and I pride myself on getting a good read on people.

Here goes nothin'..."It's a member's only erotic club. Have you heard of the Rock Hard Club?"

"The nightclub in town?"

"Yeah, that one. Well upstairs is a very different *scene* to the après ski nightclub downstairs. Members pay to watch the performers in all manner of displays; from purely exotic dancing, bondage scenes to hardcore sex. Any kind of erotic or sexual thing you can think of is performed for the visual pleasure of the patrons. Private performances are not for sale, sex is not for sale; the only staff having sex are the performers who are paid to. The guests are not allowed to touch the performers and vice versa. It is purely visual stimuli. Guests are permitted to have sex with one another and there are private rooms for them should they feel the urge to do so. Dixon Cooper, the club's owner, needs a pole dancer; someone who can make the guests hot and bothered with their moves and in between performances can help at the bar. No one would be allowed to touch you and you wouldn't be naked. Just provocative dancing in a skimpy outfit. Is that something that would interest you?"

She's silent for a long moment while she considers this. "Perhaps. Do you have a way for me to contact this Dixon guy?"

I pull out my wallet from my jeans back pocket and thumb through the contents until I find Dixon's business card and pass it to her.

"If you call him, tell him I recommended you for the position. He'll trust that you're actually there for the job that way and not just snooping around for a story."

"A story?"

"He had a bit of trouble with an overzealous reporter a few years ago – they were chasing rumors in the wind but she was persistent and hung around for a while. Made it difficult for business to continue as normal. It made Dixon a bit prickly with who he trusts, hence why you should say I sent you." Just thinking about how that reporter hung around has me equal parts amused and annoyed. I couldn't go to the club for a month until she cleared off…tail between her legs because someone had 'anonymously' tipped off her editor to the fact that she'd slept with the story in question. Dixon seduced her, fucked her seven ways till Sunday but filmed the whole thing and sent the evidence to her boss. She was pulled from the non-existent story and Dixon threatened to sue the newspaper saying that she seduced *him* and then he found out she was trying to run a story on him that would ruin him and that it was all a shady form of entrapment. The newspaper ran a mile and the story was never followed up. I'd have felt bad for the reporter but she really was an obnoxious witch who managed to alienate more than half the town with her bad attitude and passive-aggressive comments.

Maddie turns the card over and over with her delicate fingers. "I'll give it some thought, thank you." And with that, she stands and heads towards the stairs, "Night Asher, and thank you again."

I nod as she disappears back up to Katie's room and try not to think about the prospect of bumping into Maddie at the Club. All the members know each other – it's not a massive town after all – but we are all discreet and pass no judgment on each other's persuasions. But I feel like watching Maddie dance would be just a little too close to home. Luckily, my tastes run a little more hardcore than just watching a pretty body dancing around a pole so she probably wouldn't be on my radar at all.

* * *

As I return to my house the next morning after my chores down at the stables, I notice that Maddie's car is gone. She must have left early and I wonder whether Katie went with her? I bounce up the back-porch steps, keen to find out the answer.

The sound of Katie singing as I enter through the back door alerts me otherwise. Katie is here alone…and singing along to the radio. The woman can hold a tune and the melodic sound of her voice floats through the house, drawing me towards its source…the scantily-clad star of last nights' wet dreams, sauntering around my kitchen making herself breakfast.

I tried not to dream about her but not picturing her in all her naked glory spread out beneath me while my unyielding cock speared into her soft pussy was futile. I dreamed that dream and I woke up covered in a bucket load of my hot cum. Thoughts of Katie had me soaking myself and my sheets like a fucking teenager blowing his load the first time he got a good look at a Playboy centerfold.

Just like the dream, not staring at her now is also futile…I try but I fail and I'm not as distraught about that as I should be.

Katie is wearing tiny pajamas that barely cover her ass cheeks and a teeny tiny tank top that strains against the generous swell of her breasts. She's braless and either slightly chilled or aroused cause damn it, those perky erect nipples look good enough to eat.

I notice the swelling on her forehead has subsided and there's barely a bruise marring her flawless skin as she sways to the music, preparing pancakes and bacon. One of my favorite breakfast foods – I should make myself known so that I can ask if she minds making extra…and so that I'm not just some creepy pervert of a boss staring at her from the safety of a shadowy corner.

I tiptoe backward towards the back door, open it and slam it louder than necessary and walk heavily towards the kitchen to alert her to my presence. I don't want her startling and spilling hot oil on herself – she's had enough injuries for one week.

"Mornin'" I call out, just to make it really obvious that I'm in the house, as I round the corner into the kitchen.

After all that, she still manages to look startled and drops a utensil on the floor. Katie bends over to retrieve it and flashes me a generous amount of pearly white skin and that barely concealed, edible round ass of hers. There's something so utterly sensual about how her thighs, hips, and ass move so fluidly together like silk or water lapping gently on a shoreline. I want to lick my tongue along the smooth juncture between her thighs and those delectable cheeks...I wonder if she's ticklish?

"Now that is a welcome a man could get used to."

She turns quickly and her face goes up in flames, her nipples puckering to even harder points in that scrap of a top. I have to wilfully restrain myself from reaching out and rubbing my thumbs along them.

Pulling out a stool at the breakfast bar, I sit to conceal my rapidly hardening dick.

"Pancakes?" she manages to squeak. The morning sunlight streaming through the big picturesque windows frame her body and shimmer her blond bed hair like a halo. Katie is like a real-life sex angel thrown into my path to tempt me.

"Please. And some bacon if there's some going spare?" She turns and places more bacon into the sizzling pan. "Maddie gone?"

"Yes," she breathes, evidently relieved to have a safe topic of conversation. "She had to leave early, something about a tip-off for a potential job. She didn't say what though. Said she'd call later."

I'm guessing Maddie called Dix after all. Fingers crossed that works out for her.

"And how are you? Sleep well? Your forehead looks so much better today."

"I knew I looked a state in the bathroom yesterday…" she trails off at the thought and blushes at the conversation she's unwittingly started.

"You were anything but a state," I wink – yeah actually wink – at her. What the hell? My audacity is rewarded however, by the delicious deepening of her blush. So few women actually blush anymore and for someone who previously enjoyed sex on the racier side of the spectrum, the blush is, even more, a rarity.

"I'm feeling much better and slept really well thank you," she replies, blatantly ignoring my flirting…or so I thought. "Were you outside the door?"

I thought she'd sussed that from my less than subtle innuendo at dinner last night. "You need to ask?" I arch a brow suggestively. *Of course, I heard you woman, you were screaming my name*. My only regret was not staying in the bathroom to watch the show.

She considers me a moment, steel flashing in her eyes. "Well, I'm not going to deny it or make excuses. I'm a red-blooded woman with a healthy sexual appetite and you're hot as fuck. You also happened to be the one to suggest I think of you…I was merely following my bosses' instructions. So, I thought of you and came like a freight train. But don't be fooled; don't think I didn't notice you staring at me or the massively obvious erection you're trying to hide by sitting yourself that far under the kitchen island."

Busted.

My eyes widen in utter shock at this – Katie is far more observant than I've given her credit for and I'm going to have to watch myself against her penetrating eyes and sexy sass.

"Like a freight train huh?"

"Considering the sex and then the lack thereof I've had over the past few years, 'freight train' is probably an understatement. But that brings me squarely to a few points that I suppose we need to discuss."

Here we go.

"You're my boss – "

"And that would stop me because?" *Why am I arguing?* She's trying to distance herself for my overly forward and flirtatious behavior. Sure, she's receptive to it, but she's trying to rise above whatever connection is simmering between us.

"I also don't do casual, which seems to be your speed if you can go from bedding Carly to blurring the lines of our professional relationship in the space of a day…less than if we're being honest."

"Ouch." True, but sounds fucking brutal when she says it like that. I must look like a total man-whore to her. *Hmm, I may need to rethink my strategy…*

Why am I even trying to concoct a strategy?!

"Just calling it as I see it."

"Maddie gave me 'the chat' last night. I'm well aware of where you stand on casual and I'm under strict instructions not to put any kind of moves on you unless I'm serious. She didn't however, cover any boundaries where flirting is concerned." I smirk.

Katie's laugh rings out, filling the space between us with the sweetest, joyful sound. "Oh god, she didn't?" She asks while wiping laughter tears from the corners of her eyes.

"She did."

"Poor you. Take heed, do not cross her. Maddie would make an excellent Domme…there's pure steel beneath that graceful exterior."

My turn to laugh and I do…a full belly laugh from the depths of my core. From my interactions with Maddie, Katie isn't wrong; the woman would be an amazing dominatrix…commanding, elegant…deadly.

"I need to ask you an awkward question," she doesn't look too uncomfortable as she picks at her breakfast on the other side of the island so I'm not too concerned.

"Your best mate gave me 'the talk', you screamed my name while getting off to thoughts of me and now your nipples are so erect, I can barely focus on my breakfast – you really think there's such a thing as an awkward question at this point?"

Katie blushes for the millionth time this morning and glances down at her breasts to confirm my assessment of her nipples – and then shrugs. A small little gesture that tells me she doesn't give a fuck and even goes as far as to pull her shoulders back, thrusting them out in my direction. Blatantly a 'deal with it' attitude. *These are my breasts and they ain't going nowhere.*

Good.

"What kind of Dom are you? Are your subs completely subservient or just in the bedroom? And would you object to not doing it while we're housemates? It might make me uncomfortable and I don't want any more dates with doorframes."

"I'm perfectly capable of keeping my dick in my pants, especially if it saves my doorframes," I smile wryly while she just rolls her eyes good-naturedly. "I'm also not a Dom. At least, not the way you're thinking. I don't keep subs, I don't do punishments, I just like to play in the bedroom. I'm good at what – and who – I do but I want to be the one in control while we do it."

"*We?*"

"Figure of speech and hypothetical. There's something truly profound and intimate about someone giving you complete control over them sexually and I wouldn't seek control if I couldn't deliver. Giving pleasure gives me pleasure. I just like a woman tied up while I'm doing it."

"Do you not like to be touched or have some other dark emotional issue that drives you to seek control?" Her tone is light but her words betray that's she genuinely asking if I'm fucked up like her ex.

"I can show you my psyche evaluation if you like?" I joke. "It's just a kink that I enjoy; no ulterior motives."

"So, you could do vanilla then? You don't have to be kinky to function or anything?"

"Asking for yourself?" I tease.

"Just trying to figure out the type of man I'm sharing a house with for the next few weeks." Her blush betrays her yet again. She's trying to work out if she can trust her infatuation with me and if I'm any good for her, all thoughts of the boss/employee relationship apparently forgotten.

My turn for a question, "Just how vanilla are you?"

Katie laughs that full-bodied laugh once more. "I'm so vanilla I make virgins look kinky."

"Do you miss it?"

"Yes," she answers almost immediately. "But I've just pulled myself out of the tangled web that was my relationship with David and I can still feel the creepy strands of icky-ness on my skin when I let my memories take hold. I got lost in his dark mind games until I became nothing more than a vessel for his own gratification. So, for now, vanilla is as good as it gets; cowgirl, missionary – as long as I'm not too pinned…yeah, that's about it. Any position where I can't see what's happening is a no go. The same goes for a position that takes away my autonomy. I don't necessarily want control over my bedmate but I have to have control over myself. Being comfortable enough to try and trust someone again is a big thing for me. It's something I don't suspect will come easily to me and that I'm going to have to work on."

That all sounds reasonable to me so I answer her question I dodged. "I don't need kink to function. I could do vanilla…for the right woman." I can't help myself; I stare shamelessly into her vibrant blue eyes and watch her rosy blush creeping across her cheekbones and spreading down her neck to her chest. Even without a bra, she has an amazing cleavage…a blushing cleavage that I want to kiss the soft undulations of.

Katie Morgan is my Kryptonite; I get the sinking feeling that she is the one girl I'd be tempted to have a non-kinky sex life with…to start with anyway.

Chapter Six

Katie

"Get dressed," Asher orders once we've both finished breakfast and he's loaded the dirty plates into the dishwasher.

"Why?" I have every intention of getting dressed, but I still wonder what he's planning.

"As you're feeling better, it's time for the grand tour. So, unless you want to ride a horse pantie-less and bra-less, get dressed. Assuming, of course, you can ride?" The cocky tone I'm starting to become familiar with is evident and amusing. I bite my bottom lip to stop the smirk his cocky attitude threatens to steal from me.

"I can ride. Have a little faith, you're insulting me here!" I mock outrage. Little does he know that I'm a pretty good rider...and little does he know that ninety-nine percent of the time I'm bra-less – I just prefer it that way, it feels nicer and less restrictive. Having my boobs jiggle around while on horseback isn't going to phase me...it might be a little distracting for him though, given the way his gaze frequently drops to my chest. Normally that would piss me off but something about Asher's perusal of my body has my blood fizzing in my veins.

I run upstairs and quickly dress in jeans and a shirt that I tie around my belly button, exposing a band of skin around my abdomen and lower back. After rolling the sleeves up to my elbows, I tie my hair up in a loose ponytail and finish my look with a quick swipe of light pink lip gloss. Practical with just a hint of sex appeal and with Asher's words about being bra-less and panty-less ringing in my head, I leave my room without either undergarment.

There's something freeing and exhilarating about going commando.

Asher is waiting for me by the back-porch door, "I'm impressed, I was expecting you to take at least twice as long to get ready."

"Does this look like a time-consuming look?" I arch a brow at him, daring him to dig himself deeper into the women-take-forever-to-get-ready pit. I'm a feminist at heart and I believe that it takes a person as long as it takes them to get ready. So, if I feel the need to spend an hour on hair and make-up for a special occasion then fuck it, I will. It's my body after all and I'm the one living in it.

"Hey, I have no idea what it takes to make yourself look as good as you do – I was merely impressed that you could look *that* appealing that quickly." And there's that smile of his again. You know, that one that melts panties…good thing I'm not wearing any.

"Your eye-fucking at breakfast would suggest I look appealing even when I've made zero effort and am sporting a serious case of bed head." The flirty little smile I flash him is almost unconsciously done…almost.

Driving him a little bit wild is my new favorite game.

His expression is unapologetic, dark, hungry and well, dangerous to my health.

"So, can you really ride, or you just sayin' that to save face? It's perfectly fine if you need to ride with me, Sunshine." *Oh, that wicked grin.*

"You're more than a little arrogant, you know that right?"

"You love it." True, I was starting to. His confidence and cockiness were infectious. Today is going to be a good day.

"I'm perfectly able to ride on my own, sorry to disappoint you. Guess you won't be having my body pressed against you as you hoped." My tone is light and flippant but my body has betrayed me slightly and we're standing closer than is strictly acceptable in polite company.

Still, that doesn't seem to be close enough for Asher who leans in so close to my ear that I can feel his hot breath on the sensitive skin of my neck, raising tiny goosebumps and sending shivers fluttering to my core. "Sunshine, you have no idea what I'm hoping for," he whispers in a low gravelly voice that screams sex and has heat pooling and throbbing between my legs.

Jesus. I can feel the ache in my clit already. I revise my previous estimation, today is going to be a *hard* day.

I wonder how long it will take before I soak through my jeans with the juices of my arousal.

I'm already feeling slick.

"No, but I know what you're getting – you're riding alone, cowboy."

This back and forth banter continues all the way down to the stables in the bright warmth of the morning sun and it's refreshing. Laced with sexual innuendo and chemistry for sure, but still light-hearted and fun.

"Well that decides it then," he announces as I follow him inside the large rustic, but well-maintained red timber barn.

"What does?" I pause as I spot the problem. "Ah, I guess it does." The stables are empty except for one gigantic horse. Hmm.

"Sorry boss, guests went out with Mike on the Southern Trail," a voice calls out as its owner approaches us.

"Katie this is Josh, my stable hand," Asher indicates with his chin at the slightly shorter and leaner guy that has just joined us. "Josh, this is Katie, our new administrator."

"Pleased to meet you," he says shaking my hand with a warm smile. "Brute is still good to go, boss," motioning to the black and white behemoth of a horse in the end stall.

"So, all the other horses are out?" I ask even though it's kinda obvious they are.

"All except Asher's boy there," Josh confirms.

"You're riding with me, Sunshine," whispers Asher from behind me, once again tickling my neck with his warm breath and warming my body with his proximity.

"On a giant named Brute?" I try to keep the alarm out of my voice but Brute is a big boy – figures really, given the size of Asher. His six-foot-something frame can hardly ride around on a pony. But this creature looks like an old English Shire Horse. Large, intimidating and literally out of my reach.

"He's ironically named. Brute is the biggest teddy bear there is. He's all size and softness…with a deceptive dose of speed for a big guy. Come on," Asher takes my hand and leads me to Brute's stall. The warmth from his work-roughened hand sizzles through my veins and I consciously try not to swoon. Like an actual damsel swooning over a cowboy. How am I going to survive a day pressed up against Asher Scott on the back of his mammoth horse? I try to focus on the horse in question instead.

59

I still remember the first time I came into contact with horses; it was later in my life than I'd have liked but their eyes blew me away. There are such depth and intelligence to them. They look at you like they can see through you to your soul and only if they find you worthy are you permitted to ride them. Looking at Brute now, I can see from his big doe eyes that he's a beautiful, gentle giant and as reassuring as that is…it's still not going to make my climb up to his saddle anymore ladylike.

Asher mounts Brute effortlessly while I'm still figuring out the logistics of getting myself up that high…please don't tell me I'm going to have to use the wooden steps they reserve for the kids who can't ride. That would be humiliating, which I guess is nothing new.

Asher's smooth-as-honey voice brings me back to the problem at hand where I realize, he's chuckling at me. "Thought you said you could ride, Sunshine?"

"I can. I've just never had to mount anything so big –" I stop mid-sentence when Asher roars with laughter at my accidental double entendre.

"I'm sure you haven't sweetheart." Is he actually wiping laughter tears from the corners of his sexy brown eyes?

"I meant I've never ridden a horse so large let alone figured out how to climb on the back of one with another body already in the saddle," I huff but there's very little conviction to it; Asher's laughter is the sweetest music and I want to hear much more it.

Asher leans down towards me, "lift your leg." I do and with one arm, he grabs hold of my left arm while the other hand snakes around the thigh of my raised left leg. My thighs have never felt as small as they do with Asher's paw of a hand wrapped around it. Then, as if I weighed nothing, he lifts me off the stable floor, giving me enough clearance to swing my right leg over Brute's formidable body.

We shuffle around for a moment to make sure we're both seated comfortably and evenly balanced and predictably, my chest ends up flush against Asher's solid back, my thighs encasing his sculpted ass and muscular thighs.

"Are you sure this isn't too much weight for Brute?" I ask to distract myself from the feeling of Asher's body against mine.

He snorts and I can practically hear his eyes rolling as he leads us out of the stables and into the bright sunlight of a spring mountain morning. Not a cloud in the sky to dare rain on our parade.

We spend the morning riding around Asher's land, talking and laughing like old friends. He's surprisingly easy to talk to when his smoldering eyes aren't pinning you to the spot and melting your synapses. Instead, that honor went to the picture-perfect alpine scenery. There were a couple of times where I zoned out of my conversation with Asher completely – I didn't think that was possible either – to stare off at the rolling green hills framed by jagged granite peaks rising up to dominate the blazing blue sky. A smattering of leftover snow still to melt at the highest peaks. Aspen glimmers in the distance through the midday sunshine haze and I wonder what Maddie is up to and if she had any luck on that work tip-off. Birds sing-song in a thick cluster of pine trees ahead of us at the northernmost border of the ranch; an elevated position that Asher brought us too so that I could take in the wonder of his property and land and well, the awe-inspiring vista in general.

"Are you listening to me City Girl? Or did I blow your mind

with what the world actually looks like away from all your strip malls?"

I nudge him playfully in the back, as I'm guilty as charged but not likely to admit it to him. I'm also not going to admit how solid and arousing his back felt beneath my hand. Like a solid statue – broad, marble hard and hot to the touch.

I'd been doing a good job, up to this point, of ignoring the way his body felt between my legs as we undulate in an almost sexual rhythm to Brute's long, capable strides.

Who am I kidding? I've not ignored it at all. The ache in my core is radiating through my body with hot, desperate tendrils igniting my skin at his every touch and movement. When Asher commands Brute to pick up the pace I'm forced to grip hold of his muscular body and feel the iron cords of those muscles tensing and rippling with his movements. I try not to gasp as my arousal begins to spiral out of control. My pussy throbs with white-hot need and there's an ache in my clit that is becoming impossible to ignore. I ache to have this man inside me, those strong muscles coiled to unleash himself on me as he takes my body and bends it to the will of the deliciously huge cock I saw him sporting at breakfast.

Yeah, I saw it.

And it made my mouth water and nipples tense with hopeful anticipation.

Think of me.

That's what he told me and it's like the command has taken hold thoroughly and I can't *not* think of him unless he commands that too. I want him to command me. In any way he wants.

Wait. What?

Since when do I want to give myself to yet another dominant male?

Asher rides us faster; Brute really can move when he's told to. The pleasant breeze whips past my face and loosens tendrils of my hair from my hair elastic. I'm forced to grip Asher tighter with both my hands and my thighs and I swear he's doing it on purpose. Anything to force my body closer to his…not that I'm complaining.

The medley of sensations rioting through me means the only thoughts I'm capable of are ones on autopilot. The scenery, the sunshine, the breeze in my hair, the feeling of Brutes steady movements, the sensation of Asher's powerful body rubbing against me…it's peaceful, it's bliss, it's fire, it's torture.

Without permission my right-hand snakes it's way upwards across the ridges and valleys of Asher's abs and I curse the feeling of his shirt preventing me from feeling the silken heat of his skin against mine. If that wasn't embarrassing enough, my left-hand drifts downwards, caressing his side and coming to rest on the steel of his thick thigh. The punishing speed of Brute's gallop has me resting my forehead against Asher's back to avoid the slap of the fresh air blowing past us. Feeling his hot body through nearly every inch of my own and the exhilaration of galloping on horseback has me gasping, my pulse pounding.

A tiny voice fights to bring me back to the here and now, futilely shouting that I'm caressing my boss in an all too intimate way but I can't help it. Something about him draws me in. He's magnetic and I'm caught in the pull of him. His gravity overpowers my better senses.

Asher confidently holds the reins in one hand while the other reaches down and engulfs my hand on his thigh. For a heart-stopping moment I realize I've careened so far past the line of what's appropriate, I can't even see it anymore; Asher is going to remove my hand and fire me on the spot.

And I'd deserve it. What has possessed me? I know the answer but it's still no excuse. I know that I'm trying to work on putting my past well and truly behind me but this desperation for a man I barely know is taking that desire to the extreme. I'm surprised I have this level of arousal for him *and* the confidence to roam his body with my hands…without his permission.

What have I done?

I brace myself for the inevitable let down but instead, Asher moves my hand up his thigh and places it on the bulging, burning heat of his massive erection.

My god.

He's huge.

Thick, hot, rock hard and all for me…the thought has me rubbing his epic-length through the thick denim of his jeans, his clothing inhibiting my fingers from curling around the entirety of his impressive girth the way I want to. Asher laces his fingers with mine and lets out a low groan that hotwires its way to my dripping core. He presses his back into my chest, my tight nipples digging into him, the new angle exposing more of his glorious cock. My hand is eager to feel the hard satin of his skin there but it's not exactly possible while mounted on Brute.

Asher slows him to a stop behind a copse of trees, concealing us from view and he leans back and to the side, wrapping one strong arm around my waist while the other grips my thigh like a vice. Before I can figure out what's happening, he's lifted me from the saddle behind him and pulled me around to straddle his lap, the ridge of his throbbing erection pressing enticingly against my aching clit. I gush liquid desire as he snakes his hand into my hair and wraps my ponytail around his hand to hold my head mere inches from his. I can feel his hot breath tickling my lips. Locked in place like this, with his other arm still banded around my waist like a steel cable, his eyes bore into mine. Pure molten heat blazing. My lips part on a gasp and he takes the opportunity to steal a kiss from my over-primed body. His lips are velvet-soft but unyielding as he demands access to dance his tongue with mine. I'm hardly likely to decline his demands – I'm sexual mush in his hands.

The intensity of the kiss climbs higher and higher; I drink him in and meet his probing tongue thrust for thrust, nipping and sucking and just generally losing my mind to the sensations he's wracking my body with. His hands begin to roam my body, tickling up my sides until they come to rest on my breasts, his thumbs circling and pinching the puckered peaks of my nipples. I throw my head back gasping and moaning and arching into his touch and rolling my hips to grind myself onto his diamond-hard dick. I need the friction so badly. I start a rhythm of bucking and grinding as he groans, his nimble fingers unbuttoning my blouse until my breasts spill free, the crisp breeze further hardening my nipples into painful peaks throbbing with my need for him.

"No bra?" he grunts in approval. All I can do is nod my head as he brings the wet warmth of his mouth to clamp over my breast, sucking the nipple between his teeth, eliciting a scream of pure pleasure from me.

"More. Please…more," I beg. He clamps his teeth down harder on my tender point and I feel the pleasure shoot straight to my core where I'm grinding frantically against him, needing the friction to relieve the burning ache building in my poor desperate clit.

Asher turns his attention to my other breast, sucking and biting me while I squirm and moan like a wild animal. I vaguely register that Asher is holding me up in his lap, acting as a shock absorber between me and poor Brute; I'm surprised I've not startled him with the noises I'm making.

I run my fingers through Asher's thick hair and pull his mouth from my full, heaving breasts, tipping his head back to crash my lips against his, claiming him in another frenzied kiss. I used one arm around his neck to hold myself to him and keep my mouth anchored to his. The other takes his hand and brings it to the front of my jeans, his fingers tickling the exposed skin of my abdomen as we go. With his fingers entwined with mine, I pop the button on my jeans and unzip them enough for Asher to slide his fingers down over my mound and into the slick folds of my pussy. His thick fingers feel so good probing my wetness until they find the tight cluster of nerve endings that shoot fireworks across my skin. I shudder into his delicious touch and roll my hips seeking more of him.

"No panties?" he murmurs against my lips. "Commando somethin' you normally do, Sunshine?"

Between gasps of pleasure, he continues to stroke my clit in gentle circles, I find the will power to form words. "Bra, yes. That's normal for me as I hate wearing those contraptions. Panties? No. That's all for you," I moan as the first spasms of my orgasm sneak up on me.

I don't normally come from just clitoral stimulation alone; my pussy likes something to clamp down on when I climax. Asher certainly has magic fingers…fingers I want inside me when my orgasm goes off completely. I pull myself up out of his lap to give his fingers space to explore where I want them.

Using my free hand, I try to guide his fingers to sink through my folds and into my sopping slit. "Finger fuck me while I come," I half beg, half demand.

Asher obliges and thrusts two thick digits knuckle deep into me, driving them in roughly over and over as I shatter around him, my cunt quivering around those magic fingers. I cry out as he wrings every last dripping ounce of my climax from me.

"Fuck. You're so gorgeous when you come, Katie." He sounds almost as breathless as me as he presses his lush, full lips to mine in a flurry of soft kisses.

"More," I gasp. It's the only word I can articulate but that orgasm wasn't enough. I want him balls deep in my pussy and I'm impatient when I'm horny.

Holding me tightly in his lap, he spurs Brute on towards the stables.

In no time we come to an abrupt stop at the stable entrance. My shirt is still open, my rosebud nipples and ample breasts on display and my jeans undone. Mercifully Josh is nowhere to be seen, the stables are still empty and in an instant Asher has dismounted, lowering me gently to my unstable feet, securing Brute in his stall before rounding on me and backing me into another empty stall – one that has already been mucked out and is full of fresh hay.

I can't help but giggle at the notion of literally going for a roll in the hay. But I stop short when I see the dark, hungry and predatory look in Asher's eyes penetrating the very depths of me. This man, this glorious specimen of all things exquisitely male, wants me, desires me…and is going to take me. That notion is an aphrodisiac to my body that is already saturated with an unquenchable, burning need to have him take me.

I shudder under his heated gaze, discarding my shirt and shimmying out of my jeans as he closes the stall door behind him.

A moment of hesitation hits me and it must flicker across my face, rearranging my expression. Not because he's my boss and this is unwise or because of the suddenness of my desire for him – there's no going back from either of those now – but because I'm standing before him completely naked and exposed while he is still fully clothed. There's an exchange of power here that is pushing the boundary of what I'm comfortable with. A level of vulnerability I didn't think I could be capable of anymore.

Asher must sense this; immediately his expression softens. The heat is still there, fuelling his very obvious desire for me but something in his demeanor changes in a soothing response to my sudden apprehension. I dare to believe that he truly understands me and hope swells in my chest, constricting my windpipe around a sob of relief.

In seconds Asher sheds his clothes and stands before me gloriously naked; every spectacularly chiseled inch of him on display for my viewing pleasure. He's leveled the playing field, making himself as exposed as me. I wouldn't go so far as to say he's now as vulnerable as I am, as the man has boundless confidence – and rightly so given the body he's rocking – and no one as self-assured in their own skin as Asher is could ever be considered vulnerable.

Surely?

If Asher does have any vulnerabilities, they aren't the obvious kind – they're the type you have to dig deep for and may still never unearth unless he reveals them to you. I wish I was that self-possessed. But one step at a time. For now, I'll settle for having all-consuming sex with a man guaranteed to occupy every part of me, leaving nothing left to dwell on my baggage.

I tear my gaze from his to peruse the masculine beauty of his body; the guy doesn't have an ounce of body fat. He's all delicious hard ridges, bulging and flexing with his heavy breathing. Sexy sinew and smooth tan skin sheathing a perfect body of steel muscle. He's not bodybuilder bulky, nor is he the lean muscular type. He has the large, dominating body of a man who's worked hard labor every day of his life to get the sex-god physique he's displaying for me. There's nothing gym induced or artificial about him. Just raw, primal, barely contained strength. And now that I can see *all* of him, his cock is a thing of beauty. Bigger than I anticipated – long, thick, proud and ramrod straight pointing all the way up to his belly button. It's the dick that male porn stars dream of. I'm determined to fit all of him inside me.

Fixing me with his penetrating stare, his luscious lips part. "If you want this to stop, tell me now, Sunshine. There's no stopping once I lay my hands on your perfect curves." The low rumble of his voice tells me how hot he is for me and ensures I'm not going anywhere but on his cock.

My mouth is parched from desire and it takes several moments for my sex addled brain to catch up to the fact that he asked me a question and is waiting with bated breath for the answer. All I can do is shake my head to convey that there's no way in hell I want this to stop.

That small movement is all it takes for Asher Scott to unleash the full devastating force of his sexual prowess upon my needy, overwhelmed and frankly desperate body.

He closes the distance between us in two long strides,

wrapping me in the metal grip of his powerful arms; his full lips crashing against mine as one hand snakes downwards to grab a handful of my ass while the other wraps around my neck. Both holding me firmly in place – lips to lips and hips to hips.

The silken heat of his body burns through mine, scorching every nerve ending with liquid fire and a bone-deep need for him. The power of the connection I feel for him is terrifying and exhilarating in equal measure. I don't know this man in the superficial way you get to know someone on a first date with the usual trivia-style questions about their life, family, friends, etc. But my *body* knows Asher Scott. Something in him calls to me on a deeper level and I'm happy to park my brain and enjoy the ride my other senses are insisting on. You couldn't pay me enough to be anywhere else in the world, other than where I am right now; naked in Asher's arms, being devoured by his lips and the talented dance of his tongue, and thoroughly prodded in my stomach by the impressive feat that is his steel hard cock.

All of these sensations drive me into a hungry frenzy. I don't feel like I can get enough of him inside me; I cling to his shoulders to pull myself closer to him, melding our tongues together and drinking him in as deeply into my mouth as I can and moaning in pure bliss. He pulls my head back by my hair so that he can deepen the kiss and expose my neck to the soft yet firm touch of his lips and the sharpness of his teeth as he grazes them down my neck, causing my entire body to shudder at his touch. He bites me firmly on the super sensitive and underused spot between my shoulder and neck, softening the sting with the warm lapping of his tongue. I cry out in utter pleasure; how does this man know my body so well? It's like he knows every intimately secret spot on my body capable of making me scream...or cum in my pants...if I were wearing any.

Asher's breathing is as ragged as mine, his voice making these low, sexy-as-hell groans and grunts and I can't help it, I hook my leg around his – as best I can; I am short and he is massive after all – and arch back to roll my hips into him, his solid cock providing some sweet friction for my needy clit. My breasts no longer press against the heat of his body, allowing my nipples to peak further in the cool air of the barn. The sensation only heightens the longing ache in my clit and I can feel the wetness dripping from my slit.

Arousal is a strange thing for a woman. Most of the time you live your life without even noticing your vagina – like most bodily functions, they just happen without you even feeling them. The vagina is an empty chamber that you don't notice, don't even realize is empty...until something turns you on. As soon as your body enters that state of arousal, you feel it – that emptiness. It's part of what arouses you more; this strange aching pull to be filled. If you clench those intimate muscles it only heightens how empty you are and how desperately you need something – anything – to fill you and make the empty feeling go away. The higher your arousal climbs, the needier your cunt becomes. It's all-consuming, obliterating all rational thought.

Just fill me up.

That's all your body is calling out for, sweet relief and the fullness of a thick, pulsing cock.

Intuitively sensing what I need, Asher places both hands on my ass and lifts me effortlessly up so that I can wrap my legs around him, increasing the pressure of his cock pressed against my soaking slit, and walks over to a pile of hay and sits so that I am straddling his lap but still held up out of reach of his delicious cock by those muscular arms of his. I place my hands on either side of his face, looking down into the swirling depths of his eyes and placing a softer but no less desperate kiss to his sensual lips. His sexy voice groans my name as he lines up his dick with the sopping wetness of my opening. I've never been this soaked in my own juices before.

"There's no time for foreplay this time Katie. Only the hard fucking I *need* to give you…but, um, I don't have a condom," he looks pained at the realization but my mind has already gone there and made the decision.

"I'm on the pill and I'm clean." I was tested after my crappy one-night 'getting-over-David' stand.

"Me too. I've never gone without a condom."

"Until now…I'm going to be your first," and with that, he slides his huge thickness past the wet folds of my pussy lips and breaches my entrance. The feel of his hot skin on mine, spreading me is beyond bliss. My body goes liquid and arches for more of him. He feeds a third of his hard length inside me and I shriek at the fucking amazing sensation of his cock stretching me and filling me. My cunt quivers around him and my whole body shakes with the need to be impaled by the rest of him.

He's giving me a moment to adjust to the sheer size of him but I don't need it – all I need is him…all of him.

"Fucking fuck me already," I beg. "I want you to fill me up." I barely finish the words before Asher grips my hips and pulls me so that I slide down his glorious length to meet his powerful thrust. I scream again, nearly coming on the spot.

He's in me. All of him. His thick, fat cock is splitting me in half and nothing has ever felt so fucking good. Right here and now, Asher becomes my drug of choice. I don't just want that gigantic cock impaling me...I *need* it. I never want it to stop.

"Katie," he breathes against my cheek, "are you okay?" I see a flash of concern in his eyes. He thinks I screamed in pain, not the epic pleasure his pulsing cock triggers in me.

I clench around his hard shaft and begin rocking my hips. "Never better," I gasp against his lips.

"Katie," he says softly, "this is all you, baby. Take me how you want me."

And just like that, he gives me control. Again, he knows exactly what to say and do to put me at ease. Every touch, every kiss, every move he makes he considers me and what I need. I've never had that before and it tugs at something deep and intense in my chest, leaving me breathless.

Asher moves his hands gently across my body, trailing his fingers delicately, as I set a gentle rhythm rocking my hips back and forth, grinding against him before rising up the length of his steel shaft and thrusting back down, taking him to the hilt. He slides effortlessly in and out of my soaked, clenching core. He feels sublime. He doesn't hold me in place or try to set the pace; he follows my movements, my rhythm, all the while his hands worship my body with feather light caresses. His lips trail down my neck, my collarbone, my chest, settling between my breasts. Instinctively I arch backward, presenting myself to him and tilting my hips to take him deeper still. He trails kisses from one breast to the other before settling his mouth over my aching nipple and biting – the sharp sting of his teeth just the right side of pain so as to send a bolt of white-hot heat to my throbbing clit.

"Asher. Oh god. *Fuck*." I groan, unable to form a coherent

sentence. Can you blame me though, with a man as glorious as Asher Scott between my thighs, filling me to my very limit? Pushing me to the end of my sanity and driving my body to accept pleasure I never thought I'd be capable of.

My sex life always used to be vibrant and exciting, prior to David, but nothing has ever felt as good as riding Asher. Our coupling is frenzied and desperate but somehow passionate and reverent; worshipping each other's bodies – I marvel at the satin-smooth feel of his skin stretched over the iron core of his biceps as I cling onto him for dear life, my thrusts gaining momentum as I drive us closer to the obliterating abyss of climax.

The sounds of sex fill the air – gasps, groans, panting each other's names, the gushing sounds of my sex slapping down onto his – the symphony of our fuck drives me wild. I lean back, balancing one hand on his thick, muscular thigh while the other tugs and teases his balls. The reward is two-fold; the look of pleasure on his face as his climax builds spurs me to take him harder, faster, deeper but this leaned back position opens me up to the sheer scale of his hulk-worthy cock and I feel him reaching places within me that no man has ever been before, nor I suspect, will ever be again.

This is the fuck that ruins me for all others. I can feel it – *literally* – in every part of me. Every cell of my body is alive with the feeling of Asher's body on me and within me.

I can feel my climax beginning to build, coiling my muscles tight with the desperate need to unleash and explode. Electricity crackles through my veins as my body climbs higher and higher towards the peak of pleasure. A clenching need drives me on as I thrust and grind myself along the length of Asher's mammoth cock, his eyes glued to the juncture where his thick meat sinks into my slick, soft flesh.

"That's so fucking hot," he grits out between clenched teeth, his whole body taut, a sheen of sweat on those beautiful muscles beneath my spread thighs, as he fights to control his climax.

I want him to let go. I want his cum so deep inside me my pussy will be coated and dripping for hours.

"I want to feel you come," I moan, practically begging him to fill me.

"Not before you," his deep gravelly voice growls. And then his thumb is on my clit, rubbing the glistening nub in tight circles as his thick cock massages my g-spot with every gyration of my hips.

Once...twice..."Oh. My. Fuuuuck," I scream, my body exploding in the hottest orgasm I've ever had, obliterating all rational thought and the ability to speak sentences. My coiled muscles snap, radiating white-hot heat from deep in my clenching core, vibrating through every fiber of my body like an incendiary device. I'm momentarily blinded by the brightness of my pleasure as my body continues to quake, "Yes. Oh God yes. More...more."

And more is what I get. With a guttural roar, he floods my cunt with his hot seed. His cock jerks with every spurt that empties into my spasming core, milking him desperately and sending mind-blowing aftershocks rocking through me.

"Fucking hell, Katie. Just, wow." He gasps, looking as blindsided by the intensity of our fuck as I feel. Our juices mingle together and seep out of me despite still being stuffed full of Asher's dick. Our breathing ragged as we both float back to earth. He pulls me down to him where he kisses me sumptuously and thoroughly, taking the last of my breath away.

Chapter Seven

Asher

Holy. Fuckin'. Shit.

I'm still trying to scramble the remnants of my brain together to form somethin' resembling coherent thought. But currently, it's as empty as my balls. I don't think I've ever blown a load so big but Katie's sweet cunt is pure magic and milked me drier than the damned Sahara.

Watching her work us both to explosive orgasms was the sexiest thing my eyes ever beheld. I didn't go back on my word; it was all her. Katie needed to know that she could have sexual control, that I wasn't going to take it away from her like her fuckin' ex. And she mastered my body like no woman before her. I'm not used to giving up my power and control, to submitting in the bedroom, but damn if I won't do that again.

I get the sense that she wants her body to be mastered but we will work up to that and in the meantime, giving up control to her is no hardship if she makes me come like that. Watching her take her pleasure from my body was equally arousing. Knowing that my cock can satisfy her without me being able to work her with it as fully as I normally would, has my blood pumping south again. The sounds she made are going to fuel my erotic dreams for the next decade, they were so fuckin' hot. So hot, I'm pretty sure Josh came into the stables but wasn't in much of a rush to leave. He wouldn't have seen anything from outside of our stall but the soundtrack of our sex was erotic and loud enough for all to hear.

Thankfully no one was around when we left the stables – I wouldn't be embarrassed but I have a feelin' that Katie's not one for an audience. On the walk back to my ranch house, I marvel at the feelin' of Katie's soft hand in mine and how natural it feels to have the warmth of her small frame next to me.

Maddie's words have been ringing in my head since our conversation yesterday...*was it only yesterday*? I've thought about nothing other than if I'm sure enough to be pursuing Katie this way and the truth is, I am. I imagine that when Maddie told me to think very carefully, she probably thought it would take me a lot longer than a day but I've always trusted my gut instinct and that's not gonna change now. I've always been a quick and accurate judge of character and even if my conclusions of Katie are quicker than normal, that in itself tells me that my instincts for this woman are right. We fit.

It's remarkable. It's fast. But it's true.

Her delicate fingers laced with mine give me hope that she feels a fraction of the same for me. She didn't bolt out the stable door the moment she came down from her orgasmic high, clothes in hand, half-dressed and desperate to flee her fling...I wouldn't have let her even if she had tried mind you.

No, everything with Katie feels natural, the only point of concern for me is Carly. And specifically, that Katie saw me with her yesterday and the last thing I want is for Katie to view me as some sort of cavalier man-whore. I've had my fair share of sex and I won't apologize for it but there were never any expectations or emotions involved and that was always established at the onset so everyone knew where they stood. So, even though my arrangement with Carly means nothing, I worry that Katie will be wondering how I can go from one woman to the other. The timing isn't ideal and as a rule, I'm not one for regrets, but I'm starting to wish I'd passed on my romp with Carly yesterday.

There's really no comparison between a woman who's an occasional sweet distraction, but who I have no romantic feelings towards and the goddess who just took me into her and made me hers. Feelings are definitely in play now and I like the way it…well…feels.

I'm not a callous man; I'm aware that while I've stuck to the no emotion rule with Carly, her heart has started to blur the lines for her and I'm going to have to address that and in an ideal world I'd have done that before starting anything with Katie. But Katie has hurtled into my life like a category five hurricane and there's very little you can do to withstand the onslaught of power like that. And I don't want to; I'm more than happy to be blown away by the force of Katie.

But Carly is a good woman and I don't want to – didn't set out to – hurt her in any way. She's a total native; born and bred here and never left. Whether she's too nervous to leave or realizes the beauty of where she lives is far superior to other towns out there, either way, the local men have grown up with her and don't view her seriously or sexually. She was an awkward teen, a late bloomer and combined with her bright ginger hair and lack of feminine curves, she didn't get much male attention.

My family moved away for a long while before my late

parents and I decided to buy the ranch and move back. By that time, Carly was all woman. It's like her body compensated for all the years she went without boobs and a waist – she has one of the wickedest bodies around but guys still see her as the gangly teen, not the sensuous woman she grew into. The only attention she gets is from vacationers, which doesn't help her on the relationship front, or guys who move to town and in recent years they've tended to be coupled up family men. Carly frequents Rock Hard and that's where we decided upon our arrangement; instead of her having no option but to sleep her way through the tourists, she got to have the regular sex she enjoyed with the same guy and I got the same benefit. But where that was enough for me, Carly has always been a deeply caring person and wants more...I should've spotted that.

A gentle squeeze of my hand brings me back to the here and now.

"Are you okay? You zoned out there for a moment," Katie's gentle voice is a balm for the guilt I insist on carrying around.

"More than okay," I say and bend down to kiss her full lips that I've noticed sit in a slight natural pout – nothing over the top, just beautiful and plump and begging to be bitten.

I suck on her bottom lip gently, pulling it between my teeth and biting down just enough to tease the sweetest gasp from her. The sound stirs my cock to life again and in no time at all, I've swept her through the back door and up the stairs to my room.

It was one of those conscious/unconscious moments – the sort where I have full control of what I want but I want it so badly that my body does everything necessary to facilitate that desire on autopilot. So, before I'm fully aware of how we got here, we're standing in front of the door to my suite.

I pause, knowing the significance of bringing Katie here instead of downstairs to my sex room (not that she'd readily go there after yesterday anyway, but there are other rooms downstairs at my disposal).

I chose my room for a reason.

"Another first," I smile tentatively, suddenly nervous but she returns it, her bright eyes questioning. "I've never brought a woman to this room. It's my sanctuary. I've never cared enough to share it with someone," I elaborate.

Her answering smile is dazzling. "Are you saying you care?"

I nod, not wanting to say the words out loud. Fearful that it's too big, too much, too soon. By some miracle, despite everything she's been through, the memories and fears that she must still be living with, Katie seems to trust me to some extent. I'm not going to give her any reason to doubt that or herself, especially by getting all romantically intense before she's ready. "Enough to ensure we have a shower…we stink of horse," I tease.

She giggles the sweetest sound, "Yeah, we're pretty potent."

"Katie," I say, going all serious for a moment, "I've never had sex in this room so there are no toys or restraints or anything remotely kinky in here. I'm not sure if that's something you needed or wanted to know but I don't completely know the things that will set off your worries or anxieties just yet. And I didn't want you looking over your shoulder wondering if I'm about to pull out handcuffs or something. No toys. Just you, me and a whole lot of vanilla."

Her smile beams up at me, cracking my chest open a little further.

"Thank you," she whispers, rising on her tiptoes to brush her lips against mine in a delicate flutter of a kiss, which sets my pulse blazing and creates a very obvious tent situation in my jeans.

She's mine.

I need her now.

Sweeping her up into my arms, I hold her tightly to me while I walk us over the threshold, across my room to the bathroom and straight into my spacious walk-in shower. In what feels like mere seconds I've stripped us both bare and gaze adoringly at her petite, sexy-as-fuck naked body. Her curves could drive a priest wild. I literally don't know how I'm restraining myself from just plunging straight back into the welcoming warmth of her wet pussy.

Somehow, I focus long enough to wash both our bodies, enjoying the feel of her silken skin beneath my fingers. She feels like perfection. Her skin flushed from the hot water sluicing down her body and the caress of my hands. She's burning up against my skin and letting out the sexiest little gasps. I'm so fucking hard for her it hurts. The ache in my balls actually fucking hurts despite shooting my cum into the depths of her cunt less than an hour ago. This time though, I'm determined to take my time, to draw out the pleasure for both of us.

I trace my lips along her jawline and down the hollow of her neck, further south so I can fill my mouth with the ample flesh of her breasts; flicking my tongue across her pebbled nipples, sucking them into even harder peaks. Her moans of ecstasy swirl around me like the steam from the shower, doing nothing to soothe my painful erection.

Kneeling in front of her, I pepper kisses down her abdomen, heading for the sweet spot I'm aching to taste. Katie braces one arm against the tile wall and the other clings to my wet hair in a death grip as my tongue makes the lightest contact with her clit.

"Yes," she gasps, throwing her head back in pleasure.

The scent of her arousal is intoxicating, driving me wild with the need to taste her essence. I take one last glance upwards to where the water runs in rivulets around the fleshy globes of her bouncing breasts before hooking a leg over my shoulder to open her pussy wide for me, and delve into her sensual depths, running my tongue from her glistening slit to her clit and back again, spreading her juices around her swollen lips before plunging my tongue inside her tight pussy.

"Oh my god," she shivers against my face as I continue to suck, lick and probe.

Katie tastes like a woman; a real woman and none of that romantic 'tastes like strawberries' bullshit. Honestly, who has a cunt that tastes like a strawberry? The tang and musk of Katie's arousal is pure feminine lust; all raw and carnal and one hundred percent compatible with my taste buds. I could drink her for days but before long I feel her legs clenching and her body shivering harder as she grinds her sweet cunt against my face. My woman is close.

"Come on my face," I all but growl at her but it's not a demand, I'm not ordering her like a dominant might do if he's controlling the climax; Katie is going to explode with pleasure regardless, I just want to be eating her delectable pussy when she does.

"Ash...*Fuck!*" She cries as her cunt gushes onto my waiting mouth and her wet, slippery body writhes in the grip of my arms.

I love how she called me 'Ash'. Not many people abbreviate my name, not sure why, but on her lips, it sounds perfect. So perfect, she deserves another orgasm.

Before she has a chance to come down from the clouds of her climax, I sink two fingers into her still spasming pussy as deep as I can and curl them until I can feel the little rough nub of her g-spot. Her body jerks instantly and I know that she's right back on the edge once more. I seal my mouth around her beautifully erect little clit and suck hard in time with my fingers massaging her internal sweet spot. She goes off again, bucking and grinding while her screams of ecstasy ring out.

Music to my ears.

If I could hear this woman screaming my name every day as I wring climax after climax from her tight little body, I'd live a happy man.

"I need you to fuck me, Ash...fuck me hard."

I don't need telling twice. I stand, lifting her so she can wrap her legs around my waist as I go, and gently press her to the cool tiled wall. She seems okay with this position but I'm careful not to crush her and make her feel trapped.

The tip of my pulsing cock lines itself up perfectly with her juicy opening and I ease her down slowly but firmly onto my throbbing rod, sinking myself completely into the paradise that is her hot cunt.

She feels amazing wrapped around me and if the blissed-out expression on her face is any indication; she feels the same.

It's not long before our steady, passionate rhythm morphs into a purely primal, animalistic coupling.

It's loud.

It's frantic.

It's fucking everything.

Katie bucks like a wild thing around my waist and I'm so close to blowing my load but I'm becoming concerned about my grip and balance in the slipperiness of my shower. The last thing I want to do is slip us over and give her *another* head injury to contend with. So, I slide out of her – her pussy fighting it every inch of the way as it grips and clenches and tries to hold me in place. She moans her protest but I can assure her, I hate the separation as much as she does.

I stand her up gently so that she doesn't slip over and begin to slowly turn her around to face the wall, keeping eye contact with her the whole time so that I can see if this position is pushing past her limits. All the while remembering her comment this morning; 'so vanilla I make virgins kinky'. This isn't a particularly kinky position but she won't be able to see everything I'm doing; that might be too much for her but I'm hoping not.

So far, she seems relaxed but multiple orgasms will do that to a woman. She relaxes into my arms as I stroke my fingers from her hips, up her sides and down her arms to her delicate hands, which I place on the tile in front of her face so that she can brace herself against what's to *come...*

Gently I push on her back to encourage her to lean forwards. This is the point where we'll lose the eye contact we've been maintaining. I look at her questioningly, giving her the chance to shut this down if it's too much for her. She takes a small, unsteady breath and gives a little nod to continue. I smile and kiss her tenderly before grabbing hold of her hips once more and arching them towards me as I use my foot to knock her legs into a wider stance.

Katie is now perfectly positioned for me to take her. She's displayed gloriously and glistening and I can't help but groan at the stunning sight of her. I line myself up and thrust into her waiting flesh roughly and fully.

"*FUCK*," she screams.

"Too much?" I'm not even trying to be cocky, I lost control of my restraint for a moment and I'm not a small man by any means. But that's what Katie does to me; makes me lose my carefully constructed control.

"Not even a little bit. More. I want more. Fuck me, Ash. Show me how bad you want me."

Christ, this woman is going to kill me. I may like to tie my women down but I sure as hell love to hear them talk dirty.

I pull out a little before slamming back deeply to the hilt, my balls slapping against her clit.

"YES…just like that…fuck…you're so deep."

"How deep you want it, baby?"

"So fucking deep I can't breathe. Fuck me the hardest you've ever fucked. Now. I *need* it."

And I do. I fuck her so goddam hard it's brutal. But she takes it, all of it, meeting me thrust for thrust, shouting my name in pleasure. I love the loudness, how unrestrained she is; like she trusts me enough to lose her inhibitions and unleash herself with me. This is truly the hottest sex I've ever had.

I fight the roiling urge in my balls to come, not ready for this to be over with yet. I almost lose it though when Katie's body quakes around me and falls apart in another shattering orgasm.

She's so responsive, I love it.

Wrapping my arms around her body, I pull her upright and step us closer to the wall until her breasts are pressed against the coolness of the tile. She yelps and jumps a little as the cold bites her nipples but I've no doubt the contrast between the wall and my hot body pressed against her back is a pleasurable sensation.

This is one of the many things I enjoy about having a long cock as well as a girthy one – I can change positions without slipping out of her pussy. Credit where it's due though, her greedy little cunt helps out by keeping me caught in its death vice; my cock is going nowhere without this pussy's permission.

"No more," she gasps.

"You really want to stop?" She shudders as I trace my hands up her sensitive sides.

"I…can't…" she trails off as I kiss her neck behind her ear, nibbling on her supple skin.

"Can't what baby?" I murmur in her ear.

"Orgasm. I can't come again."

"Says who?"

"I've never come more than once," she whispers.

"You've never had a man who knew what he was doin'. I do. You can take more. I've got you." She sighs, relaxing into my embrace. "But you can stop *this* anytime you want"

"Stop wh – "

Swiftly I lift her arms above her head and hold both her hands in one of mine. My other arm hooks under her thigh and lifts her leg off the floor so that she's once again open for me and I start thrusting again, slowly at first.

"Ash…Don't stop," her gasp comes out a plea and I'm happy to oblige. This position has her pinned by my will more than any other so far and I'm pleased that she's in the moment with me, taking the pleasure I want to give her.

I pick up the pace, very aware of my growing need to find release and even though it hurts to hold it back, I'm determined to because I'm also aware of how this position has my cock head constantly rubbing along the front wall of her pussy…right across her g-spot…

"ASH…FUCK…AGH."

Her body sags against my chest as her climax pulses around my cock, she can barely stand on her own two feet.

I switch the water off, pick her exhausted body up and carry her to my bed, not caring that we are soaking wet. The room and our bodies are hot enough to ensure we won't get chilled.

"Did you come?" she asks sleepily and with lust glazed eyes.

"You couldn't tell?" I tease.

"I was a little pre-occupied with all of my many orgasms. I'm so wet I can't tell if it's all from me or you too."

"It's all you baby, I've not come yet."

"Fuck, you must have blue balls by now!"

I can't help the surprised laugh that breaks free at her exclamation – she's dead-on; if the color of my balls matches the ache then they are definitely blue. "It's been pretty *hard* but I'm certain you can help ease the discomfort." I lay her down on my bed and she instantly spreads her legs wide for me, displaying her glistening folds and that tight little core that's all mine for the fucking.

Blushing, swollen, wet labia greet the head of my straining dick as I slide home deep into her hot velvet depths.

"So good. So deep," she murmurs and bites down on her plump lower lip as I rock into her.

"You like it, baby? You like how I fuck you?"

"I'm so full…I love it. You're so fucking huge, I could cum just imagining how hot it looks to see your fat cock spreading me wide. Ah, oh god. Yes…YES. Right. There."

I know exactly what she means; the sight of my dick coated in her juices every time I withdraw before thrusting back into her, her cunt stretched to its limits is the hottest fucking thing

I've ever seen.

She's my dirty, sexy fantasy.

On instinct she raises her hands above her head, crossing her wrists in the perfect position for me to restrain her. I can't help it, she's been fine with everything else we've done, so I grab them firmly in one hand while my other hand grips her hip. My body is pinning her down as I fuck her relentlessly.

Katie can't move. She gasps and her eyes fly open and lock with mine. For a millisecond I panic –

"I'm gonna cum so hard," she gasps and then screams so fucking loud that Josh should be able to hear her from the stables. Her body convulses in the throes of the longest, fiercest climax I've ever seen, her body slicked with sweat and shaking in my arms as she screams my name over and over.

I fuck her hard through the endless waves of her orgasm, driven on by the fire in the base of my cock and the goddess of a woman falling apart with bliss in my arms. Knowing that I'm the cause of the pleasure splintering her body sends me soaring over the edge into the most powerful climax of my life. White-hot lightning shoots up my spine while my balls erupt and my seed rips through my cock and coats Katie deep inside.

"Holy fucking shit," I groan, rolling onto my back and taking Katie with me so that she's on top and flopped across my chest listening to my rapid heartbeat and ragged breathing. We lay this way until Katie's soft, even breathing tells me she's fallen asleep. In this moment, there's nowhere in the world I'd rather be.

Chapter Eight

Katie

A gentle burst of air fluttering across my face rouses me from my incredibly comfortable napping spot.

Cracking my eyes open I realise that I've been sleeping on Asher's seriously sculpted chest while he has propped himself up and is reading a book with one hand while the other idly strokes delicate patterns over my back, leaving a blazing trail in their wake, the puff of air coming from the turning of pages. It feels sweetly domestic and it pulls at a tender spot behind my chest.

My body feels languid and comfortable.

I feel relaxed.

I feel content.

I feel...*full...still*?

Huh?

That's not a sensation I'm used to...most flaccid cocks slip out. I can't help but wriggle slightly to establish that I am indeed feeling what I thought I was feeling. Asher's cock is still inside me.

"How are you long enough to still be in me soft?"

"I feel like you've sort of answered your own question there,

Sunshine," he smirks. "I'm long, so even when I'm soft I don't necessarily slip out. Plus, your pussy is pretty tight so it's getting help to stay put. And as for the how, good genetics I guess?"

"Superhuman genetics more like."

"Are you saying that having a big dick is a superpower?"

"As far as yours is concerned it is," I giggle, causing my pussy to clench, which leads to Ash's cock being less soft. If I'm not careful, we'll spend all night fucking, which ordinarily would be amazing but I'm aware we skipped lunch and I'm getting hungry.

Right on cue, my stomach growls.

"Looks like we've worked up your appetite. Shall we go out for dinner?" He asks hopefully.

My heartbeat stutters for a moment and I try not to get my hopes up, but I can't help it…is he asking me on a date? Could this more than just one-night chemistry? Christ, I hope so.

"Like a date?" I blurt because I'm not one to beat around the proverbial bush. I need to figure out what this is between us and it sounds like my brain wants the answer now.

"Yes, like a date," he grins that panty wetting smile at me and I exhale the breath I didn't realize I was holding. "Hey," he says while gently lifting my chin so that he can look me in the eye, "did you think this was it? One afternoon and I'd be done?"

"I'm not really sure," I answer honestly. "I was hoping it was more but we never discussed it before-hand, so I wasn't sure if I was just another Carly-type arrangement."

"The casual arrangement I had with Carly was something we both mutually agreed on and we discussed our expectations at length before we had sex. You and I had no such conversation. What we did is what happens when two people feel something significant for one another and take the leap of faith to do something about it. Two completely different scenarios. I rarely ever want more than the casual arrangements I make for myself, but Katie, you compel me to want more."

"I can live with that," I grin and internally do a geeky little happy-dance.

"Besides, Maddie gave me 'the talk' remember? I was under very strict instructions not to do anything with you unless I was serious. Do you not remember the conversation from this morning? Maybe you hit your head harder than I thought…," he teases and earns himself a swat across the chest for his efforts. "Ow, easy little spitfire," he chuckles.

"Joking aside, you're serious?"

He nods and lowers his lips to my forehead for a gentle kiss. It's such a sweet and intimate gesture that any reservations I may have had regarding my trust issues evaporate leaving nothing but a burning desire in its wake. "I imagine Maddie thought it would take me longer to fall for you but she clearly underestimated your appeal, Sunshine."

"Clearly," I agree and clench around his hardening rod to make my point.

"Mmm, I thought you were hungry?"

"Oh, I am."

And with that, Asher fucks me thoroughly once more for good measure.

* * *

As first dates go, dinner with Ash was amazing. The food was delicious, my date was charming, funny, intelligent and attentive and the conversation flowed freely. I'm astounded by how at ease he makes me feel and I'm pleased there's more to our connection than just the burning desire to fuck each other's brains out. Not that you'll ever hear me complain about his ability in the sack. I've lost count of the number of orgasms he's given me already and I'm still throbbing for more. Every part of me is alight with anticipation; I can't wait to be alone with him again. Even though he's been the perfect gentleman and not touched me suggestively all night, dinner has still somehow ended up as foreplay.

Patience certainly isn't one of my virtues.

Judging by the scorching eye-fucks being flashed my way, it's not one of Ash's either.

The sexual energy crackles around us the entire drive home and just when I'm practically wriggling in my seat with need for him, we pull up in front of the ranch house, only to have my sex-fire doused by the sight of Carly waiting on the porch.

She looks beautiful in tight jeans and an off the shoulder blue sweater but she doesn't look impressed by the sight of Ash and I dressed up in the front seat of his truck. I'm guessing she saw her night ending differently…that makes two of us.

"Sorry," Asher mumbles, obviously annoyed to see her sitting there waiting for him. "I need to take care of this, wait for me inside?"

I nod in agreement but my insides feel like they need to upchuck the delicious dinner I've just consumed. I don't want to cause friction here as this is my place of work but equally, I feel territorial over Asher and our fledgling relationship and the last thing I want is the beautiful fuck buddy hanging around trying to claim him back.

It probably says more about me and my insecurities that the sight of Carly in all her sexy glory pisses me off. Still, I try not

93

to let it show.

As I reach for the passenger door, Ash leans over and kisses me delicately on the cheek.

"I really am sorry," and I can hear the reassurance in his tone.

"I'll see you inside," I manage as I hop down from the cab of the truck and walk past Carly into the ranch house, neither one of us attempting eye contact.

Yeah, so much for not being awkward.

Once safely inside – my desire completely extinguished – I have a few moments to myself to reflect. If we're really going to make a go of this relationship, it's not just Asher's baggage with Carly that needs addressing, there's some of my own that needs sifting through. Carly's appearance might well be a blessing in disguise, giving me a moment of much-needed clarity to tackle the elephant in the room…specifically, the sex room in the ranch house.

I make my way to the room where I first saw more of Asher and Carly than I ever dreamed of.

I don't like the room.

Everything about it screams at me. The décor, the memories, its principal function…the secrets hiding in the closet.

Nothing is sitting right with me and I feel uneasy being in here. This is a room that Asher has used with every other woman but me, and I sure as hell don't want to use it. Therefore, it's sort of redundant if we're committing to giving a monogamous relationship a go.

Also on the redundant list is the rack of canes and whips tucked neatly within the walk-in closet…Yeah, really not using those.

I open a distressed wooden dresser within the closet to find an array of toys and restraints – some look quite arousing but if it's not in its original packaging and unused, I'm not interested.

The front door slams shut as I pick up the new Womanizer clitoral massager – with its hygiene seal still intact…that could be fun later.

"See anything you like?" Asher gives me a roguish smile but it doesn't quite reach his eyes. Obviously, it wasn't a pleasant conversation with Carly.

"You found me quick," I deflect.

"I had a feeling we'd end up in here sooner or later."

"Not in the way you're hoping though," I sigh, "to answer your question, no, I don't really see anything I like. Except maybe this," I hold up the small, sealed box containing the Womanizer.

"Good choice. Anything else?" He sounds infectiously hopeful.

"Not really…I'm trying to figure out the best way to ask you to get rid of most of it…" I trail off at the momentary hurt in his eyes. It's replaced with astonishment and I can't help the flare of anger I feel in response. Why on earth, given my history, would he think I would feel differently about his sex room? I ask him so, as measured as I can but there's acid sarcasm in my tone that I can't hide.

"When you put it that way…" he shifts his feet and looks uncomfortable.

"Damn straight. I was beaten half to death and you told me you weren't a Dom, that you weren't into pain and punishment and then I find a closet full of whips, canes, crops, and *paddles*. Of course, it's going to be confusing and frightening and of course, I'm not going to be okay with it. And aside from your assortment of pain instruments, why on earth would I want to use *used* sex toys? I'm not going to use dildos and plugs that have been inside other women. I don't care how thorough your sterilizing techniques are, it grosses me out."

Abruptly, Asher turns and walks out of the room.

Panic replaces my frustration. While I feel somewhat justified in being honest with my feelings and fears, I'm insecure about the consequences. We've not exactly had a deep and meaningful conversation about our relationship status and I could have approached what I needed to say in a better way. I'm worried I've just overstepped and pushed him away.

A few moments later I exhale the fear-trapped breath in my throat as Asher walks back into the sex room with an industrial thickness black sack. He marches past me to the closet and begins ruthlessly chucking things into it. The paddles, canes, and whips are the first victims before emptying each drawer of his sex chest. Every now and then, he'll toss something onto the bed while I stand here astonished, bewildered and a little uncomfortable. Glancing at the bed I notice that he's separated anything that's unopened and still in its packaging.

"Do any of those take your fancy or should I chuck them too?"

I've lost the ability to speak. His tone is amicable but the words filter into my brain in a way that sounds harsh and sarcastic.

"I – I'm sorry," I whisper and look down at my feet. Too embarrassed and ashamed to meet his eyes. I've no right to waltz into his life and demand that he upends everything – literally.

I hear the bag drop to the floor as I turn to walk out the door. A strong hand grabs hold of mine, keeping me in place, while the other takes my chin and lifts it to force my eyes to meet his.

"You've done nothin' to apologize for. I'm not angry with you for being honest, I'm angry at myself for not considering how this room would make you feel *before* you had to point it out to my dumb ass."

His eyes blaze into mine and take my breath away; not for the first time today. "Some of the women who enjoy my style of dominance also enjoy pain/pleasure play and punishment. I kept the rack of whips and canes as it was convenient to have it on hand if they were in the mood for them. They do nothin' for me. Using them does not arouse me. They were merely there for convenience and it doesn't bother me to dispose of them or the used toys. You and I are new and should we decide to use toys, they should be new too. Those" – he nods in the direction of the bed – "have never been used, that's why I asked if any of them interest you. I didn't mean for it to come out so harsh though."

"You're sure?"

"Katie, my kink is a choice, not a compulsion. Right now, I chose you."

Warmth floods my body at his words and touch.

He cares.

More than I thought possible for something so new.

I'm lightheaded with euphoria and joy. No man has ever made me giddy but Asher Scott does.

Somehow, he's crept into the dark places and filled them with the brightness of profound happiness and desire.

It's too much, too fast but I don't give a shit.

I don't bother to look at the toys again – whatever they are, we'll play with them when I'm ready for it. "We can keep those," I say and plant a sweet, soft kiss on Ash's full lips.

Asher

This night might be salvageable after all.

I didn't think that was possible after pulling up and finding Carly sat on my porch waiting for me like a scorned girlfriend who just found out she's being cheated on.

Yeah, the night took a definite nosedive at that point.

Katie tried to hide it, but I could tell it bothered her. I couldn't help but feel a little smug at her jealousy, she definitely feels whatever this is between us if she's territorial already, and I sort of love that. Not that I want her to feel bad, but it's always nice to feel wanted.

Seeing Carly sat on my porch with a face like thunder really pissed me off though. That's not what we agreed going into our sex-only arrangement and I'm not thrilled at having her shift the goalposts on me.

We always agreed our hookups ahead of time, unless it was a consensual spur-of-the-moment thing. We didn't hang out in front of the others' home like a lost puppy. If she wanted to hook up tonight, our precedent would dictate her calling or messaging me to see if I was free – not that I would have been or will ever be, now that I've found Katie. Rocking up uninvited is a sure-fire way to end up on my shit list.

And she had the audacity to look pissed at me.

Yeah, that conversation with Carly definitely wasn't the nicest but it could've been worse…

"Replacing me with the new girl huh?" Her voice was stern but there was a dejected and despondent edge to it that made me feel bad. Carly does actually care about me, but I never asked her to and it wasn't what we agreed.

"Carly, we were just fuck buddies. I'm not replacing you,

because there's nothing to replace. I'm sorry that sounds harsh and I probably should've done this sooner to save your feelings but we're not a couple. We agreed to an arrangement *without* emotional attachment. I care about you as a person but not in the way you apparently want me to. And I truly am sorry that I'm not the man for you. You are a wonderful person; you're just not the girl for me. Katie isn't a new fuck buddy to replace you. There's something between us that I'm excited to explore with her."

"Well, don't mind my heart while you stomp all over it."

"Your heart was never meant to get involved. That's what we agreed on. I wouldn't be *stomping* on it if you didn't throw it at my feet."

"Asshole," she spat.

"You're right," I sighed, "that was unkind. I don't like feeling like I've hurt you but feelings were never meant to be a part of this. You promised me they wouldn't. Do you remember that? Before we did anything together, I was worried about the boss/employee dynamic and what would happen if things went sour and you promised me it wasn't about feeling anything for each other. That it was the need for sexual release. You promised me, Carly. And then you broke it and made me the bad guy because now I have to hurt you. It wasn't supposed to be this way." I'm almost pleading with her at this point, for what, I don't know.

"Right. So, it's all my fault. Like you didn't see me developing feelings for you. You could've ended it sooner before I got too deep."

"So could you."

"I was living in hope."

"That's not fair Carly. You can't tell me I should've called time on our arrangement sooner to prevent your feelings from growing deeper when you ignored your developing feelings and clung on knowing full well that wasn't what I agreed to. That I wasn't going to care for you back. You can't blame me for your decision to hold on regardless."

"So, it *is* all my fault."

"No, it's not. But neither is it all mine. I'm not really sure what else you want from me, Carly?"

"I wish you would've told me before taking her to dinner."

"That's fair. I'm sorry I didn't tell you." Not that there had been an abundance of time to have that conversation but Carly deserved better. She deserves respect even if she did complicate matters.

And you let her. My subconscious shouts at me.

"And I want you to treat her better. If you're hurting my feelings over this woman then I at least want her to be the one you marry and have babies with. I can deal with the embarrassment and hurt if she's going to be the big love of your life."

"It's new, but I think it has a shot at greatness."

"Wonderful," she said dryly, "I'll try and be happy for you but I don't want the details. See you around, boss." And with that, she stalked off in the direction of her little cottage. I let the darkness swallow her before walking up the porch steps into the house.

And just when I thought the worst of the evening was behind me, I find Katie unhappily rummaging through my sex room.

Fucking. Typical.

Of course, our first date was going to get worse before it got better.

I made an ill-advised attempt at humor and Katie's true

feelings about my sex room came tumbling out. I knew this was a conversation we needed to have but I sort of hoped it wouldn't be on the back of dealing with the Carly drama.

But I wasn't that lucky…or skilled enough to say the right things. Actions speak louder than words anyway, or so I was told. Hence my stomping off to retrieve an industrial black sack to throw away all the offending shit from my sex closet. My life was to be physically and metaphorically cleansed this evening, whether I liked it or not.

But now here I am, with the object of my fantasies pressing her luscious lips tentatively against mine.

Yeah, tonight is definitely salvageable.

Chapter Nine

Katie

The rest of the week passes in a blur of contented domestic bliss and work.

After the night of the Carly / sex room cleanse, mine and Ash's relationship became public knowledge; he's all in and it's intense but I can't help but love it.

I feel relaxed in a relationship for the first time in...well, possibly ever, which explains why, given my past, I'm able to jump into this with both feet so quickly. It's eye-opening and frightening that I ever let myself settle for less than what Asher is showing me. And it seems so natural for him, like cherishing me the way he does is just second nature requiring no more thought or effort than breathing.

His enthusiasm for our relationship – because that is what he officially calls it – is infectious. He's gentle and considerate and fierce and protective. He takes what he knows I can give but doesn't push for more. The sex is electric and so far, he's not taken my limits any further than he did that first day, which is still way further than I thought I'd get. I love the fact that I trust him enough to let him take me from behind where I can't see him or that I can let him hold my wrists down. That sort of sexual vulnerability, the willingness to submit your power to someone else, used to light a rocket in my libido. I'm so happy that with Ash I'm able to claw back some of those desires from the dark place to which David stole them.

I trust Ash, but I'm also learning to trust myself, my belief in him and in us.

Asher aside, the ranch is really starting to feel like home. I'm acing the work. Surpassing all expectations of the resort and ranch managers – maybe they never had anyone organized before? The records certainly give that impression; they're going to take a while to get in order.

All the staff have been friendly, warm and welcoming. Well, maybe not Carly, but things on that front have been better than I expected. She's not bitchy or antagonistic and she doesn't go out of her way to make life difficult or awkward. She also doesn't go out of her way to make conversation but that's understandable but she doesn't ignore me either. Normally there's a curt nod of acknowledgment from her when I see her about the ranch. Thankfully though, our paths don't cross much as I spend most of my time in an office in the Lodge.

Ash explained his arrangement with Carly and how things were supposed to stay platonic but I can see that she's hurting and although you can't force someone into a relationship, I can't help but feel responsible for her pain. Like I'm some sort of man-stealing homewrecker who just showed up and immediately ripped her heart out by taking her man.

Except Ash wasn't her man. He was a single man, I was a single woman and I guess Carly was just sort of caught in the crossfire of our attraction. Logically I know it's not my fault, but I'm still happy that I have an office to hide in most of the time. Until her hurt and my misplaced guilt pass, I don't need to keep bumping into her.

A knock on the office door brings me back to the task at hand – an unorganized pile of customer receipts from last year.

"Makin' headway, Sunshine?" I smile at the sound of Ash's deep voice. I swear it's so low that it physically vibrates through me...well, my clit at least.

"A little. It'll take a while to get everything organized and filed away but I'm definitely not going to be defeated by your mountain of disarrayed paperwork."

"Hey, this mayhem isn't *all* my fault." He casually leans against the door, arms crossed, stretching the tight fabric of his shirt. The perfect fit of his worn jeans draws my eyes to the hardening bulge between his legs. How is he always ready to go?

"You're my boss' boss. Ultimate responsibility falls to you," I tease.

"Well as your boss' boss I feel it's my duty to tell you how impressed I am with you."

"You're only saying that because I'm the best at sucking your cock," I wink.

"You are very talented where my cock is concerned but I was being serious, Bill and Moira are impressed with your work and you seem to have settled in really well. Are you happy?" It's hard to answer his question when I'm distracted by the tent in his jeans but with a monumental effort, I focus on his face and to what he asked.

Bill and Moira are the Ranch and Lodge managers respectively and are important to Ash, so their approval means a lot. Ash bought this place with his parents as a joint venture but they were killed in a car accident shortly after. Even though

Ash was a fully-grown man at the time, Bill and Moira took him under their wing and over the years have become sort of surrogate parents to him. He has a lot of love and respect for them and because of that, this place has a real family-run vibe to it. The guests really respond to that feeling of family and I'm thrilled to feel a part of it.

"More than I can say," I answer honestly.

"Good." And with a dangerous twinkle in his eye, he closes and locks the office door.

Wetness floods my core. I know that look. That heated gaze melts my synapses in seconds leaving me ravenous for his touch.

Asher picks me up from my chair, wrapping my legs around his waist and crushes my lips with his; his tongue demanding entry and taking it…claiming me with masterful strokes. He lowers us onto a soft rug in the corner of the office. I'm so desperate for him already even though he took me thoroughly this morning. It seems my addiction to his lovemaking needs sating every few hours. Frantically, I tear at the buttons of his shirt to feel the hot, hard ridges of his muscles before trailing my hands lower to tug open his belt and jeans. His fingers have already found my soaked, aching core, having lifted my skirt and pulled my panties to the side to expose me. This need is furious and desperate; there's no sensual foreplay or removal of clothes, only the pure, carnal need to fuck.

Freeing him from his boxers I line up his massive cock head with my slick opening and he drives home with one powerful buck of his hips. Having that beautiful, thick cock of his slamming forcefully into my shaking pussy is like nothing I've ever experienced. All conscious thought flees my mind and I'm nothing more than sensation and need.

Ash sets a furious, punishing rhythm that has me arching into him, clawing at his back and screaming like a woman possessed. A woman possessed by her man and his gigantic cock. A woman fucked to an almost painful climax in the best quickie of the goddamn century.

When he takes me like this, so utterly and desperately, I feel complete.

I need this man in me.

Filling me.

Claiming me.

* * *

Sometime after dinner and yet another amazing fuck on the floor in front of the fire in the lounge of Ash's ranch house, the topic of the weekend comes up.

I don't know why this makes me nervous. We are a couple but we've made no plans so far so I don't know what the status quo is supposed to be. Do we spend it together? Does he need some space? Does he already have plans? What do I do about the text Maddie just sent me? I've not seen her all week so should probably make time for her this weekend.

I needn't have worried though; like everything Asher does, the weekend conversation was covered with confidence and ease.

"Unless you have plans baby, this Sunday you are all mine."

"You have something in mind, Cowboy?"

"Maybe somethin' that involves not leaving the bedroom ma'am," he leans down and kisses me suggestively. Deep, long strokes of his tongue that have me worked up and ready to go again in seconds.

"Fuck waiting till Sunday," I murmur against his plush lips. He groans and pulls my body flush with his so I can feel the hard length of his erection.

That thing is barely ever flaccid.

"Baby, I would fuck you all weekend, believe me, but I have an appointment that I can't get out of tomorrow. If I could, I would." He looks genuinely upset that he can't spend the whole weekend inside me. The man has an insatiable appetite...lucky for him, so do I.

"Don't worry about it, Cowboy. I need to see Maddie tomorrow anyway. We can meet up in the evening and fuck like uncontrollable, horny teenagers then."

Ash's laugh echoes through the large lounge and the sound feels like home.

I snuggle in closer to his side, the heat of his skin and the pure masculine scent of him calming me to my core as the log fire crackles next to us. I'm not sure why we even lit a fire; our sex is hot enough to keep my body blazing all night long.

Just as I think we're going to drift off to sleep in the tangle of soft blankets right here on the floor, Asher breaks the silence with his deep voice.

"How did you discover it?"

"Huh?" I'm not sure I follow as I rub the sleep out of my eyes and try to focus.

"Your kink. When? How? I'm basically asking what led you to my bed," he winks.

"I'm guessing you mean prior to David?"

"Definitely. I'm talking about when you were first curious; what did you do on your path of sexual self-discovery?"

I sit up so that I can look him directly in the eye. "I'll tell you mine if you tell me yours?"

"That's generally how a relationship works," he teases. I love playful Asher. It's a side he doesn't show many people and I can't help but take comfort in the knowledge that he shares that part of himself with me.

"I was very lucky growing up. I had the loving support of my parents and a great set of friends – no fake bitches in sight. My formative years were blessed with positive reinforcement and confidence. I grew up knowing myself and being unafraid of it. My mother always said 'if it brings you pleasure and happiness and it doesn't cause harm or hurt to others, then it can't possibly be wrong'. I took those words to heart so, when I met Maddie at college and we started confiding in each other about the sort of things we liked, I didn't feel judged or conflicted. I felt empowered to explore because I truly believed that it couldn't be wrong. I didn't have to worry about some hypothetical moral dilemma, I had the confidence to just go with it.

"We discovered a sex club not far from campus and started exploring our sexuality. I caught the eye of a senior Dom early on and agreed to try subbing for him. I learned a lot about what I liked under his tutelage but also a lot about what I didn't. He was into exhibitionism and although I've done it a few times, it's not really my scene. One night he really wanted to play in public and I *really* didn't. He felt that my disagreeable attitude was my way of crying out for a good spanking, to be reminded who was in charge. The spanking was also to be done in the public section of the club while I was tied to a bench. I let him hit me once before I realized that it would never have the desired effect on me; I felt pissed off that he got to decide what arbitrary line I'd apparently crossed and earned myself a punishment for. Who was he to make that sort of decision? I know that some women get off on it but I've since realized that I'm the sort of feminist who believes in equality and having my ass spanked raw because of some rule made up on the spot by my lover isn't equality…not when the sub never gets the chance to punish her Dom when he's acting like a dick. It's not a power exchange I can get behind; I realized that pain and punishment weren't my kind of kink so safe-worded then and there. He untied me so quickly and was attentive and concerned about my welfare but I nearly punched him in the face with how angry I was. I think I told him if he ever laid a finger on me in punishment again, I would rip his balls off and feed them to him while I paddled his ass until it blistered."

At this, Ash roars with laughter. "You actually said that? What did the poor guy do next?"

"Poor guy? Why on earth is he garnering sympathy here?" I shove him playfully.

"Because you are one hell of a catch and you publicly dumped his ass and humiliated him."

"After he tried humiliating me."

"Yes, but you were still discoverin' your limits and instead of saying 'yellow' or whatever and talkin' him through what you were feeling, you ended it. Publicly."

"Yeah, I figured he'd appreciate the audience," We chuckle at my joke.

"You still haven't told me what he said," he probes.

"He diplomatically told me that he didn't think our kinks were aligned."

"Poor guy."

"After I spent some time reflecting on the whole thing, I realized I could've handled it better and I did apologize to him for not communicating better with him. He was gracious about it; he was really into the lifestyle and I think he was looking for a 'round-the-clock' type sub and that's just not me. I like the freedom of being tied up and having my sexual desires fulfilled without me having to think about them. That doesn't include spankings for being a 'naughty girl.'"

"Baby, I have to ask – and please don't be mad – but, how did a woman so self-assured and fiery get snared by a loser like David?" I can see the hesitation in his eyes and the worry that this may be one question too far but it's not like I haven't asked myself this a million times.

I take a calming breath, the warm scent of hot male and musk, the remnants of his aftershave and the potent smell of sex envelop me. It's a powerful combination and gives me the courage to answer. "Shortly after I graduated, my parents took a sailing vacation with two of their friends. Their boat was lost at sea in an unexpected storm. All four bodies washed up a couple of days later and I officially became an orphan."

"I'm so sorry, Sunshine. I know how it feels to lose your parents and I hate that you have to live with that pain."

"It's definitely something I wish we didn't have in common. They were all taken before their time and it's just another reminder that sometimes, the world really sucks.

"In the months that followed their deaths, I spent more time at the club where I felt comfortable and safe and that's when I met David. In hindsight, I think he chose me because my defenses were down and, in my grief, I couldn't see him for what he really was. He gave me the security I'd missed since my parents died but it blinded me to the true extent of his toxic depravity."

Asher holds me close throughout, stroking my skin with his

rough fingers, swirling delicate patterns across my sensitive flesh.

"He's never going to hurt you again, you know that right? Not on my watch. I'll kill that fucker before I let him lay a finger on you." His voice practically growls his assertion. I believe him. David would be a fool to track me down. A dead fool.

"I've told you mine, tell me yours."

There's a momentary pause. Hurt flashes through the golden depths of his eyes. It's brief, but it's there.

"I had a girlfriend, Sylvie, Freshman year of college. She was a virgin. Completely inexperienced. Was too afraid to even touch herself. She didn't know where to start, what she wanted, what she liked and would get upset if I asked because not knowing the answers, to her, just highlighted her inexperience more. She told me to take control and enlighten her because she didn't want to keep overthinking and worrying about it. So, I took complete control of our sex life and I liked it. More than liked it. I can't describe the thrill it gave me to be the one responsible for her pleasure. For her to trust me so intimately. It was a heady combination and I fell in love with her fast and hard. Slowly we introduced toys and eventually bondage. I thought we were on the same page but it turns out she only let me tie her up to make me happy, not herself. Bondage is for the enjoyment of both parties but she didn't enjoy it and she didn't tell me. Eventually, she unilaterally decided that I couldn't live without kink and she wanted to, so she left me. I'm not ashamed to say she broke my heart. I didn't see it comin'. She didn't talk to me, so I had no idea how she felt until she stormed out of my life. Katie, that's why I need you to know that I *can* live without kink and

I would rather do that than lose you. Do you understand?"

I answer with a searing kiss. I can't stand to think about Ash broken-hearted. I understand Sylvie's fear but the bitch broke *my* man's heart. I suppose I should be grateful that she was too stupid to talk it through with him because now he's mine and not hers.

Shit, I'm territorial over him.

Doubt pierces my heart in a flash. What if she did want him back? He loved her; she'll always hold a spot in his heart even if it's a painful one. Knowing what I do now, I realize that Asher is my first true love and it sits like lead in my stomach that I'm not his. I'm too terrified to admit out loud to him how deeply I've fallen but my face must betray my inner turmoil and like always, Ash reads it and gives me exactly what I need.

"Baby, look at me," he holds my chin between his thumb and forefinger and tilts my head back and locks me with his gaze, his thumb gently caressing my bottom lip. "Sylvie wouldn't even register in my mind if she passed us in the street because all I can think about is you. She and I were an adolescent kind of love; yeah it hurt that she didn't trust me or talk to me, but she's nothing more than a memory; she's not the woman for me."

My chest tightens at the prospect that maybe *I'm* the woman for him but he doesn't say any more. I exhale the tight little breath I was holding and swallow the lump of disappointment.

"Is that why you only did casual affairs?" I ask instead.

"Yeah. Can't get hurt if you don't care in the first place."

Yeah, Sylvie left her mark alright. I'm the first girlfriend since her and intend to be the last; I vow to never hurt him the way she did.

* * *

The next morning, we oversleep slightly so there's not enough time to satisfy each other before we separate for the day. This leaves me antsier than I thought it would and once again, a little bewildered at how quickly Ash got under my skin. I also notice that despite the epic amounts of sex – I don't think I've ever been fucked so thoroughly or so much – I'm surprisingly well-rested.

I managed to get over the worst of my nightmares in recent months; their severity had lessened massively and I no longer wake up screaming and swimming in sweat. But they haven't left completely. I still have a couple a week but on a much smaller scale. They're the kind that if they wake me, I can roll back over to sleep reasonably quickly or they don't wake me at all, but I know I've had one because I'm exhausted the next day from all the tossing and turning I did in the night.

This week I've had none. Perhaps my body is so exhausted from all the sex with Ash that I physically can't have a nightmare? Or perhaps it's something more profound keeping my darkness at bay? I suspect it's the latter.

Either way, I'm awake and energetic – if not a little horny – and ready to head out and see Maddie. Her message was a little cryptic. It didn't say what she needed me for, only that it was really important for me to be at hers for ten a.m.

Considering she's a half-hour drive from here, I'm only just going to make it.

With a minute to spare I rock up at Maddie's apartment and she buzzes me in.

She really is the queen of apartment Tetris. Her place is small but looks like one of those chic little apartment displays they set up in Ikea. Her interior design skills amaze me but I guess she's had time to work on it as she's not mentioned anything working out on the job front.

"I see how it is," she says in that suspicious tone of hers as she closes the apartment door behind me and I flop down on the small sofa. "You've replaced me with a certain cowboy's cock, haven't you?" Her teasing causes me to blush deeply. "Otherwise you'd have been calling and texting your best girl but aside from a few messages it's been radio silence."

"I have been messaging you," she arches one perfect eyebrow at me and I admit defeat. "Okay," I sigh, "not as much as normal, but there are only so many hours in the day for work, messaging and fucking," I grin.

"Girl, if all you needed was cock, I'd have bought a strap on and pleased you myself."

I laugh and throw a cushion at her. The funny thing is, she probably would have and deep down I'm kinky enough that I probably would have let her. Maddie and I are super close but not in a sisterly way where we can't talk about sex in front of each other. We've never been uncomfortable with each other's sexual exploits. In college, we both went to a sex party and I watched her getting thoroughly fucked on the kitchen counter by two guys and it was one of the hottest things I've ever seen. Watching Maddie in the throes of ecstasy is something to behold. It was so fucking arousing that I stuck my fingers up my skirt and into my panties and got myself off...until someone knelt down in front of me and ate my pussy until I came all over their face. It's one of the few times I didn't mind getting off publicly. I remember gripping their hair as I came hard and realizing that they had soft, long hair and that the person with the talented tongue going down on me was a woman. Maddie told me later that night that she couldn't tear her eyes away from my girl on girl action. That it was just as hot watching me as it was for me watching her. Maybe that makes our friendship weird but we wouldn't have it any other way. We are who we are.

This was before David; when I was more sexually open and it was the hottest experience of my life…well up until Asher fucked his way onto the scene. Nothing competes with him. Not even the vaguely arousing notion of Maddie with a strap on.

"Sorry to disappoint Mads, but it's the man attached to the cock that I'm addicted to. Or at least I'm as addicted to him as I am his massive dick."

"I'll put the strap on back in the closet then," she grins.

"Probably for the best. I'm the monogamous type."

"How would you know unless you've tried polyamorous?"

"If you really want to be my girlfriend Mads, I can ask Ash if he's up for it."

"I love you but no. Thanks for the offer but I want a big cock of my own," she laughs.

I've missed her banter.

"Seriously though, you are happy? He treats you right?"

"I am Mads and he really does. I never knew a relationship could be so good. I don't know how he does it but he's protective without being overbearing, cherishes me without smothering me and takes care of me without making me feel incapable or pathetic for wanting it. And the sex…fuck me it's so hot."

"I offered already," she smirks. "I'm glad you're happy Katie. This relationship seems to suit you; I've not seen you so relaxed and contented for years. But if he goes all asshole on you, you tell me. He's a big guy but he's not bulletproof and I know people."

"You're strange Mads."

"The strangest," she agrees

"But you're my kind of strange and I love you."

"Do you love me enough to come with me on an errand that you might not like?" she asks hopefully.

"Of course," I answer automatically and hope I don't regret it. "What is it?"

"So, Asher gave me a tip for a job and I made contact with the owner of this club. He's been busy all week so he's not been able to see me for an interview until today. Will you come with me?"

That is odd. Why on Earth does Maddie – my amazingly confident Maddie – need a chaperone for an interview?

"Um, okay? I'm a bit confused as to why you need me with you?"

"Okay, don't freak out, but it's for a dancing position at a sex club."

"There's a sex club here in town?" I ask incredulously.

"It's sort of an exclusive club. You know, high paying members, exclusivity and secrecy, that sort of thing. Dixon, the owner, says it's on the level – employees aren't paid to have sex with the clientele. Guests can have sex with each other and some performers are paid to act out sexual scenes on stage but I wouldn't be doing any of that. I would be purely dancing on the pole and helping out behind the bar."

"Wait. Back up. Asher told you about this exclusive sex club?"

"Um, yeah. He didn't mention it to you?"

"That he knows about the town's underground sex club or

that he recommended you for a job? Pretty sure he didn't mention either." I breathe heavily for a moment, trying not to get eaten up by anger and insecurity.

"Okay Katie, let's think the problem through," she soothes. "Asher didn't tell you and that sucks but let's consider perhaps why he didn't?"

"Because he thought a club full of bondage and sex would upset me. If he mentioned it though, he'd find out it doesn't."

"It doesn't?"

"No. I know it's quick but I feel safe with him. I've let him restrain me a bit and control our sex. I'd be up for going to a sex club with him. Color me intrigued."

"Wow. I think he really is good for you."

"I think so too. He should have told me though, especially the part where he suggested you work there."

"I agree with you, in the very basic sense of not keeping secrets from your partner. But if he told you about helping me with the job then he'd have to tell you about the club, which brings us nicely back to the original point where he probably didn't tell you about the club to avoid upsetting you. But he's a man and they don't always see that omitting information to protect someone causes just as much upset as being honest with the painful truth."

"I really admire your ability to think situations through logically Mads."

"Sometimes you just need someone to take a step back and point out the argument without the tangle of emotions. Definitely bring it up with him though. Work through it and then have epic make up sex."

"Sounds like my kind of plan. Thanks, Mads. I mean it." I'm not thrilled that Ash kept this from me but Maddie raises a good point. He's been very respectful about things that could upset me and he probably thought to mention a sex club was a conversation too far at this stage. He's not malicious, just misguided.

"Care to show your appreciation for my wisdom by coming with me?"

"What's the name of this club?"

"The Rock Hard Club. I'm sure it's on the level, considering it was Asher who told me about it, but I'd rather have someone with me until I know first-hand, you know?"

"Yeah. Of course. Let's go check out the kinky sex club," I grin.

Half an hour later we arrive at a non-descript warehouse looking building where a burly looking security guard lets us in.

"Downstairs is apparently just a regular club. Alcohol, dancing and lots of tourists. Upstairs is where it gets interesting," Maddie whispers.

The burly security guard gestures for us to walk down a dark, innocuous corridor and through a door that when closed, I imagine blends with the wall to be almost invisible unless you know it's there. Behind the door is a staircase to the upper floors. Everything is painted the typical burgundy and black colors you'd imagine a sex club to be but it's not over-the-top or in your face. The tones, detailing and lighting give off a sumptuous and sensual vibe.

We exit the stairs on the next floor and walk into a sex enthusiast's wonderland. It's truly decadent and amazing and instantly has my skin prickling with goosebumps. The main space is dotted with stages and exhibition cubes for the sex performers and poles and hoops for aerial dancers. Plush chairs and couches surround the small stages, gauzy wisps of material drape strategically to divide the space to give it an enclosed and intimate feel. There's an elegant looking bar in one corner and a series of smaller, private rooms along one long length of the club. The room has a circular vibe with the stages loosely arranged around an intimate dance floor for guests. I'm not sure what's upstairs but if it's anything like this floor, it'll be amazing.

"This is seriously cool," I whisper to Maddie as a tall, dark and tattooed hunk of man-godliness approaches. Not my type but definitely Maddie's. I see her blush in the dim light as Mr. Handsome locks eyes with her and extends a large hand in her direction.

"Maddie, I presume? I'm Dixon Cooper, the owner," his voice is deep and gruff. Definitely Maddie's type. Except she's not so fond of fucking the boss like I am – she's smart.

"You presume correctly. Nice to meet you, Dixon," she shakes his hand and I swear her blush deepens but it is hard to tell in this light. "This is my friend Katie. I asked her to come with me until I knew this place was legitimate. I hope you don't mind?" She's not really asking if he minds; it's one of those polite Maddie questions where your answer doesn't count for shit because she's going to do whatever she wants or needs to. But Dixon doesn't know that.

"Not at all, that's a smart move, especially when you are new in town." He turns his attention to me and shakes my hand firmly, "It's a pleasure to meet you, Katie. Ash can't stop talking about you so it's great to meet you in person. You should go say hi while I speak with Maddie," he jerks his chin towards a small lit stage on the far side of the dance floor that I hadn't focused on before.

As Maddie and Dixon walk off in the direction of the bar I look closely at the stage and notice there are a small group of naked female performers practicing their bondage skills and...holy motherfucking Christ...

Ash is their instructor.

Chapter Ten

Asher

I look up from my handiwork to see Dix heading towards his office with Maddie. Wasn't Katie supposed to be spending the day with Maddie? I get that sinking feeling in the pit of my stomach.

"Ash, your girl's here," he calls over his shoulder.

What?

I glance towards the staircase and see Katie, my woman, looking at me with confusion and distrust while I stand here surrounded by naked and bound performers.

Fuck. Fuck. *Fuck.*

I knew in my heart of hearts that it was the wrong move not telling her what I had to do today. She acts so confidently but she has to work damn hard at it and I didn't want to give that hard-fought confidence a knock. But omitting the truth has done it anyway.

Hindsight is a bitch; a bitch with twenty/twenty vision.

"Katie," I breathe as I bolt across the club to her. The performers are fine to be left; one girl isn't tied up so she can undo the knots binding the others.

Katie doesn't run or turn her back on me. She's rooted to

the spot with a warring expression of her face like she can't decide what reaction I deserve. But I take the fact that she's still stood here as a good thing.

"Let me guess, it's not what it looks like?" she says sourly.

"Clichéd but true. Can we talk?" I gesture towards one of the private rooms and Katie nods, allowing me to take her hand and lead her to the nearest.

Another good sign. I dare to hope that I can dig my stupid ass out of the crater I've made for myself.

Her small hand feels warm and tender in mine as I close and lock the door behind us and turn to face her. She eyes the decadent room and despite the anger I see in her eyes, I swear there's a flash of desire too. The room is decorated much the same way as the rest of the club; burgundy and black with a sumptuous bed and sofa and a crystal chandelier casting fragmented shards of light. Satin and lace drapes cover the walls, hiding the assortment of equipment and toys behind them. There are strategic hooks and restraints throughout all of the private sex rooms. I desperately want to tie Katie up beneath me and fuck her so hard until all the doubt and fear leave her and she knows exactly what she means to me but that's not the way to go about it.

"Go on," she snaps. "Explain to me how it's okay for you to be tying up naked women who aren't me. Tell me why it's okay to keep your membership to an exclusive sex club a secret despite hooking my friend up with a job here. I can deal with many things, Asher – I *have* dealt with many things – but lying isn't something I'm willing to tolerate. I'd rather take uncomfortable truths over the hurt and humiliation of having my trust misplaced."

"You're right – "

"I wasn't' finished. Wait, what? I'm right?"

"You sound surprised to hear me admit I was wrong? I'm not an idiot Katie, well I sort of am, but I can admit when I've fucked up. I didn't trust that you could handle the truth but that wasn't my call to make. I should have given you the opportunity to decide for yourself instead of stubbornly insisting that I protect you from everything that could upset you. I'm new at this Katie; after Sylvie and before you, I only had unemotional sexual arrangements with women. I never had to take their feelings into account before. Now I have someone who means the world to me, who I want to protect, whose feelings are more important than my own and knowing that I have the power to hurt those feelings is pretty fucking daunting. I hate that I don't have all the answers, that I'll make mistakes and that those mistakes could upset you. I'm learning how to build a relationship but I'm not perfect. Today is a prime example of that."

"No one is perfect Asher. I sure as fuck am not. But we can choose to be better and to be honest," she looks expectantly at me.

"Dixon and his brother Max are my oldest friends so I've had a membership here since the club opened. Despite what you must think, I don't frequent this place all that often. Over the past year or so when I have visited, I've only been watching the performers, not hooking up with other patrons. Given my work on the ranch and my proclivity for tying women up, I'm pretty handy with ropes and knots. Every now and then Dixon asks me to come in to teach bondage to the new girls or to teach the experienced girls some advanced techniques. I already told him that today will be my last session but this one was already organized so I couldn't get out of it. I didn't want to bail on my friend but I should have told you."

"Yes, you should have. Because you'd have found out that this whole thing is actually a little hot. Watching you tie someone up with those capable hands of yours was a shock. But as uncomfortable and unexpected as it initially was, it was a shock because it was hot watching you."

I was not expecting that.

"You never fail to surprise me. I thought you'd scream and shout and accuse me of cheating or somethin'."

"Such little faith," she teases dryly. She's not moved from her spot in front of me and despite her stiff posture, I can see the anger dimming in her eyes.

"Having a relationship is new territory for me, I'm not sure what to expect."

"My default would be to be angrier with you but I'm trying Maddie's approach to things," I furrow my brow in question. "Maddie is logical," Katie replies. "She takes a step back and tries to look at the bigger picture. She's pretty good at seeing more than just her perspective. We already had a conversation about why she thought you didn't tell me about the club and her job. She concluded that you were misguidedly trying to protect me and I was inclined to agree. That doesn't mean lying by omission is okay, but it means that I understand your motivation. I've gotta say, Maddie is your biggest advocate. She thinks you're good for me."

"She does?"

"And I do too. As long as there are no more secrets."

"I promise I have no other secrets and I'm so sorry that I hurt you by keeping it from you."

"I trust you, Asher. That's why a club full of bondage equipment isn't freaking me out. I feel safe with you. Safe enough that I think I want to come here with you sometime. I never thought I'd be able to say that about a sex club but that's how much you've changed me for the better. I'm not going to throw that away just because we're still learning how to have a relationship and communicate with each other. I can't imagine there are many things I wouldn't forgive you for; please don't test the limits of that though," she smiles softly at me.

All I can do is kiss her. Kiss her for being amazing and willing to forgive my fuck-ups. Because let's be honest, there are many ways this situation could've been viewed; and in many of them, it would've ended with a dick punch and the words 'it's over' being screamed at me. Not many women would be prepared to let me explain and to calmly look at this for what it really is…an explicit job on the side. I love that Katie is kinky enough to find me tying up other women sexy – that element alone would've been a deal-breaker for many. And she wants to come here with me sometime; I didn't see that coming. Katie is definitely opening up to me sexually; I'm so proud of her courage and happy that she chose me to join her on her sexual journey.

As usual, it does not take long for our kiss to combust into something insatiable but I'm aware that I am supposed to be outside giving a tutorial. For a minute I'm torn about what to do next.

As if sensing my conflict, Katie pulls back slightly. "I think you should finish your lesson…while letting me watch." Desire and intrigue flare in the depths of her sparkling blue eyes and I get a thrill thinking about her watching me bind those girls. I grab her by the hand and pull her back into the main room of the club and deposit her in one of the sofa's next to the stage I'm working on. She giggles a little at my caveman manhandling and the sound sends a shiver straight to my cock.

I spend the next 20 minutes demonstrating and assisting the girls with their bondage attempts and fighting a raging hard-on. Katie has been watching me intently the entire time, apparently mesmerized by my hands restraining the performers. I feel like I'm the one performing for Katie. She watches every touch I make, every knot I tie, every gasp as rough rope gently chafes soft skin. All the while her cheeks are flushed a rosy pink, her eyes wide with anticipation, her lush bottom lip bitten between her teeth as she subtly squirms in the chair, clenching her thighs together for some friction to relieve the tension she's obviously feeling.

Maddie is still being interviewed by Dix when I finish.

Good.

I coil up the last of the rope while Katie waits patiently…well as patiently as she can for being as aroused as she is. As I place the rope in my bag, I spot something…a length of red, satin ribbon. I snag it and stuff it in my jean pocket before taking Katie's hot little hand and leading her wordlessly back to the sex room from earlier.

As soon as I have the door locked and turn to face her, she leaps into my arms, kissing me urgently. I give my cock permission to go full salute and it feels so good not to have to fight it. Grabbing handfuls of Katie's ripe ass, I keep her legs locked around my waist as she drags her fingers through my hair, gripping tightly and then pulling it back so that she has space to bite the sensitive spot of my neck below my ear. I grind my erection into her pelvis giving her the friction she needs to moan loudly. My woman is never quiet when I pleasure her and I fucking love it.

I pin her to the wall, nuzzling the column of her neck with my teeth, lips, nose, and tongue and feel her shiver in my arms.

"Oh god, Ash," she gasps.

Reaching into my pocket, I pull out the satin ribbon and dangle it in front of her, making my intentions clear.

"Strip. Now." This is the moment of truth. I've restrained her movements a little during our lovemaking but I have never been controlling and told her what to do. I am curious to see how far being in this club and watching me has loosened her up. Looking at her intently, I convey my demand with my eyes but give her the opportunity to say 'no' if she needs to.

After the longest moment known to man, she frantically undoes the buttons of her shirt, throwing it aside and peeling off her jeans before all that is left is her underwear. White. Lacy. Underwear. She is the embodiment of an innocent angel about to be thoroughly fucking corrupted by my devious desires.

"Good girl," I breathe through gritted teeth as her bra slides down her arms and onto the floor followed closely by her panties. She is completely naked before me and the sight blows my mind. How did I end up with someone so beautiful, so willing and so trusting in me?

The last time I was fully clothed while she was naked there was a glimmer of fear in her eyes, but not this time. Right here, right now, she's lost to our desire and there's nothing holding her back.

Katie holds her wrists out before her like a perfect little submissive and allows me to tie the smooth satin around her silky-soft skin. "This ends whenever you want it to or when we come screaming each other's name. Do you understand?"

"I understand," she sighs with pleasure.

"I'm only tying it in a bow so you can pull the end and release yourself whenever you need to or you can use our safe word."

"Which is?"

"Sunshine," I can't help my smirk at using my nickname for her as her safe word.

"Sunshine," she repeats smiling.

I finish the satin bow and walk her back to a height-adjustable carabiner, lock it around the ribbon and adjust it so that Katie's arms are raised above her head. The sight of her stretched and balancing on the balls of her feet, her tits bouncing with every deep gasp she makes, has me so hard it hurts. I palm my cock through my jeans trying to get some much-needed relief but nothing helps. My entire length aches for her to the point of pain, causing my eyes to roll with the need. I wanted to drag this out, tease her and make her beg but it's my cock doing the begging. I need her body wrapped around mine. Now.

I discard my clothes as quickly as humanly possible, suck a plump rosy nipple into my mouth and push my fingers through her wet folds. She's soaking. Her juices coat the inside of her thighs where it's dripping from her. I don't stop at her entrance, running my hand underneath her to her ass instead, gripping her pale flesh tightly and hauling her off her feet high enough to impale her with my impatient cock.

Katie

"YES," I scream at the top of my lungs as I slide down his hard length until he's seated fully and throbbing inside me. I can't control any of my movements with my arms bound above my head and that makes me wetter. My arousal is dripping out of me I want him so bad and we both know it, which makes me hotter again for him.

Any residual uncertainty I had about being here evaporated in the heat of my desire while I watched him teach those girls. Their sensual naked bodies trussed up beautifully by his large skillful hands. The entire time I was desperate for it to be my body smothered by his touch. I couldn't follow him to this room fast enough. And when he told me to strip with the intention of tying me up, the only reason I paused was that I noticed I didn't feel insecure about giving him total control at all.

No fear. No memories. Just the insatiable burn to have him take me however he wants.

And take me he does.

I love that he used 'sunshine' as my safe word - I prefer lighter and playful safe words as opposed to 'red' or other words associated with pain. I also love that he tied me up in a way that I can free myself, but I'm excited for the day when I'm confident enough to have him restrain me where I can't escape.

He's more thoughtful than he realizes. Yes, he fucked up earlier by keeping things from me but it wasn't out of malice, his heart was in the right place and we all make mistakes especially when it comes to things we're particularly protective over. But Ash knows me, knows my body…knows what I need…and boy does he deliver.

His lips crash against mine, his tongue lashing mine with deep, wet strokes as he thrusts deep into me. His hands grip my hips moving me up and down his thick length slick with my juices. Ash makes me ride him mercilessly; driving upwards every time he slams me down on him. His bulbous head hitting my g-spot every time. I'm a ragdoll in his control, my body boneless and melting with the fire raging inside and radiating out from my core yet at the same time my muscles tense and coil in desperation. The pressure building, the tension unbearable. Something needs to snap, to explode, to release me from the all-consuming insanity of my need to be pummelled by his punishing cock.

"Harder. Fuck me harder. Please," I whimper. I have nothing left to give. My body can do nothing except what he makes me. He's burning me up; my mind is blank and frazzled simultaneously. Utter desperation and intense pleasure bring tears to my eyes as he works my body impossibly higher.

"I've got you, baby. I've got you," he grunts between thrusts.

"I need it, I need it, I need it, I. Need. It," I mumble repeatedly and incoherently, praying that he knows exactly what I need because I'm not sure I do. My mind and body are lost to the pleasure. I only know that it needs something desperately.

Out of nowhere, he bites my nipple hard as he slams my g-spot with his magnificent dick and the pain shoots straight to my clit as pure unadulterated pleasure. I shatter into a thousand orgasmic pieces around his thick shaft as my body finally explodes into the most blissfully intense climax. He rides each wave of pleasure, prolonging the beautiful agony until his cock throbs and swells impossibly and he pulses jet after jet of hot cum inside my shattered cunt. Just like he promised, we scream each other's name.

Chapter Eleven

Katie

The weeks pass and finally, things seem to fall into place in my life.

By the time the flood damage to my little cottage was fixed, it seemed almost pointless moving in considering the amount of time I spend in Ash's bed. We sort of fell into the routine of living together and I briefly wondered if it was too soon but Ash successfully argued that even the short amount of time traveling between the cottage and his place was time better spent fucking. Who was I to argue? Especially when he hid my suitcases in the attic to prevent me from packing; I wasn't *that* desperate to leave that I was going to go crawling around up there. And despite it all, it felt natural to live with him.

Maddie got the job at the Rock Hard Club and seems to be enjoying it, although she has made a few comments about Dixon not being friendly towards her. I'm not sure what's going on there but she seems reluctant to talk about it.

The lodge is thriving and at max capacity most weeks. Ash and I continue to go from strength to strength…and the sex is still insanely explosive. The red satin ribbon has become my new favorite toy…amongst the other toys I've found the confidence to try with him.

We've still not gone so far as to restrain me in a way where escape isn't an option. If my wrists are tied then it's normally a knot I can undo or my ankles are bound but my arms are free. I'm excited about being totally restrained by him and although I trust him, I'm still not quite there yet. Ash has mentioned it a couple of times, but never in a pushy way. He's mentioned it more recently because I think he senses that I have no reason to hold back with him anymore because I love him – not that I've told him that though. I just need to let go of that final little piece of resistance, the dark piece that reminds me of what happens when I'm not in control. I'm slowly overpowering the last of the bleak negativity because I trust Asher with my life and I have nothing to fear from him and I refuse to let fear be a part of my new life.

Just when I think I'm ready to take that step with Ash, a knock on the ranch house door one Friday evening shatters the little world of security I've built for myself.

"Detective Jones?" I ask as I open the door to reveal the aged appearance of the Detective who worked my assault case. He looks somber and tired in his crumpled suit.

Shit.

"How are you, Katie? May I come in?" He asks gravely.

"I'm doing really well thank you," I answer as I open the door wider for him and lead him into the kitchen. "Would you like a drink?"

"No, thank you, I won't be staying long as I'm needed elsewhere. Are we able to talk privately?"

"Um, yes, my boyfriend isn't home from work yet."

"You have a boyfriend?" He asks somewhat surprised.

"Yes, Asher Scott, the ranch owner."

"That's wonderful Katie. I hope he treats you right?"

"He does. Better than I ever thought possible. Detective, I don't mean to be rude but what's all this about?" It's not that I don't mind small talk but this feels stilted and awkward.

He sighs and looks utterly defeated. "Does the name Elsie Cade mean anything to you?"

Dread swirls suddenly and violently in my stomach. "That's...David's new girlfriend...isn't it?"

"Yes, it is. Phone records show you calling her shortly before you moved out here. Can you tell me what you spoke about?"

"I tried to warn her. To get her to leave him. Why are you checking her phone records? What's happened?" I'm starting to panic now.

"The inevitable," Detective Jones sounds angry now. "David beat Ms. Cade the same way he did you but she wasn't so lucky. I wish I didn't have to tell you this but he killed her and then he fled. He's wanted for murder and the DA is reopening your case and will likely contact you for a testimony once he's apprehended. It's too late to help Elsie but he's not going to have the opportunity to hurt another woman again. I will see to it that he spends the rest of his days rotting in maximum security."

"When you find him," I add, feeling the strength in my legs failing.

"Yes, once we find him," he admits darkly.

"Am I in danger?" I whisper, barely able to breathe.

"It's unlikely. He's not a stupid man and he'd have to be to try and track you down, knowing that I'd notify the local police department and have you watched. It strikes me that he wants to avoid jail time, not get caught. I've already spoken with the local sheriff but you should probably mention the latest development to Maddie; he wasn't her biggest fan and saw her as an interfering trouble maker. Again, it's unlikely that he would try to find either of you but she should be made aware of the situation."

"So, that's it?" I choke out, feeling my world disintegrate around me. In he walks and detonates a fifty-megaton nuclear bomb in the middle of my blissfully rebuilt life and that's it? Elsie Cade is dead. Tell Maddie.

What. The. Fuck.

"I can sense your frustration Katie and believe me when I tell you I'm right there with you. That twisted bastard should've been locked away forever after what he did to you and the skills of a smarmy-assed lawyer cost Elsie Cade her life. Nothing about this is right. An investigation is also being launched into the handling of your case by the DA and the legal firm that represented David. Other than that, I have nothing else I can tell you. And it fucking frustrates me that I can't stand here and reassure you he's already behind bars. Elsie's case is an active murder investigation and you're not family so I can't disclose too many of the particulars. All I can tell you is what I have. You shouldn't have faced the horrors you lived through and you sure as hell shouldn't have to live through this asshole's manhunt.

"The local sheriff is aware and patrols around the town and surrounding area are being increased. He's a wanted man; his mugshot has been circulated nationally. All I can do is keep you notified and tell you to stay safe." Detective Jones sounds exhausted. It's not his fault this situation exists. He was my champion in the aftermath of my attack. One of the few who really pushed for my case to see the inside of a courtroom. I can see that it burns deep that justice wasn't served and that an innocent life has had to pay the price.

I want to cry for Elsie. I can imagine the fear she lived through when she should never have been in that position in the first place.

My fear crystallizes to white-hot fury on her behalf. She was such a sweet-sounding person on the phone and she didn't deserve to be left at the merciless hands of my fucking ex.

What must her family be going through? Out there somewhere is a parent whose little girl is never coming home. They will never walk her down the aisle, never be grandparents to her children. Never see her smile again or hear her voice. The knowledge pulls at my chest and my eyes sting with unshed tears.

I should've done more.

I should have saved her.

As if sensing the direction of my thoughts, Detective Jones grips my shoulders in both hands. "You tried. There was nothing more you could've done. You were strangers to one another and you had the decency to warn her about the man she was getting involved with. I can understand why she didn't heed your warning; to her, you were the crazy ex-girlfriend who tried to have her boyfriend arrested. She was never going to listen to you but you still tried. Short of kidnapping her, you had no power over her decision to be with that scumbag. Do. Not. Blame. Yourself." He enunciates each word to drive home his point and then marches to the door, clearly a determined man on a mission. He turns just before he leaves, "I'll be in touch."

The door slams behind him, leaving me in ominous silence with only my chaotic thoughts for company.

I fumble with my phone with shaky fingers, eventually connecting the call to Maddie and briefly relay the conversation I just had with Detective Jones.

She sounds mildly concerned but there's an edge to her tone, one that I know means she's trying not to freak out on my behalf. The last thing she wants is for me to panic. But the absence of words can be just as terrifying as speaking a painful sentence out loud.

I end the call before I can read too much into Maddie's responses and wait in the eerily silent house for Ash to come home.

It's not unusual for me to finish before him and to be in the ranch house alone but after Detective Jones's bombshell, the quiet calm doesn't feel friendly.

It feels menacing.

Chills ripple down my spine as bone-deep unease claws at my chest from the inside. My mind is turning my safe and familiar surroundings against me and I don't know how to stop the spiral. I want to be strong but I know that Ash is going to come home to a girlfriend-shaped, crying and crumpled heap on the floor. I can feel my legs failing me as the last of my strength vacates my body.

The shrill sound of the doorbell tears me inside out, ripping the air from my lungs and forcing my heart into the confining space of my throat, choking me. Its beat is so violently rapid that my pulse deafens me and blackness creeps at the edges of my vision.

I grip the countertop for dear life, white-knuckled as I clumsily reach for the knife block to arm myself.

The logical part of my brain has been forced into a faraway corner so its voice is barely discernible when it tries to reason that if it were David, he's hardly likely to ring the doorbell.

I clutch the knife to me and stumble towards the door as the bell rings out again, echoing around the empty house like a taunt.

The front door is surrounded by slender glass panes allowing me to see who's on the porch – another reason why David would be unlikely to ring the doorbell; I'd see it was him, call the cops and leave him on the porch until he was arrested…or shoot him through the glass…one of the two.

I sag with full-bodied relief when I see it's just a delivery man. Being as far out of town as we are, and depending on who we've ordered from, we get deliveries at all hours of the day.

Hiding the knife in the back pocket of my jeans I open the door and sign for the slightly elongated box. The guy looks at me curiously; I'm guessing my face is still white as a ghost and my fingers definitely shake as I sign his handheld device but I'm in too much of a rush to slam the door and lock myself safely inside to care.

I relax a fraction more as I hear him descend the porch steps. Moments later, a door slams and his van rumbles as he pulls away. On still-wobbly legs, I walk to the kitchen with the package and discard the knife from my back pocket onto the countertop within arm's reach. That's when I notice the discreet little symbol stamped unobtrusively on the side of the box…the symbol of the online adult website that Ash has bought a few sex toys from.

That's enough to distract me momentarily but not enough to relax me – the box is too big to be a dildo or vibrator and anxiety gnaws at my already fraying nerves. *What has he been buying?*

And why the secrecy? He didn't tell me he was purchasing

anything else for our sex life…so that would suggest something that he wants me to work towards…because I'd probably not be comfortable with it currently…

This is the absolute worst day to be buying boundary-pushing sex gifts.

I tear into the box, not caring that it's addressed to Ash and gasp, nearly dropping the contents with a clatter.

A spreader bar.

A fucking spreader bar.

Any other day I'd have been apprehensive but intrigued. Today I'm just freaking the fuck out.

My mind is awash with memories I didn't give permission to run riot and they are mingling, distorting and twisting the device in my hands into something sinister.

It's fine, it's fine, it's fine…

It's. Not. Fine.

A scream bubbles up and I bite my lip and swallow it down like a painfully trapped hiccup. I try to reason that it's no different to having my ankles restrained in the cuffs we attached to Asher's bed but it *is* different. My legs would have less scope to wiggle even a bit and he could move me into whatever position he wants with this; I wouldn't be restricted to being tied up on my back – we'd have more freedom to move but I'd have less control over that movement. He could put me in any position he desired without any input from me.

Instead of arousing me like it would have this morning, the thought has me hyperventilating.

Air barely makes it into my lungs and conscious thought has flat out fled me. I'm teetering on the edge of a very dark precipice; weak, vulnerable and shaking with sobs when large, rough hands clamp hold of my shoulders out of nowhere.

I full-on scream at the top of my lungs. Blood-curdling and terror-filled as I gasp for breath and try to shake off the hot hands caressing me…

Caressing?

That's when my eyes fight to focus on the man in front of me. The beautifully familiar and clearly alarmed man who lifts his hands in surrender to show he means no harm.

Every inch of him is coiled and tense, the veins on his thick forearms bulge with the effort of not reaching for me. I want to run to him. To bury myself in the safety of his massive body, enclosed by the strength of his muscles protecting me from the dark world that's crept up on me.

I want to. But I don't.

His lips are moving but the sound is obscured by the frantic beating of my heart in my head. I focus harder on his deliciously full lips, but still can't tell what he's saying until he reaches his hands towards the spreader bar that's still clasped in my hand.

"It's okay, Katie," he soothes, his voice finally registering.

It is very fucking far from okay and the panic he fails to keep from his voice just reiterates this.

I pass him the bar on autopilot. I feel like I've been sucked into a vacuum and none of my senses can function. I'd be numb if it weren't for the fear wreaking havoc and causing my brain to misfire.

I need to tell Ash exactly what's happened and why I'm on edge and reacting so badly to something that this morning wouldn't have phased me half as much. I want David out of my head, out of my life, buried in my past where he deserves to stay. Not ruining the one good thing I've found for myself.

But I can't speak the words I need. Everything is failing and

139

falling around me. The darkness has seeped into my heart and oozes its way through my veins with every labored beat, thick and suffocating. I can't focus. I can't feel the love that would ground me and keep me here with Ash and keep me safe. It's being consumed and twisted. I can't focus on anything except what's right in front of me...the surprise spreader bar.

"Talk to me, Katie," he pleads.

"Why?" I barely whisper.

"Why talk to me?" he looks hurt and confused.

"No. Why did you buy *that*?"

"I bought it for us, for when you're ready. There's no pressure, baby."

"Then why didn't you wait until I was ready before buying it? Why are you always trying to push kink? Aren't I enough for you?"

"Of course, you are enough for me." He says earnestly but I'm so shocked it doesn't register.

"If that were true then you wouldn't need to keep trying to push my boundaries, you'd just accept them."

"Where is this coming from, Katie? We've been exploring together and you've been fine and I've always been respectful of your needs and told you a million times that I don't need the kink but it's obvious we both enjoy it. I've never hurt you baby, so I'm just really confused at the minute. I just want you to enjoy yourself."

"By doing something you want." In its terror addled state my brain isn't hearing any of his words of comfort. It's on a twisted self-preservation rampage.

"No. By doing something that we will both enjoy. I'll say it again as you're obviously not hearing me, I would never hurt you. I thought you knew that? I'd rather die than see you hurt.

Katie, I love you. And it's killing me that you don't trust me. Everything I am, all the love I can give, you hold it in the palm of your hands. You can crush me, my heart, or you can have it all. I love you, trust me."

He said it.

Those beautiful words I've been so desperate to hear. The words I'd hoped would calm me but apparently, I'm too far gone. The twisted place in my gut won't let me separate my fear of David-the-murderer-at-large and my love for Ash.

I panic. It's all too overwhelming, I can't think straight so I do the most stupid thing I can think of…I run.

I run from Asher.

I run from the man I love.

Just like Sylvie did.

Chapter Twelve

Katie

I rush to my car and drive to Maddie's as fast as is legally possible. For a BFF she seems remarkably irritated to see me.

"Let me get this straight," she sounds like a schoolteacher, "he professed his love for you and you ran away? Like a coward?"

"Hey! That' not fair."

"You're right. It's not fair...on him. I love you Katie, but I won't stand by and enable your bullshit and watch you screw up the best thing in your life. You get that right? Tell me you know you made the wrong choice here. Tell me you're not so completely wrapped up in your own crap that you can't see the damage you've just done to the both of you? I know you were thrown for a loop after Detective Jones dropped by and that it brought some scary as shit memories to the forefront but you didn't even tell Ash, did you? You didn't give him a chance to help you. Instead, you hurt him and yourself."

I try to hold it in but this is why she's my girl after all. She can call it as she sees it...and what she sees is my bullshit. I start to cry. Big, fat, ugly tears. The kind that makes your face completely wet, red and blotchy. I know the truth and I'm terrified I've just fucked everything up but I just didn't know what else to do at that moment. The words I wanted to say were stuck in my throat. The 'I love you' I so desperately wanted to say was trapped behind the bile that was rising at the thought of truly letting my guard down and trusting him…even though I already do, I just have a problem admitting it. And Maddie's right; I didn't even explain why I'm such a fucking mess. I'm not liking the lack of control I currently have over myself.

Surely Ash would be better off with someone else?

"I know. I…I love him and I'm scared. I'm scared and I don't know how to fix it and make it so that I'm not. I'm scared that David is out there and I'm scared that he will never be just a memory that I can shut down and forget about."

"Of course, you're scared sweetie," she says and holds me tight in a bone-crushing hug. "Big love is a big deal. Allowing yourself to be that vulnerable with someone, giving them your heart – especially after what you suffered – is a big fucking deal, but you're ready. Don't underestimate the progress you made. Don't let one conversation with a detective take that away from you. They're handling the David situation so it's out of our hands and we have to trust them to do their jobs. You've come so far sweetie, so let's help you go a little further. Let's break it down and come at this bit by bit."

"Okay," I sniff miserably.

"He loves you?"

"Yes."

"You love him?"

"Yes," I don't even hesitate.

"Do you trust him?" I take a deep breath and consider this. "Think about whether you believe he could ever truly hurt you emotionally, mentally and physically."

"No, he wouldn't hurt me. Yes, I trust him."

"With your life? If David found you on the ranch and came at you with a baseball bat to finish you off, would Asher Scott give his life to save yours?"

"Yes, and yes."

"Would you let him die for you?"

"Fuck no," I scream. The thought of Ash hurt causes my chest physical pain. Maddie just smiles.

"So, we've established that you love him and trust him. So, if you don't want him – as indicated by you running away – how will you feel when another woman comes along and tries to fix his broken heart?"

I basically just scream at this point. He's my man and no other woman is having him.

"Thought as much," she smiles smugly.

"But what if another woman can fulfill him better? What if I'm not enough?" I cry.

"That's for him to decide and he's already made that choice. Which brings us nicely back to the elephant in the room…or the spreader bar in your relationship. Sex. Asher loves you. If you asked him for a purely vanilla relationship do you not think that he would?"

"I thought so, but if he could do vanilla then why is he buying spreader bars and always seeing how much control he can take from me during sex?"

"Katie, anyone who knows you can read you like a book. You wear your heart on your sleeve and your expressions all across your pretty face. Whenever you talk about your more erotic, pre-David, sexual experiences your eyes light up with pure fire. It blazes through you leaving you scorched and hungry for it – it's obvious you like it. We've established that David

144

is just some psycho blip in the grand scheme of your life so don't let him ruin the things you take pleasure from. I know what you went through was seriously, seriously fucked up so I don't mean to sound flippant about it, I'm just trying to get a point through to you. Think about the rest of your life; don't think about Asher, just concentrate on what you want and answer me honestly. Can you really spend the rest of your life without kinky sex? There's no right or wrong answer here Katie, but I do expect you to be honest."

I mull her words over for a long moment. The rest of my life will hopefully be many, many years so when she puts it like that..."No, I can't. I don't want to deprive myself just because my ex was a goddam sadist."

"Then you have your answer. You're in love with Asher Scott, you trust him with your life and you don't want to live without thrilling sex. So, get your fucking ass home to his bed, beg, grovel and promise to never hurt him again because that man is never going to hurt you...unless you ask him to," she finishes with a wink. "Your pussy has well and truly whipped that cowboy so go home and claim him."

The tears are flowing faster now – I didn't think that was humanly possible – but everything Maddie has said is true. Sometimes it takes a neutral – or almost neutral – party to point out the obvious to you. I just hope that I haven't done any lasting damage to mine and Ash's relationship. I love him and want him so badly. And now that I've admitted that to myself, the words just want to keep flowing through my mind like the smoothest silk and tumbling out my mouth for the world to know.

I love Asher Scott.

I give Maddie a quick hug and head for the door.

"One more thing," she calls after me. "Asher has never had his own satisfaction at heart Katie. Before he bought the toys, he contacted me. He was pretty sure he knew you and your desires but he just had to be sure that what he knew was true and that he wasn't just projecting his sexual desires onto you. The very thing you accused him of – of pushing your boundaries for his own pleasure – was the very last thing he was trying to do. He worries about being enough for *you*, about being able to satisfy you because despite your protestations otherwise, he knows you much better than you believe he does. He could see you selling yourself short in the bedroom department and knew you needed his dominance to be fulfilled. You just keep living in denial because of fear. Talk to him. Take the leap Katie, he'll catch you."

"He's worth the risk," I choke out between sobs. I can't believe he checked with Maddie first before buying all those sex toys. I now have two people in my life who can see through my bullshit and help me to the other side. I just hope that Ash still wants me; I don't think he would instantly fall out of love with me but I know him, and running out on him while he put his heart and soul out there would've cut him deep. Just like it did with Sylvie.

I swore I'd never hurt him like her, but I did anyway.

Fuck.

"I'm not sure I deserve a man as good as him," I sob, my selfish shortcomings becoming painfully clear to me.

"You deserve to be happy. Asher makes you happy. Everything else is irrelevant. Do not be some pathetic woman who pushes a wonderful man out of her life because of some crazy-ass bullshit that's all in her head. And if you can't shake the crazy out of that brain of yours, *talk* to him about it. And then let it go. Asher is more of a Dom than he realizes; he may not live the lifestyle as such but he has that protective, alpha streak down. You're his woman and he would move heaven and earth to keep every single facet of your emotions and body safe from harm. But he can't protect what he doesn't know. Let him in."

"Thank you, Maddie. I love you."

"I love you too, now go get lost in Asher's bed...I have a date with my vibrator."

* * *

I drive back to the ranch in record time. I'm not sure how I manage that considering the swollen puffiness of my eyes from all the crying I've done, but I do.

As I pull up in front of Ash's ranch house it dawns on me just how big a mess I created by running away to Maddie's – even if it was for the best because she was able to give me the verbal kick up the ass I needed. Still, Ash doesn't know that; all he knows is that he said those three magic words and I turned my back on him and left. Actions speak louder than words...and that was a pretty bad action on my part. I'm going to need something truly spectacular now to erase that memory and show him how I really feel about him.

I can't breathe at the notion of him hurting over something I did. I need to fix this and I think I know just the way.

I rush up the porch steps and through the door.

"Ash," I call out, the desperation clear in my voice. I move through the cavernous entryway and movement in the living area catches my eye. My breath catches too, as the image of my tall, broad, overwhelming cowboy with a scotch in his hand

and gleaming wetness in his beautiful eyes punches me in the gut.

I did this to him. I reduced this beautiful, powerful man to tears because I can't get my own shit straight in my head. I hate myself in that second.

I don't go to him; I want to but I don't. My plan to give him all of me won't work if I fall into his arms the way I want to.

I look longingly into his eyes in the hope of conveying what I feel. Neither of us moving, barely breathing as the tension winds tighter and tighter. I snap first, toeing off my sandals and pulling my dress off over my head leaving me in my, thankfully matching black underwear.

Asher's eyes widen at the sight of me but still, I don't go to him; I make a dash for the stairs and hope that I have enough of a head start for what I have planned. I look over my shoulder at him as I'm halfway up and unclasping my bra, but I needn't have bothered; the sound of his heavy footfall tells me he's following me and my trail of lingerie. I drop my bra right there on the stairs and move a little faster – Ash has large strides and I don't want him to catch up with me. I shimmy out of my panties, discard them in the upstairs hallway, and run the rest of the way to our bedroom.

He's not far behind me so I need to be quick – hopefully he stopped to pick up my panties, buying me a few more seconds.

I find the right spot in the middle of the bedroom and turn to face the door so that as soon as he enters, all he'll see is me…knelt down…submitting myself to him.

I remember the position from some of the sub scenes I dabbled in college with and of course David was always keen to have me kneel before him. But that is the last time I will allow myself to think about him in this context. This is for Ash, to show him I do trust him and that I give myself completely to him. This is our clean slate; this position will no longer be tainted with bad memories or fear.

Sinking to my knees I spread my legs wide enough so that I am open and exposed for the man I love; the notion makes me wet and knowing he'll be able to see my arousal dripping from me, makes me hotter and wetter again. I sit up straight with my palms facing up on my thighs and look down to the floor. I've never been as elegant looking as some women in this position, but I think I get it looking good enough to convey what I want it to; *I'm yours, I'm sorry...I love you.*

I'm so lost in my thoughts and getting the position right that I don't notice Ash enter the room until I hear his sharp intake of breath at the sight of me naked and presented to him.

There's a beat where my heart doesn't work and my lungs refuse to inflate. What if he rejects me for what I did? I've just made myself completely vulnerable to this man and he could crush me...the way I did to him.

Karma can be a bitch like that.

I'm not sure what I'm expecting but it's certainly not what happens next. I hear the sound of Ash removing his clothes quickly but still, I don't look up – he's not given me permission to do so and that's the level of power I'm giving him over me. I need him to know I trust him. Suddenly, he's kneeling in front of me, mirroring my position, telling me the level of power I have over him. The power to love and trust and the power to hurt, which is what I did earlier when he laid himself bare to me. The tears begin to flow silently down my cheeks and splash onto my breasts and thighs. His head must not be that downcast because he sees and with one hand cups my cheek and tilts my chin up in the same motion so that I am looking into his fiery molten eyes, bloodshot with emotion. He brushes my tears away with his large, calloused thumb and that one act of tenderness tells me all is not lost. I finally find my voice and the courage to fight for the man I want, for the life I want, for the pleasure we both deserve.

"I love you, Ash, so much. I'm so –," he cut's my apology off with his mouth, soft and tender at first, like I'm breakable glass that he's afraid to shatter with the force of his emotions. His thumb gently grazing my cheekbone, cupping my face before trailing his fingers into my hair and gripping the back of my head. I push up on my knees for better access and demand more from him, my lips and tongue moving desperately to convey that I won't break, that I can handle all he has to give.

"You love me?" he questions as he pulls away from our kiss for breath.

"More than I can ever show you, more than I ever thought possible," I cry but this time the tears are happy.

Chapter Thirteen

Asher

She takes my breath away. This woman – *my woman-* – actually takes my breath away. I thought that was just over-exaggerated romantic bullshit but since Katie barrelled into my life like a tornado, I know the expression to be true.

I can't believe the gamut of emotions I lived through in the past few hours. When I told her I loved her, I knew it was risky – given the state she was in after finding that damned spreader bar – that maybe she wouldn't say it back and that maybe it was too fast for her but I genuinely never expected her to actually walk out on me.

That blindsided me for sure.

And the things she accused me of; of only buying the toys and pushing her limits for my own gratification at the expense of her feelings…yeah, that stung.

A lot.

She couldn't have bitch slapped me harder if she'd actually hit me. Especially after I checked in with Maddie first; she wasn't wrong and neither am I, Katie needs to learn to let go and let me in. We both know that Katie likes the same kink I do but that she's clinging to her fear like a protective blanket. Lord knows neither I nor Maddie can truly comprehend the horror she lived through but it's slicing me alive that she couldn't bring herself to trust me – it's almost like she's saying I'm no different to *him*.

When she fled out my front door, Katie ripped open my chest exposing every soft, vulnerable and breakable part of me I've spent years hiding and protecting; she flayed me alive and didn't give me so much as a backward glance in her urgency to flee. She left me bleeding, scared and cold in the darkness she created. Like she took the sun when she ran; sucking all the light from my life and leaving me empty and alone in the dark. And I couldn't help but think *not again*.

The second the door slammed I called Maddie but the line was engaged – a good sign as it meant Katie was calling her and would probably go there; I wouldn't be panicking about her whereabouts or tearing up the mountainside looking for her. Eventually, my call to Maddie connected.

"Maddie, I fucked up. Is she coming to you? Is she okay? Tell me how to fix it." I begged.

"You didn't, she did. These are her issues Asher and she just needs a moment...and a verbal kick up the ass. I'll talk to her. Try not to worry."

Easier said than fucking done.

She sighed down the phone then said, *"It's a little more complicated than just the surprise of finding the spreader bar. The detective that worked her case back in Colorado Springs came to see her before the package arrived. Her psycho ex is wanted for murdering his new girlfriend."*

"Fuck."

"Yeah. It gets worse. He evaded arrest. There's a manhunt underway. I'm feeling uneasy about the whole thing, which means

Katie is definitely struggling."

"Christ! And then the package arrived. No wonder she was freakin' the fuck out."

"Yeah, but she could've talked to you. Explained why she's afraid. I'll talk to her and send her back to you once she's calmed down."

Fucking David. Will that specter ever leave my woman alone?

I paced and paced until it felt like I had worn a groove into the hardwood and when I couldn't take any more of that, I grabbed a stiff drink. My plan was to have several to try and obliterate the pain shattering my insides but instead I sat in my favorite chair by the fireplace and did something I hadn't done since I was eight...I cried.

Big, stupid, fat tears that splashed down my face like the traitors they were. How could it have gone so wrong? I honestly thought I was good at reading people – I prided myself on it. How could I have miscalculated so badly with the one person most precious to me?

I don't know how long I sat that way. It felt like forever and then, in the gloom of my despair, the voice belonging to my angel ripped through my pain haze.

I'll never forget the sound; the panic, the fear, the desperate need that saturated the syllables of my name on her tongue.

I vaulted from my chair and made for the door to meet her as she looked for me.

The look on her face hit me hard. The uncertainty and the unwillingness to move a step closer to me. And then, with a suddenness that knocked me sideways, something in her solidified, her body language shifted...like she finally knew what she wanted.

I stood mesmerized as she undressed and raced up the stairs, casting me one sultry look over her shoulder to ensure I was following her. Of course, I was; I'd follow *my* woman to hell and back if that's what it took to keep her, cherish her and make sure she knew how loved she was.

I wasn't expecting to find her as I did.

Sprawled on my bed?

Yes.

Kneeling at my feet, the picture of perfect submission?

No.

So here I am, standing over the naked perfection that is Katie, breathless.

I've been with women before who were more into the lifestyle, who wanted to act out scenes that involved this submissive position but it never did anything to stoke my desire – I was aroused because they were naked not because they were kneeling at my feet.

But seeing Katie that way? *That* does something to my arousal…fires it into the stratosphere like a fucking space rocket.

The elegant lines of her glorious body enthrall me. The glistening juices of her arousal on display possess me. I never considered myself a 'shaven haven' man, but with Katie? Fuck yeah, I am.

But there's something not quite perfect with this situation. I get what she's doing – she's showing me what she couldn't say with words. She's giving her whole self to me, entrusting me with every fiber of her being.

Trusting me.

It's time for me to show her that she has *my* trust; that she has *my* whole self.

So, I strip and kneel in front of her, mirroring her, giving her my submission.

"You love me?" I ask as I brush away her tears, barely daring to believe the words she just whispered softly.

"More than I can ever show you, more than I ever thought possible," she breathes, tears of joy staining her beautiful, flushed cheeks and filling my soul.

This is my woman and I am never letting her go.

"Oh god, Katie, I love you so much," I manage to breathe before crushing her lips with mine. I savor the soft fullness, the delicate flicks of her tongue against the demands of my own. I almost lost this so I take what she's offering and drink her in until we're both gasping for air but reluctant to stop and draw breath.

"I need you," I whisper against her lips. She groans as her fingers trail all over my body, leaving a wildfire in their wake.

"You have me. I'm sorry I put you through that. I should never have walked out. I'm yours – only yours – for as long as you'll have me. No more holding back. No more fear."

"Careful, Sunshine, I want it all and I want it forever. Tell me now if that's not what you want."

"I want it. Take it all. Take *me*," she barely finishes her sentence as I wrap her body in my arms, lift and take the final few steps to my bed. I'm not restraining myself anymore. She's mine and I'm claiming her.

"I need to be inside you. Now," I basically growl like a Neanderthal.

"Yes. Yes. *Please*," she begs.

I spread her thighs beneath me with my knees and my fingers plunge into her wet heat. It's been an emotional few hours for us both but I love how ready her pussy always is for me. Soft and pliable, hot and soaking wet.

I fist my aching cock and feed her the first inch. Her tight little channel parting and molding itself around me. Her arousal glistening on the bare skin of her stretched opening. I'm not a small man, but watching her stretch to capacity to fit me makes me feel enormous. I still can't get over how easily she takes every solid inch of me; nothing feels as exquisite as bottoming out in her pulsing pussy.

I've been with women who weren't as tight as Katie and they've struggled to fit me, but with the goddess beneath me, it glides like a knife through butter.

I sink further into the velvety depths of her, feeling every pulse and squeeze of her delicious cunt, every shake of her muscles as the pleasure builds, every shiver as she gasps my name and claws at my skin. I watch her glorious tits bounce with every thrust, her eyes dilating with desire and love. I want to stay buried in her all night and I might just be determined enough to make it happen.

Lacing my fingers with hers, I set a slow but powerfully deep, grinding rhythm.

"Where's the spreader bar?" she asks as I sink fully into her and force the air out of her lungs.

"Not tonight, Sunshine." Her eyes search mine, a little confused and if I dare to believe it, a little disappointed. "It's just us tonight baby. No toys."

"No toys?"

I shake my head no. "Just you, me and a whole lotta love makin'," I thrust hard to drive my point home and her lips part on a truly erotic gasp that makes my balls tighten and threaten to blow.

"Right there. *Oh, God. Right. There.*" She pants, moans, writhes and cants her hips up to meet mine, driving me to hit that delicious little spot of ecstasy over and over.

"Look at me, baby. I want to be the only thing you see when you come on my cock."

Her blazing baby blues burn into mine as we collide. I grit my teeth to hold back but her sweet little pussy incessantly tries to milk me; every time my cock drags along her g-spot she squeezes tighter. The sensation is blinding.

I kiss her passionately because I love her and I can't not. She tears her lips away on a moan that increases in volume, her body bucks and then every muscle shakes.

"Ash! *I'M COMING!*" she screams...and screams. Katie is so fuckin' hot when she orgasms.

"That's it, baby, come for me. Who owns this pretty pussy?"

"You do!" she sobs in ecstasy.

"Damn straight," I growl. "Your cunt and climaxes belong to me."

"Yes," she whimpers, her body trembling as another fast orgasm tears through her. I can't hold back anymore, my own pleasure surging through me as I shoot my white-hot seed deep into her core. For a brief moment, I hope it finds its mark; my alpha streak wanting to put my baby in her and watch her sexy curves grow and swell with our child. We're protected by her pill though, so I know it won't happen and that disappoints me more than I thought it would. After Sylvie, I never thought I'd open my heart up to another woman again, let alone love her enough to want to impregnate her and build a family. But that's what I want with Katie. We've fallen fast and hard but I'm sure. As sure as the sun rises and sets and the thought doesn't fuck with my head as it would have before Katie.

I guess we're both making progress.

Her cunt continues to quiver in orgasmic aftershocks, milking me to perfection, demanding every drop of the seed I want to fill her with.

"I love you," her breath tickles my lips and she looks fearlessly into my eyes.

Katie Morgan just seared herself into my soul.

Chapter Fourteen

Katie

I wake the next morning cocooned by the smooth heat of Ash's body and a delicious soreness deep between my legs. The kind of sore that makes you want to do it again. My sex could manage another punishing round from Ash's pounding cock. The man is seriously, mouth-wateringly hung. Nine girthy inches of pure orgasmic perfection that I need to feel inside of me.

I don't normally wake up this aroused – even with Ash – but last night the sex was on a whole other level. It was just the two of us, making love in the purest of forms. It was true intimacy.

The connection was so intense, the orgasms so powerful. Just being with him, being held by him, feeling his powerful body on mine, fills me with a need so overwhelming that I don't think twice about waking him with my lips around his morning wood.

"Damn baby, that's so good," his voice gravelly, thick with sleep.

I deep throat his mammoth cock as best I can but I think I'm going to need to practice to fit *all* of him down my throat.

Placing my hands around his steel shaft to join the fun, I take him into my mouth twice more before he pulls me off and up to straddle him. He deftly finds my already soaked entrance and slides straight home. Nothing has ever felt as good as being speared by his thick dick. I'm not known for waking up this aroused and I'm also not known for sleeping naked…but it sure has its advantages, when the sex god between my legs can just slip easily between my folds and bury himself to the hilt.

He bites down hard on my right nipple, sending a violent shot of pleasure to my clenching core, and I melt for him, for us and for the future within our grasp.

* * *

Eventually, I spot the time on the clock on the nightstand and my heart jumps double time. We're so late.

"Baby, we need to get up."

"Relax, Sunshine. You're not needed anywhere," that sensual smirk of his sending me off-kilter once more.

"It's Saturday…the day that most of our guests' check-in and out on! I'm definitely needed somewhere!"

"Baby, it's the 19th. Remember? Our last guest checked out last night, that's why I was late coming home. We're closed for the week to refurb the plumbing."

Of course. Even though it's nearing high season, this was the only week where we didn't have as many bookings and the contractor could to the work so, reluctantly, we've had to close the lodge for the week while the work is done. We're even paying extra to have them work on it over the weekend to ensure it's completed on time.

160

"Aren't you needed at the stables?" I ask just to cover all the bases before I snuggle back down in his arms.

"Josh is working the stables this morning. I'm all yours, Sunshine...do your worst," he smirks that sexy-as-sin smile and I melt all over again.

* * *

Later in the morning, I wake again – I must've needed the rest; my boyfriend is an insatiable sex god after all.

The sun shining through the floor to ceiling windows is high in the sky and my body needs a few moments to adjust; I don't normally sleep in...I also don't normally have so much sex that I need the extra sleep. My life really is different these days and I love it.

I also love the huge, sexy cowboy sleeping next...*not* sleeping next to me.

I stretch my arm across his empty half of the bed as if the gesture alone will make him reappear. The sheets are cold so he's been gone for a while. I grab one of his t-shirts from the closet and pull it over my mussed-up mass of hair and go in search of my absent lover.

He's so broad and tall that on my short stature, his t-shirt is basically a mid-thigh length dress.

I wander down the hall to the stairs, my footsteps following the sounds I can hear below me. In my sleep befuddled state, it doesn't register that there is more than one male voice coming from the kitchen and too late I remember that David is on the loose...I'm already around the corner and in full view of everyone in the kitchen...

...Everyone being Ash, Dixon, and Jack. I breathe a sigh of

relief but it's momentary; with all the high-intensity emotions we went through last night, we never got around to having a conversation about David and the danger his wanted-by-the-law status presents. It's not a conversation our current house guests need to be a part of so instead of finding the courage to bring it up now, I allow myself to get distracted by their presence and the numerous boxes and plastic packaging strewn across the shiny countertops.

What are they up to?

Why are they all here?

Sensing my presence, Ash look over his shoulder, turns and then thoroughly looks me up and down with his smoldering gaze.

Now I'm distracted by the unimpressed look on his face as it dawns on me that *all* I'm wearing is his t-shirt – a white one that probably looks a little see-through in the light streaming in through the windows…and no underwear. With my un-showered and bed-head appearance, I must look thoroughly fucked.

"I didn't know we had company," I say uncomfortably and tug on the hem of the shirt. The action may cover an extra inch of my thighs but it tightens the garment around my breasts. Not the look I was going for.

Asher lifts an eyebrow and his lips twitch with the hint of a smirk at my awkwardness. His eyes still look unimpressed that I'm displaying myself for anyone but him and I have to admit that I sort of love that possessive streak in him. I've dabbled with exhibitionism but it never thrilled me the same way a possessive alpha does, so I'm more than happy to go upstairs and change – Jack and Dixon don't need to see my state of undress. But judging from Dix's expression, he doesn't mind so much.

As I begin to back out of the kitchen, Ash strides over to me.

"Sorry I wasn't there when you woke. I had to go into town to buy some supplies," I eye the boxes behind him and again wonder what he's purchased – the last item having not worked out so well for us. "I asked Jack to stand guard while I was gone so you weren't alone."

Stand guard?

What the…?

At my confusion, Ash elaborates. "I called Maddie last night and she explained what happened with that detective droppin' by to tell you about David."

I draw in a jagged breath at the mention of my crazy-murdering ex-boyfriend, my nerves pinch uncomfortably and my skin feels three sizes too small. A tiny whisper in my mind is thankful that I get to chicken out with a get-out-of-jail-free-card and not have to explain the situation.

Ash closes the remaining distance between us with one stride and envelopes me in his massive, solid arms. Holding me up with his strength when I need him the most and I can't help but whisper *I love you* into his fabric-covered chest – it's the highest bit of him I can reach.

"I love you too, Sunshine. You don't have to worry, you're safe here with me. I spoke to Detective Jones this mornin' and got the details from him so there's nothin' you need to say."

"Okay," I mumble, relieved. "Why did you need Jack to babysit?"

"I went into town to meet Dix. He helped me pick out some extra security gear for the house. She's already pretty well alarmed but I figure it couldn't hurt to put some security cameras and motion-detecting lights out front and back. I also picked up a bunch of Echo smart speakers to put around the house so you can sync your phone and use the Alexa Voice Service to call for help if you can't get to your phone."

The thought of needing to call for help and having something be so wrong that I can't get to my phone sends a tremor through my body and I shake in Ash's unyielding arms.

"Shh, baby, it's okay. I'm not tryin' to scare you. I'm just covering all our bases and makin' our home as safe as possible."

Our home.

Hearing those words spoken with his deep timbre makes my heart flutter.

He loves me. This is *our* home.

For the rest of the afternoon, Ash and Dix work on installing all the security gear and I keep them supplied with food and the occasional beer. By the time they finish, the sun has long since set so I prepare dinner – nothing spectacular as my mind isn't in it – before Dix head's back to town to take a late shift at the club.

That night I'm restless. Deep sleep evades me. I'm nervous and tense, despite being curled up safely in the warmth of Ash and the monumental fuck-fest he put me through. Honestly, that alone should've knocked me out for a week but all I can seem to do is snatch small amounts of disturbed slumber between bouts of anxiety and nightmares. At one point I sit bolt upright, the hairs on the back of my neck on end and adrenaline coursing through me putting my whole body on high alert.

Someone's here.

"Katie?" comes Ash's groggy voice.

"I feel like someone's watching me," I choke out.

Needing nothing more than my panicked worlds to fully

wake him, the lights flash on and he's on his feet and reaching under the bed to grab a baseball bat.

That wasn't under there before.

How'd I miss him storing that thing underneath our bed?

"Stay behind me," he growls out before I can ask.

I follow him from room to room while he checks every window and door and closet to confirm that we are indeed alone and I'm just being all kinds of crazy. He assures me that he's not pissed and that it's understandable, but I still feel stupid.

"Why didn't you tell me there was a baseball bat under our bed?" I finally ask as he climbs back into bed and folds his arms around me, one hand lightly stroking the curve of my hip in that gentle yet possessive way of his.

He takes a deep breath and audibly exhales an awkward sigh. "I didn't want you to know. Not because I didn't want to worry you, but because I didn't want you using it."

"I don't get it. Why wouldn't you want me to defend myself if it came down to it?"

"Firstly, I'm always in bed with you so you shouldn't need to defend yourself and not to sound big-headed, but there are few men out there who can take me in a fight, even with the element of surprise. I've always won the fights I've had and I can promise you that compared to how hard I'd be fighting to save you, I was barely tryin' in those other fights.

"And secondly – please don't be mad – you're tiny, Sunshine. I'm all for feminism and equality, but in a fistfight with a guy twice the size of you, you're not going to come out on top. You're going to get hurt. Bad. You try to defend yourself with a baseball bat and you'll be overpowered and then *they'll* have the bat. You'll have handed them a weapon to beat you with.

And their muscles will have the capacity to swing it harder."

I huff at his remarks and he has the good grace to look uncomfortable and apologetic but I can't deny his reasoning. I'm not a strong, powerful woman in stature. I'm petite and sure, given my past, I'd be damn determined to be scrappy in a fight but that wouldn't be enough to overcome a man who meant to cause me harm. I hate to admit that he's right; if I had to defend myself with that bat, it would be ripped out of my grasp and the tables turned.

I sigh and admit defeat. The feminist in me is chagrined but the bigger part of me that wants to live acknowledges Ash's infallible logic.

He continues tracing his calloused hand from the underside of my breast, down the curve of my waist, to my hip and back again while his other hand fingers strands of my hair, lulling me into a fitful sleep.

I don't wake rested, but I do wake up next to the world's sexiest man; *my* cowboy. Thinking of him as mine sure doesn't get old. The rough and rugged, melt-your-pants, swoon-worthy specimen with a heart of gold, lets out an adorable little snore and I find myself watching him sleep, unwilling to leave the bed and break our little bubble of momentary bliss. I only say momentary because as soon as I get up, I'll be confronted by the knowledge that David *still* hasn't been apprehended and the thought sits like lead in my gut.

I want to be done with the cloud of my past looming overhead like a churning thunderstorm, rolling through my veins until I'm thick with its poison. I have a bright future with the man lying next to me and I want to grasp it with both hands and no backward glances.

Just then, Ash's phone vibrates on the nightstand.

Ugh. Why can't the world leave us alone for a little longer? Why isn't the damn thing on *silent*?

I suppose until David is apprehended, it's probably a good idea to make sure we're always contactable, in case we need to be notified of anything.

Knowing what I know about my cowboy, that's probably the reason he set his phone to vibrate and why I now have to listen to it buzzing like the world's angriest mosquito. Incessant, annoying buzzing.

Buzz. Buzz. Buzz.

Ash's huge mitt of a hand grabs at it, fumbling as he comes to.

Bleary-eyed and barely coherent, this man is still the sexiest thing on two legs I've ever seen.

"Yeah?" he grumbles, gravelly husky voice sending shivers through me.

A male voice mumbles in response, but as the phone isn't on speaker, I can't hear what's being said, only what Ash says. He looks at me then with frustrated eyes and an exasperated set to his lips.

"Seriously?" he growls. "Fine. I'll be there as soon as I can." He hangs up with an angry stab of his thumb before dialing another number.

Anxiety starts to bloom in my chest, gnawing at my nerves. *What's happening to make him so angry?*

"Bill? Sorry to be callin' you on your Sunday but I need a favor. The contractor called and there's some kinda complication they need me to come and look at. Can you come by the house and keep Katie safe for me? No, they still haven't caught him. Yeah, don't want to leave her alone. Thanks, Bill. See you shortly."

I feel my hackles rising and I try not to be petulant, I really do, but I don't like being talked about like I'm not sitting *right* here. Ash didn't even take the time to talk to me and tell me what's happening before calling Bill to come and babysit me.

I'm frustrated.

Frustrated that for the second day in a row, I won't get any real-time with Ash.

Frustrated that someone else has to have their Sunday ruined in order to 'protect' me.

Frustrated that I'm a burden on the people around me.

Frustrated that David is yet again fucking with my life.

There's probably a healthy dose of exhaustion in there somewhere thanks to my nocturnal paranoia. All in all, I'm now in a bad mood.

And as usual, Ash can read me like a book.

"I'm sorry, Sunshine, I've got to head over to the lodge. There's some issue the contractor needs me to oversee. Bill will be here shortly though, so you won't be alone." He gets out of bed and walks to the closet, pulling out clothes in an aggravated fashion. Short, jerky movements making his displeasure obvious. I should take comfort from knowing that it pisses him off to leave, but it makes me no more amenable to the situation.

"On a Sunday?"

"We're payin' them to work on a Sunday, so, yeah."

"And now poor Bill has to ruin his weekend plans? Moira won't be happy. We could've called Maddie you know; if you'd bothered to talk to me *before* calling Bill and talking about me like a child who needs to be babysat. And since when does the entire ranch know about my ex?"

"Firstly, it would take too long for Maddie to get here plus she was working last night and the club is open late, she's probably still asleep. Secondly, your ex is a psycho wanted for murder, of course, everyone got told. It's not just a matter of your safety, Katie, it's theirs too. We're half-hour from town and if David came out here to find you, there are a number of other people who live here who could get caught in the crossfire. They had a right to know."

Great. Now I feel fucking wonderful knowing that I may be the cause of someone else getting hurt.

"Not sure it's wise to call Bill then. Wouldn't want him or Moira to be *caught in the crossfire.*"

He shoots me a dark look as he pulls a shirt over his rippling muscles. I'd be mesmerized if I wasn't so pissed off.

"Bill and Moira will be just fine as long as they know you're safe. Stop being a petulant brat and be grateful that there are people who care enough to want to protect you."

"Excuse me? Who the fuck do you think you are? You don't get to control my emotions or dictate what I feel. Yes, I'm angry, but I'm angry at the circumstances. I'm well aware that everyone is in danger until David is caught and I'm the reason for it. As you so rightly pointed out, people are at risk because of me and on top of that, I'm a burden that they have to babysit. I don't want to be a burden on people. I don't want to be a *petulant brat* they're obligated to protect. All I wanted was to spend a lazy Sunday with my boyfriend." I stomp past him and slam the bathroom door behind me just as he finishes buttoning up his jeans.

He looks damn fine and all I want to do is curl up in bed with him. Instead, I'm tired, anxious and hungry...all of which is a bad combination if you're me.

"Baby," he sighs from the other side of the bathroom door.

"I'm sorry. I didn't mean to make you feel bad about any of this. I want to spend my day with you too, but I can't so I'm not going to leave you here on your own. I won't apologize for that. I gotta go, I love you."

With his big strides, he's out of the bedroom before I've even opened the bathroom door. He's gone and that pisses me off even more. A few angry tears spill down my cheeks as I hear him greet Bill downstairs and then the front door closes.

This morning needs a do-over.

* * *

The day drags.

I try not to sulk and mostly pull it off but when Ash is late for lunch, which is then followed with a phone call to Bill explaining that he's needed at the lodge for the rest of the day, I regress.

Bill is polite enough not to comment on my mood but he definitely notices. I miss Ash and I feel like shit after the way things were left this morning. Not to mention last nights' lingering paranoia still has me on edge. I can't shake the feeling that something isn't right.

Moira joins us for a couple of hours after lunch and that helps my mood, marginally, but I'll take it. Anything to help shake the cloying feeling of hurtling towards something bad and unavoidable.

With nothing else to do, I fall asleep on the sofa and have a nap. I sleep for longer than intended, thanks to the shitty nights' sleep last night, and when I wake, Moira has gone again.

I feel bad for not making more of an effort considering they've been stuck with me all day thanks to Ash's contractors.

And at the expense of any plans they might've had.

Bill and Moira are the quintessential farming-type couple. Both in their fifties with greying hair, weather-beaten skin with fine wrinkles but the warmest eyes and kindest natures of anyone. They have a surrogate parent quality about them and I can see why they are so important to Ash. Maybe one day, they'll be that important to me and be people that I can turn to for support and guidance. Today though? Today, I feel like an awkward imposition.

Wandering back into the kitchen, I spot Bill sat at the island counter with cartons of take-out food.

"How long was I out for?" If it's late enough for dinner then I slept *way* longer than I should have.

"Hours sweetheart. I'd have woken you but you were deep asleep and I figured you needed the rest. Stress can really take it out of a person and the way I see it, you must be stressed to hell and back." I simply nod. He's not wrong. "Amazed you don't have a crick in your neck though – sleeping that long on a sofa? I was sure you'd wake up feelin' it, even if you are the tiniest person on this ranch."

I quirk a brow at his teasing tone. "Who bought food?"

"Jack came back from town with it. Said Ash asked him to pick it up."

"Ah, guilty conscience food. Guessing he's no closer to coming home and spending any time with me today."

Bill shifts awkwardly but is saved from responding to my snarky comment by the shrill ringtone of my phone, amplified due to being connected to the Echo speaker in the kitchen.

Glancing at the caller ID, I see it's Detective Jones and my stomach plummets through my body to the floor. Just like the lurch of a rollercoaster as it takes you over the edge into a terrifying freefall.

The call connects and the beat of silence before he speaks twists a tight knot in my gut.

"Katie, I have news," his grave voice finally booms over the speaker. "David was spotted at a gas station on the outskirts of town. The local sheriff is on route and he's sending someone to check on Maddie. I want you to keep yourself securely locked inside and with someone at all times until this is resolved. Do you understand?"

"Y-yes," I stammer through the shock. "How did he find us?"

"I'm looking into that Katie but the priority now is catching him and keeping you and Maddie safe. Is there anyone with you currently?"

Bill speaks up at this, "Yes, Sir. Bill Shaw, ranch manager here at Diamond Peak."

"Good. Bill, make sure all the windows are secure and the doors are locked. Don't let Katie leave the premises, even escorted. Understood?"

"Absolutely."

"I'll keep you updated with any developments. Keep yourselves safe."

"Sure," I whisper, shell shocked and with that, the call disconnects and Bill jumps into action.

"Call Ash, I'll check the windows and back door. You check the front."

Holy. Fuck.

He found me. How the fuck did he find me?

I stumble towards the front door in a haze of terror, thoughts racing through me a million miles an hour.

How?

Over and over again I ask myself this.

How did he find us? How did I miss his true nature? How did he hide his true self for so long?

The 'how's' don't matter, only that the front door is as dead-bolted as Fort Knox. He's not getting in this way.

I walk my way back to the kitchen, feeling a little calmer knowing that the house is secure, and call out to *Alexa* to phone Ash. I feel equal parts idiot and awe when I ask an electronic device to do something for me. I also feel old – this shit was science fiction when I was a kid. The rate of technological progress is astounding and probably outpaces my ability to keep up.

As the dial tone rings through the speaker I hear a disturbing thud from near the back porch. It sounds heavy and that sets me on edge.

"Bill?" I call out, trying to keep the edge of panic from my voice.

The house is secure. Of course, it's him. He just bumped into something.

My mind plays these thoughts like a mantra, trying in vain to keep my heart rate down but my gut must know something my head doesn't and refuses to co-operate with the keeping-calm program.

Bill doesn't answer and that makes my stomach cartwheel into my chest, leaving less space for my lungs and their oxygen requirement.

The silence stretches on and feels eternal but in reality, it can't have been more than a few seconds; somehow my brain has registered only two rings through the Echo speaker.

Ash will pick up. Bill will answer. Everything is okay.

Everything. Is. Not. Okay.

I know it the second I spot the eerie shadow that precedes

the looming figure about to round the corner into the kitchen.

I'd know this shadow anywhere and it's *not* Bill's.

It's David's.

He's in the house.

Terror grips me, keeping my body frozen and locked with shock while my mind falls over itself.

How did he get in? How long *has he been inside?*

My gut clenches and my stomach lurches, causing me to question my grip on its contents. Maybe I wasn't being paranoid last night? What if he really was there, in our room, watching up sleep?

Three rings...

A violent shiver shakes me to my core at the thought.

David rounds the corner and for the first time in a year, I lay eyes on the man who nearly ended my life...and left me fucked up about it ever since.

The specter of him has been replaced by the real thing and my knees nearly buckle at his proximity, the calculated yet deranged look in his eyes and the menacing way he stalks closer.

Four rings...

Oh god. My brain is a jumble of thoughts; how to escape, is Bill okay because the thump was obviously him falling to the floor, will Ash ever pick up the damn phone?

"There you are, princess. I've been looking everywhere for you," David's tone is silky yet deadly. A slow, sinister prelude to whatever he has in store for me. Right now, he is the epitome of a true psychopath; superficial charm with an undercurrent of ominous intent. Callous and manipulative and not caring enough to stop. There's not a shred of remorse or empathy in the depths of his dark eyes. He's the predator...and I am very much the prey.

Several things happen at once. Ash picks up on the fifth ring, just before his phone switches to voicemail, and David lunges towards me.

Despite my shakiness and nausea roiling through me, I'm able to dodge away from his grasp.

"Katie?" Ash's voice booms through the speakers.

"HE'S HERE," I shriek at the top of my lungs as I flee from the kitchen. I don't stop to grab a knife as Ash's words about handing a weapon to your attacker flash in my mind. I just sprint as fast as I can towards a downstairs bedroom on the opposite side of the house. Heavy footfalls tell me David isn't far behind so I don't think he paused to pick up a knife either.

Not that he needs a weapon to do damage; the man looks bigger than he used to. Not Ash big, but big enough and certainly bigger than me.

Vaguely, I register Ash's voice shouting through the speaker that he's coming, but as I'm running flat out away from the kitchen his voice disappears all too quickly. I don't run for the front door, knowing that it's locked up tight and that I'd be caught by David by the time I'd unlocked it. Instead, I lock myself in the first guest bedroom I come across.

Mercifully, this buys me a few seconds to plan my next move. Adrenaline burns through my veins, replacing my nausea with a jittery determination to survive.

The lodge is a ten-minute walk from here, which at the rate I move, is a five-minute run. However, Ash is on his way here; should I wait it out or make a run for it and meet him partway between the house and lodge?

The bedroom door creaks dangerously on its hinges as David slams into it from the other side, making my decision easy; there's no way that door will still be standing by the time Ash gets here. A few more blows like that and it's had it – *I'll have had it*.

I bolt for the window and squeeze myself through it and land on the wrap around porch with a loud thud that echoes through the empty night. The sun has disappeared behind the mountains, casting long, obscure shadows into the darkening twilight. The dimming light makes it difficult to see, but I don't have time to worry about it – I can hear the clunking of the locks on the other side of the front door. David must have heard the window sliding open and my heavy landing onto the wooden porch and figured he would have more luck with the front door than trying to squeeze out of the window after me.

I sprint along the porch, down the couple of steps and into the inky night, not pausing to mourn the fact that I'm barefoot. I'm not a shoes-in-the-house kind of girl, but I'm starting to regret that decision each time my soft pedicured feet hit the rough grass and dirt of the ground and gravel track connecting the house with the lodge. My life depends on my ability to reach Ash before David reaches me; my feet are just going to have to put up with it.

The muscles in my legs scream as I push myself as fast as I can go. My lungs heave with the exertion of sprinting uphill to the lodge, which is hidden behind the gentle curve of the hill I'm running up. The lights of the lodge illuminate the surrounding area, giving me a spot to run towards through the encroaching darkness.

My heart beats frantically as I hear the sound of heavy footfalls gaining on me. David was always faster than me. His long stride no match for my shorter frame, but I've got undiluted adrenaline and panic on my side and that drives me forward. Forwards to safety. Forwards to Ash.

David's heavy breaths creep ever closer. He doesn't scream or shout. There's no sound but for our labored breathing and pounding footfalls.

I keep my eyes fixed on the spot of the dirt track where Ash will appear from behind the hill. *Any second now. Any second now.*

He has to be there.

He's going to appear.

He *will* save me.

I *can* make it to him.

"AAARGH," I shriek as white-hot pain slices through my right foot. I don't know what I've stood on but it's sharp and it hurts so fucking bad that I stumble to the ground, unable to weight bear on it. Whatever it is has jaggedly torn through my soft flesh to leave a deep wound dripping blood. The burning pain radiates from the point of impact, nauseating me as my body fights to deal with the shock. Dizzy, stomach-churning and clammy skin from a cold sweat. I try to scramble forwards and attempt to get upright.

I didn't have much of a chance before and now I can't run, but I refuse to give up without a fight.

Just hold on.

Ash will be here soon.

Just as I make it to my toes, a brick wall of a body collides with mine, lifting and slamming me in a full-body tackle to the solid ground, knocking the air from my lungs and bruising me from impact. My head cracks against a rock and powerful fists begin to repeatedly connect with my sides. I feel as well as hear the sickening cracks of my ribs fracturing, my re-inflated lungs having the air forcibly beaten out of them again.

I curl into a ball as best I can. Shrinking away from the onslaught of punch after punch after punch. My legs thrash and kick at any part of him within reach while my arms wrap around my torso and head, trying to protect my vital organs.

"Stop! Please stop!" I beg as I gasp and force air back into my lungs, my sides splintering in pain as I do.

David's eyes flash with fury and menace. The look is cold and murderous. His face contorted with contempt. There's no sympathy or empathy to be found in his soulless gaze. This man never loved me. I'm in a real-life *Sleeping With The Enemy* situation. The man I shared my bed and my life with was a controlling psychopath; capable of faking love long enough to snare his victims before revealing the monster beneath. How could I have been so blind? I know it's not my fault but I'm still angry with myself that he could fool me and angry with him for being the worst thing to ever happen to me.

"Naughty girls who run away need to face the consequences of their actions," he sneers. "Your punishment stops when I say it does; when I'm satisfied you've learned your lesson, Katie."

A fist drives into my face like a brick. The asshole's been working out that's for damn sure. The hits are definitely harder this time – and they were bad enough last time to land me in critical care.

Shit.

I start to mentally catalog my injuries:

Head injury and likely concussion. Check.

A black eye, split lip, and a bloody nose. Check.

Foot laceration. Check.

Broken ribs. Check.

My rage boils over, the adrenaline mercifully numbing some

of the pain, and I start to fight back in earnest. Clawing and scratching at his face and arms. Screaming and thrashing wildly. Sinking my teeth into any bit of him that's stupid enough to get close.

He grunts and groans with the effort of fighting through my defenses, wrestling with me in the dirt and gravel that scratches at our skin. Dust kicking up around us. Veins popping in his neck and forearms, his face red with fury.

Just hold on.

Help is coming.

And that's when I make the error that will end my life.

I wince as my injured foot scrapes across the gravel, shooting spikes of fire up my leg, causing my guard to drop a fraction. That's when David back-hands me across the face, stunning me and forcing dark splodges into my vision. In that dazed moment, he straddles my torso, putting painful pressure on my damaged ribs, grabs hold of my wrists and pulls them above my head. He pins them both with one of his brutal hands while the other snakes around my throat and squeezes. Not a warning squeeze. A squeeze intended to close my airway.

I can't breathe.

The pressure increases and my lungs pound in my chest, straining for oxygen. Tears spring from my eyes, my whole body strains against David's body trying to loosen his grip. My throat feels crushed, my mouth dry. The world is eerily silent as I slowly suffocate.

I have one last burst of fight in me and I channel it all into my hips and, ignoring the pain in my foot, I brace against the ground and buck my hips with all my might and roll to the side to dislodge David.

It works for a brief moment and I'm able to draw a ragged

breath through my raw throat but David is too big, too heavy to roll completely off me. He mounts me again but this time he grinds his weight down harder, pinning and suffocating me worse than before.

With what little air I have left I try to do the math. Do I fight and burn through my oxygen quicker or do I go still, conserve the air and hope that Ash gets here before it's too late?

How long does it take to asphyxiate?

How many minutes away are we from the lodge?

I didn't get very far before David caught me, which means Ash has to run nearly the full distance to get to me. I imagine I'll be unconscious within a couple of minutes and dead a few after that.

In theory, Ash should be able to get here in time, so I stop fighting and try to control my rapidly beating heart. My panicky pulse is burning through my oxygen reserves.

David's vice-like grip tightens and the burn for air amplifies. Black spots start dancing before my eyes while the edge of my vision goes blurry. I'm not in pain anymore and that's how I know I'm in trouble.

Pain is good. It means you're still alive.

All I feel is fear.

Fear that this truly is the end. Fear that I'm dying alone with this monster. Never to see Ash or Maddie again.

My throat strains and tries to gulp. It feels like trying to breathe underwater. Drawing a breath and getting nothing. Lungs empty and confused.

Oh god. This is it.

No one came.

But I will fight to the end and even though I don't want the last thing I see to be David's maniacal face, I force my eyes open and look him in the eye. I refuse to give him the satisfaction of seeing me broken *and* afraid so I stare that motherfucker down with a grin on my face.

You can take my life but not my spirit asshole.

You lose fucker.

A loud noise cracks like thunder through the silence and a millisecond later, the light in David's eyes vanishes as part of his head explodes. The sadistic satisfaction replaced with nothing but glassy emptiness. A dark red hole blown into his forehead oozes thick blood. An inhuman wound not conducive to life dominates David's face. His expression distorted, pupils blown, slack-jawed, body slumping forwards and covering me with the blood spilling from his split-open head.

I'm able to breathe again as his hand slips away from my neck; it burns and stabs sharply, like trying to swallow a large, angular rock that's stuck. I cough and gasp and my vision clears just enough to see Ash rising from a crouch about twenty-five meters away with a sidearm in his hands. I can just about see him through the murky twilight, which means the shot he just made was more than impressive.

Ash knows how to handle a weapon.

I see his lips moving as he sprints towards me but the sound is distorted by the buzzing in my head and the pounding of my heart. My whole body shakes with it. The pain is returning and it's everywhere. Breathing is still labored and hindered by the body smothering me. I kick my trapped legs at the slumped dead David-corpse just as Ash reaches me and shoves his foul carcass the rest of the way off, freeing me.

Ash freed me.

In more ways than one and I think he knows it.

He brushes my hair from my eyes to better examine me, his fingers delicately tracing my cheek as the world fades to black with the soundtrack of approaching sirens.

Chapter Fifteen

Asher

This night will go down in history as the most traumatic of my life. Not even losing my parents came close to the terror of seeing that fucker squeezing the life out of the woman I love.

There was just enough light that I was able to make out their bodies tussling on the ground as I rounded the hill but I was too far away to do anything about it. I couldn't take the shot from that point as it was too dark to see clearly and I could've hit Katie, especially given how hard she was fighting back. At that moment, I was simultaneously the proudest and most scared I've been in my life. Scared of losing her. Proud of her strength to fight back like a ferocious hellcat.

I had never sprinted so fast; fear of losing her pushing each step faster than the last. I got close enough to take the shot just as her body stilled and gave up the fight.

That moment.

That's the one that will haunt me forever.

Because it's the moment I thought he'd killed her.

You'd think that in the height of panic, everything would be a blur.

You'd be wrong.

It's not.

It's crystal clear, the harsh reality stamping itself irrevocably in my mind. I will remember those moments in painful high definition for the rest of my life.

I remember crouching to take the shot, trying to make myself as steady as possible despite the tremor in my body. I know I'm a good shot, but there's nothing like knowing you forfeit the life of the person most precious to you if you fuck up, to make you doubt your own skills.

Every second that I hesitated felt like a lifetime of torture. Until finally, I had him right between the eyes. A slow exhale of breath, gentle pressure on the trigger, the heart-stopping moment before impact and then it was done. Like flicking off a light switch, David's life was over.

But the worst night of my life was just beginning.

Shoving David's dead weight off my woman, we lock eyes and I stroke her hair from her face before her eyes roll back into her skull and she falls unconscious.

She doesn't wake.

Not that I expect her to, given what I know of her medical history and previous head injury, but as the sirens grow louder and nothing changes, I really start to panic.

I keep checking her pulse and watching her chest rise and fall with jagged breaths but I can't shake the feeling that something is really wrong. That I wasted too many seconds retrieving my gun and calling 911. The latter was obviously a necessity, but I keep thinking maybe I should've taken him on regardless of whether I had the gun. He wouldn't have bested me in a fair fight but I had no idea from Katie's phone call whether he was armed with a weapon or not.

Christ, the sound of her screaming when the call connected

is going to give me nightmares for years.

Chilling. Desperate. Afraid.

No matter how logically I think through my actions since that fateful phone call, none of my justifications work. I still can't shake the feeling that I've failed her. The one person I swore to protect, the one life I value above my own, is lying in the dirt, broken and slipping away from me.

Her injuries gut me as I sit beside her with the sirens of a patrol car bearing down on me. The wound on her foot looks nasty and like something stabbed her. Katie's face is mottled and swelling from the bruises forming, her lip split, a patch of dark blood in her hair, no doubt from another trauma to the head. Countless other injuries I can't see because it's getting darker or because they're internal.

I've never regretted living a rural life and living so far from town…until now. It's clear that Katie has been hurt and hurt badly; these are the situations where every second matters and I can't bear to think how far away an ambulance is. I know emergency services drive faster than the rest of us but even at twice the legal speed, they're still a good fifteen minutes away.

A firm hand lands on my shoulder scaring the shit out of me. I turn abruptly and notice a patrol car a few feet away, lights flashing but siren now switched off.

A local deputy takes in the scene before him and listens while I tell him everything, my voice working on autopilot because my mind sure as hell isn't in the conversation. It's with the woman whose hand lies limply in mine.

The deputy, Elliot I think he said his name was, turns to his radio and has a conversation with the dispatcher. He told me he was told to patrol near here due to David's sighting earlier in the day. I'm thankful that he was able to get here so quickly but there's little he or I can do until someone with medical training arrives. I look between Katie and Elliot, picking out a few words of his conversation.

"Gunshot...David Marks...Miss Morgan...critical...urgent." I stop listening then and turn my focus back to Katie's lifeless form while Deputy Elliot steps around us to check David for a pulse and confirms to the dispatcher that he's deceased.

I killed a man.

The stark truth of that hits me in the chest. It was justified; he was trespassing and trying to kill the love of my life so I'd do it again without a second thought. But that doesn't change the gravity of knowing you ended someone's life, no matter how much they deserved it. In the blink of an eye, he went from drawing breath to an empty shell of dead flesh, bleeding out over my hillside.

I did that.

If Katie makes it through this, will she be afraid of me? She's suffered enough violence at the hand of one boyfriend, could she stay in love with a man who was just as capable of causing harm? I never thought David and I would have something in common, but we do...we're both murderers.

No matter the justification, I murdered him. Because I'm a good enough shot that I could have hit him in the shoulder or leg but I didn't. I chose to shoot him in the head. Because he deserved it, because it *was* justified after everything he's done and because I wanted him gone from Katie's life forever. No trial, no jail time or possible parole, no chance that he could ever find her again. She deserves a life free from him, free from looking over her shoulder. We deserve a life without fear. In the second I pulled the trigger, I saw our future flash before my eyes and there was no way in hell I was letting him live so that he could come back to haunt or hurt us in the future; what if we had kids and he threatened them? No. I chose. I chose to kill him and I have to face the consequences of that.

"Hell of a shot," comments Elliot.

"What?" I realize he's no longer talking on his radio.

He nods in the direction I said I took the shot from. "Quite a shot to make in the fading light. Quite the marksman, if I had to guess."

"I am. I aimed at his head, pulled the trigger and hit my mark," my voice is emotionless and I'm bracing for the backlash of my actions.

"Don't look so worried. You took his life in defense of another *and* it was on your land. He was a wanted man, trespassing and inflicting harm on another. There isn't a DA in a hundred miles that would take up David Marks' case against you."

I register a flicker of relief in my stomach before more sirens blare, lights flashing on the hillside. An off-road vehicle from the Aspen fire department comes careening to a stop next to the patrol car. I knew they were quick but I had no idea they could move that fast over this terrain. The doors fly open and two medics rush towards us, followed by Max Cooper, my friend and Dix's slightly younger, firefighter brother.

"Ash," he yells and runs to me. I'm so grateful to see a familiar face as the medics move me aside and start assessing Katie's condition.

"Max," I give him a one-armed hug on autopilot.

"Don't worry man, she's gonna be fine. Smith and April are the best medics in the county. A chopper is on route to airlift her to hospital.

"We need to intubate, radio the pilot and tell him they're

going to have to take her to Denver. She needs an intensive care unit," April calls to Max. "Then radio dispatch and get a patch through to Denver. Tell them she's unresponsive following asphyxiation, her esophagus is swelling, bruising around her torso indicative of internal injuries and blunt force trauma to the head."

My face pales, bile rises into my throat and I feel lightheaded. I don't do dizzy, ever. But April's assessment has the blood rapidly draining from my face.

Sweet Jesus. What has that monster done to her?

"Sit down before you fall down," Elliot's arm grips me and helps to lower me to the ground as Max talks into his radio, relaying everything April said.

That's when I remember Bill.

Fuck.

With the shit storm around me, I completely forgot that he was with Katie and the only reason he won't have killed that fucker himself would be because David hurt him first.

God, no.

Bill is like a father to me. I can't lose another. Just when I think this night can't possibly get worse, I realize that I still have more to lose. That knowledge hurts so much.

With my heart beating rapidly enough to explode, I leap up and sprint towards the house just as Moira comes into view.

"Asher, what's going on? I can see the lights flashing from our cottage –"

"Bill," I yell at her and vault up the porch steps, heavy footfalls, likely belonging to Max, behind me. We divide and conquer; he goes left and I head right into the kitchen and then on towards the rear porch where I find him slumped against a wall, blood trickling down his face but starting to come around. David must've knocked him out with a blow to the head.

"He's over here," I yell.

Max and Moira round the corner moments later; Moira crying and running to her husband's side.

"I'm okay my love," his voice is strained and hoarse. His eyes suddenly bug and he makes to stand, "Katie, where's Katie?" he asks but pales when he looks at my face.

An awkward beat of silence follows. One I don't know how to fill. Whatever I say, Bill will feel awful for not protecting Katie. Even though it isn't his job and he was outmatched by a much younger and stronger man.

My mouth won't form words and seeing my difficulty, Max answers for me.

"She's hurt but the medics are with her now. We'll know more once we get her to hospital."

I've always liked that Max doesn't sugar-coat shit, lie or make false promises, but his honesty of the situation is too much. I turn and stride back out of the house and run back to Katie, needing to be beside her now that I know Bill is okay. The distant but growing sound of helicopter rota blades fill the dark and several things happen at once. More patrol cars arrive, including the sheriff and Detective Jones, and the chopper bears down on us, landing in a clearing not far from the house. The engine roars loudly while the rota blades whip up the wind and dust. A door on the side opens and more medics in red flight suits spill out and make a beeline for Katie. They talk to Smith and April and as a coordinated group, count down and move Katie onto a spinal board. They're careful not to jostle her and that's when I see that they've attached a neck brace, she's intubated and being given oxygen and she's attached to IV's.

The sight makes me sick to my already fragile stomach. The entire hillside is alive with chaos, but the organized type that emergency personnel specialize in. Nothing makes sense to those of us looking in from the outside, but they know what they're doing and they do it efficiently as a team.

Blue and red flashing lights cast swathes of light and shadow across the whole scene, people yell instructions over the sound of the chopper, David is being zipped into a black body bag, Max and Moira help Bill out of the house and I stand here. Frozen. Wishing I could un-see it all. Wishing that I never left our bed this morning. Wishing that the last words I said to Katie weren't huffed in exasperation through a goddam door.

If I had just stayed with her today, none of this would be happening right now. Bill wouldn't be injured and Katie wouldn't be fighting for her life and being slid into the back of a helicopter, poised to take her to an intensive care unit nearly two hundred miles away.

I start to walk towards the chopper when one of the medics stops me from climbing in beside her.

"Are you family?" he shouts to be heard.

For a fraction of a second, I think about this. If I say no, they won't let me go with her or allow me to see her once she's in intensive care. She has no other family to the extent that Maddie is probably her emergency contact, but she's my girlfriend, the woman I want to spend the rest of my life with. That is if we get to have a life together.

"Yes," I answer, "She's my fiancée." It's an almost truth. If Katie makes it through this and will have me, she *will* be my fiancée. If I get to hold her in my arms again, I'm grabbing hold of that opportunity with both hands in a death grip and never letting go.

The medic looks apologetically at me, placing a hand on my shoulder and gripping reassuringly. "I'm sorry," he says sincerely, "there's not enough space to take you with us."

I balk at his words as if they were a physical blow to my stomach, confusion clouding me. "I don't understand."

"We don't have the space for another person on board; our main chopper has a fault so we've had to use our smaller bird, leaving us no space for passengers. I really am sorry. I know it's a long drive to Denver but I promise you she's stable. I'll notify the hospital that you're on your way and by the time you get there, they'll have done scans and tests and have a better idea of what we're dealing with."

"Or she could die mid-flight," I bite out.

I see it the moment he admits I'm right. There's a sad resignation in his eyes. "It's unlikely but I can't promise you it's not a possibility."

"Let me say goodbye," I'm begging at this point.

He nods and I climb into the cramped cabin. He wasn't lying, with all their equipment and Katie laid out on a stretcher, there's barely any room for the medic who just let me in.

"We can't hang around," the pilot calls over his shoulder, "take a moment but then we need you to get out and stand back from the rota blades so we can get airborne."

I nod and look at Katie, willing her to wake up with my eyes. Not even trying to fight back the sting of tears threatening the backs of my eyes. Stroking a blond wave of hair from her cool, bruised skin, I lean close and whisper in her ear.

"I love you, Sunshine. Don't leave me. It's not your time. I'm here, waiting for you, so don't you dare go towards any fuckin' bright lights." I press a gentle kiss to her cheek and climb out of the chopper, allowing the medic to climb in so they can take off. He looks me straight in the eye, a silent promise that he has my woman and he'll take care of her.

In a vortex of wind and dust, they take off and speed into the darkened sky, taking my heart with them and leaving me an empty, broken shell.

Bad shit needs to stop happening to the people I love. I can't take much more.

"Ash," Max's deep voice draws me out of my self-contained misery, "Smith and April are taking Bill to town to get his head checked, Moira's going with them. The Sheriff and his deputy will wait around for David's body to be collected and I'm gonna drive us to Denver. Where are the keys to your truck?"

Dix and Max are my closest friends so I know when Max is on and off shift and his shift…it ended hours ago. He shouldn't be here; firefighters wouldn't be dispatched for this sort of thing, especially one going off shift.

"You don't need to do that Max, your day ended hours ago, go home to Lucy." Lucy being the super adorable girl-next-door turned sex-vixen girlfriend. She totally blew his mind this past winter when he stupidly assumed she was nothing more than a buttoned-up PA with a pretty face. Turns out, all she needed was someone to flip the switch and now *he* almost can't keep up with *her* sexual appetite. Max part-owns the Rock Hard Club with Dix and had the biggest smug face the first time he paraded his new girlfriend there; they've been going strong ever since.

"I called her on the way over. She knows and she'd kick my ass if I went home now and left you. Not happening brother, so give me your goddam car keys."

"How did you know?"

"The call came in as I was heading out. I wasn't about to ignore an emergency on your ranch so I turned around and hitched a ride out. April drives like a fuckin' beast so we made good time."

"So, Lucy is okay with you being gone all night? It's not just a little drive down the road and I appreciate the offer but you must be exhausted from workin' all day and if you come with me, you'll be up all night."

"I've done plenty worse Ash. I'm not on shift for a few days now so I can rest up later. Lucy is fine with it and most importantly, you are my friend. I'm not leaving you alone in this."

"Thank you, but I'm drivin'," I all but grunt. Max raises an *are-you-serious* eyebrow and despite the bone-deep weariness, I need to drive. "If you drive, I'll have the entire trip to mull over the worse-case scenarios. If I drive, at least I'll be focused on somethin'.

He holds up his hands in surrender and we start walking towards the house and my truck but are intercepted by Detective Jones. I know I have to talk to him but I really want to get on the road; I have somewhere far more important to be.

"Mr. Scott?" I stop in my tracks, sigh and turn to face him. "I'm sorry we aren't meeting under better circumstances," he holds out his hand for me to shake.

"No offense but I can't think of many circumstances where it would be a pleasure to meet you," sounds harsh but it's true. He's a detective working a homicide investigation, who also happened to work my girlfriend's assault case. He was never going to be someone I wanted to meet because when people like him show up, terrible shit has gone down.

"I suppose that's true," he smiles, but it's tired and doesn't reach his eyes and his graying hair looks like he's run his hands through it and pulled a few too many times. I probably look the same, minus the gray hair. "There are a few things I need to handle here and then I'll be making my way to Denver. When you're ready, I need to take your statement. A forensic specialist will also be brought in to photograph Katie's injuries and collect samples. I know you don't want to hear this but I still have to present all the evidence, even though David Marks is dead. I hope you understand?" He places his hand on my shoulder in that protective, fatherly way, which just compounds how weak and helpless I feel.

I nod once, "I'll see you in Denver, Detective."

Chapter Sixteen

Asher

Max and I speed away from the carnage on my hillside, leaving the flashing lights and dead body in our wake of dust and exhaust.

One of the many knots in my chest loosens at the knowledge I'm on my way and will be with Katie again soon. It's not much in the way of relief, but I'll take what small comforts I can get. Not knowing how she is or if she's even alive is crushing my frantic heart. My pulse pounds and I don't feel like I can breathe; like I have a thousand-pound weight squeezing my chest and constricting the function of all my vital organs.

Max looks sideways at me. I know his expressions and this one says *dude you should totally be letting me drive right now*. I glare back, a look that's somewhere between *don't fuck with me* and *I promise not to drive us off the road and kill you*. It's the best I can do currently. Max wisely decides to call Dix – who I found out was tasked with protecting Maddie – and I listen as the call connects over the truck's speakers. Apparently, I was right about Maddie being Katie's emergency contact as she's on the phone to the hospital at the same time Dix talks to us.

"We'll get on the road shortly and meet you at the hospital,"

Dix confirms. It will be good to have my friends with me as I brace myself for what's to come. All of my muscles are tense, coiled and ready to snap while my stomach has a tentative grip on its contents. I've never been scared sick in my life, but I sure as hell am now.

The drive to Denver drags despite the light traffic of a Sunday night and my inability to stick to the speed limit. It's too dark to appreciate any of the spectacular Colorado scenery, not that it would register much through my anguish. I'm good at schooling my features but Max knows me better than most and can sense my turmoil. He doesn't try to fill the painful drive with idle chatter – what would he talk about, how great his life is with Lucy? No, my friend is wise enough to sit in my darkness with me and knows that just being there brings me more comfort than I can tell him. Max was never one for dragging you to where he thought you should be physically or emotionally, he's brave enough to stand with you wherever you are. That's probably what makes him the great firefighter he is; he's not afraid to stand tall in the painful places where others can't help but fall.

After what feels like forever, the hospital comes into view.

"Pull up out front and I'll park the truck while you go and find Katie," Max instructs me. I'm not going to argue; this means I don't have to waste any more time. As soon as the truck comes to stop, I jump out and bolt towards the automatic doors of the ER, Max calling that he'll catch up.

I can barely breathe to talk to the secretary at the nurse's station my chest is so tight.

I can't lose her.

I. Just. Can't.

It's all I can think. Katie deserves to live out her days

196

surrounded by the people who love her and I don't want to be alone again. I can't face it. She's my person. The one your soul recognizes as your kind of crazy. She's can't be gone. I can't bury another person I love. *Please, God. Don't make me.*

"She's been admitted to the ICU, fourth floor." I think I manage to thank the woman as I bolt for the stairs, too impatient to wait for the elevator. Each heavy, punishing footstep echoing around me as I race upwards.

I fly through the door on the fourth floor like a man possessed and sprint my way to another nurse's station. An older nurse smiles at me expectantly as I skid to a halt in front of her.

"You must be Mr. Scott? Miss Morgan's fiancé? Follow me, she's in room six. Doctor Peterson is with her now." I relax a fraction at the nurse's use of Katie's name in the present tense. *She's not dead*. My angel managed to hang on.

I mutely follow the nurse down a pale green corridor, scared shitless of how I'm going to find Katie on the other side of the door to room six. The smell of antibacterial strong in the air, shoes squeaking on the linoleum floor.

Following the matronly nurse into Katie's room, my senses are assaulted by the bleeping and hissing of machines and the sheer number of things she's attached to. Needles pierce her, sensors attached to heartrate monitors are stuck to her skin. Tubes come out of her mouth and nose as another machine breathes for her. Something with a red light is clipped to one of her fingers and I glimpse a small tube snaking its way out of the blankets and into a catheter bag. In the harsh light of the hospital room, I can see just how badly David hurt her. Katie looks like she went ten rounds with a heavyweight boxer and lost. She couldn't have looked worse if Antony Joshua tied her up and used her as his punching bag. She looks horrific. There's barely a patch of lightly tanned skin that isn't black or that violent purple-blue color of fresh bruises. Most of the marks are swollen and tinged with crimson where her flesh had bled beneath her beautiful skin. Where she's unmarked, Katie is a pale, sickly gray color. Only a shade or two warmer than the color of a corpse.

Christ. At that moment I'm beaten. I've no more strength left. My knees feel weak and wobbly before they collapse out from under me and I slump to the floor, salty wetness trickling down my cheeks.

I'm not ashamed to show weakness and I couldn't give two fucks about people seeing me cry. This is not the moment for false male bravado. It's okay not to be okay and I'm very fuckin' far from okay.

From behind me, two firm hands help pick me up and I'm guided forwards to a chair by Katie's side. Max.

He looks to the doctor and asks for his prognosis of her injuries. I take Katie's cool hand in mine, carefully avoiding the cannula and the IV tubes connected to it, while I listen to Doctor Peterson talk about the tests, x-rays, and scans they did while we were driving here. The medic didn't lie and apparently, Katie was stable for the entire flight.

"Why is she still unconscious?" My voice feels tight and sounds hoarse.

"It's a medically induced coma. Her windpipe was crushed enough to cause her esophagus to swell, so we're keeping her intubated until this swelling goes down. It's less of a strain on her recovering body if we keep her in a coma and breathe for her, especially with the number of cracked ribs she has. Given the severity of the bruising, I'm surprised there isn't more internal damage. But there's no trauma to any vital organs and her ribs, although fractured, have not broken completely. Katie did sustain a head injury and had her oxygen supply restricted, so while there's no obvious brain injury on the scans we've done, we can't rule out brain damage. We'll know more when she wakes up. Her vitals are improving and promising; if she keeps up this level of progress, we may look to bring her out of the coma on Tuesday. That's subject to change and while we'll do everything we can for her, Katie's recovery is in her hands for the moment." With that, Doctor Peterson addresses the nurse and reals off a different language of required tests, vital monitoring, and drug prescriptions. He then pulls some of the blankets away from Katie's legs to assess the wound in her foot. The nurse brings him a tray of injections, suturing equipment, and sterilized gauze while he situates himself on a wheeled circular stool and positions himself at eye level with Katie's injury and unwraps her foot from a bloodied bandage.

"I'll go raid some vending machines for snacks," Max announces and quietly leaves the room. We didn't stop for food on the way and although I've lost my appetite, Max is probably starving after a long day.

"What do you think caused that?" I ask and jerk my chin towards the still lightly bleeding foot.

Doctor Peterson gives a thoughtful shrug. "I can't be certain but I would hazard a guess at a sharp rock. The wound isn't clean like I would expect if it were from a knife; the edges are jagged, suggesting the skin was broken by something uneven. Sprinting along barefoot like she was, she probably put a lot of force onto the object she stepped on. But she got lucky, whatever is was missed the tendons in her foot. It's just a large, slightly deep wound that requires a few stitches to stop the bleeding."

Once he snips the thread of the last stitch and bandages her foot, he gets up to leave. "Vanessa, the nurse, will conduct half-hourly observations to check on Katie's vitals. If any of the machine alarms sound, don't panic; Vanessa and her team will deal with it. Here is the call button," he indicates a red button on a corded remote that he places on the bed near my hand, "press it if you have any concerns and Vanessa or one of her team will come immediately. Unless Katie takes a turn for the worse, I'll be back in a few hours."

I'm alone with Katie then, for the first time since our argument in our bedroom this morning. I'd give anything to have her wake up, argue with me again and tell me how much of a dick I was.

It's always the small things that hit you in moments like this.

With my parents, I remember thinking how sad it was that we'd never have the epic drama that accompanied *every* game of family monopoly. Sitting here with Katie now, the rough pad of my thumb tracing the pale, silky coolness of her knuckles, I'm struck by the myriad of memories I can't bear to lose. The way her face lights up when she smiles or how her eyes sparkle and dance when she's makin' mischief. The way her body sways to songs on the radio as she cooks in the kitchen, flipping her hair around and wafting the coconut smell of her shampoo that assaults me. How my cock is strangled on a daily basis because I'm transfixed by Katie's bouncing breasts and perky nipples that pebble through her shirt because she refuses to wear a bra. God, I love that she doesn't wear a bra and that whenever I feel like it, I bend down and nip one of her delicious, rosy buds through her clothes, eliciting a positively primal moan that hardens my dick in seconds.

I even miss the mundane things, like finding her toiletries all over the bathroom and the sass she gives me when I dare to complain about it. Who knew there were so many necessary feminine products and that the struggle to find the toothpaste amongst the tampons was real? We even had an argument about her using tampons; I'm a possessive prick who hates the idea of anything penetrating her but me and the toys I use on her. I don't care if it's for sanitary purposes; I'd fuck her whether she was on her period or not and a tampon is just in the way of that. She laughed adoringly at me and said once she used them up, she would 'consider' switching to pads. Always on her terms and I love that she's secure enough with me to enforce that. Not that I would ever coerce her but I'm glad she doesn't feel the pressure to buckle to my desires over what she's comfortable with. I can be a force to be reckoned with, I know this; I'm dominant with a commanding presence and it's easy for women to get swept away in that and give me what I want. But Katie is her own powerhouse and she stands toe to toe with me; an unshakable force of nature to rival my own.

God, this woman.

My woman.

I love her so damn much.

She better fuckin' wake up and soon.

Stroking little circles on the delicate skin of her wrist I settle in for the long haul. The steady beeps and the rhythmic hiss of the ventilator breathing for Katie my only companions until Max returns with take-out coffee cups and a shit tonne of vending machine junk food.

"I couldn't find an open café as it's a Sunday night, but there are various vending machines for snacks and hot drinks scattered around. I've scouted out the best and brought you back my haul. Help yourself," he dumps his score on a little table in the corner of the room. "How's she doing?"

I wave a hand at all the machines keeping her alive, not sure what to make of it all. "She's as good as she can be, I guess, considering there's a machine breathing for her. The doc sounded positive. It's a waiting game now," I scrub my hand down my exhausted face and over the stubble that's grown the past couple of days.

I keep thinking I'll wake up from this nightmare any second and that Katie will be safely tucked into my side, sleeping soundly with that delicate faint smile her lips naturally rest in.

Reality is not so kind.

"Maddie messaged me; she and Dix will be here in about half-hour." Max sits in a chair near the door and tries to get comfortable. Leaning my head forward to rest on the bed next to Katie's arm, I zone out until I hear familiar voices outside.

I look up just as they enter and Maddie lets out a panicked sob at the sight of her best friend. She doesn't look too steady on her feet either – glad it's not just me – but Dix is there to support her before she hits the floor. Wrapping his arms around her, he holds her tight.

Dix isn't an uncaring man, but it's been a long while since a woman was able to move him enough for him to want to offer support. He's chivalrous enough that he wouldn't let Maddie face plant the floor but once she was steady on her feet, he'd put distance between them. He doesn't do that. He continues to hold her, tucking her into his side and leaving a sturdy arm wrapped around her waist. If I wasn't in turmoil, I'd be curious, but playing twenty questions with Dix will just have to wait for another day.

When Maddie has calmed enough to talk, Max and I explain her injuries while Dix looks grimly on.

"How much do you know?" Max asks.

"Only that David attacked her and that, as her emergency contact, I was needed at the hospital. They wouldn't give out any details over the phone," Maddie's voice trembles and her eyes glisten as they fill with tears.

"You should know, I had to tell them I was her fiancé to be allowed to stay with her. Please don't accidentally mention the truth," Maddie and Dix nod their understanding in unison. They both know enough about mine and Katie's relationship to realize this is just a technicality. We belong to each other and if she could talk this second, I'd come right out and ask her to be my wife.

"A deputy called to tell me I was safe and that David was no longer a threat; I take it they apprehended him?" Maddie asks.

Dix's eyes bore into mine; he sees the truth. One look at his brother, who returns his steady gaze, and he has the confirmation he needs. The Cooper brothers have known me pretty much my whole life. They know that any man stupid enough to harm *my* woman has already drawn his last breath.

"He's dead, Maddie. I shot him," I answer bluntly. My earlier unease of taking a man's life is long gone. One look at what he's done to my Sunshine is enough to erase any misplaced guilt. Fucker had it coming and I'd gladly do it again.

"You sure? David is as wretched as a cockroach and it's always the assholes who survive –"

"I blew a hole between his eyes, Maddie. Unless he can survive without half his brain, which is splattered across my hillside, I'm fairly confident I ended his reign of terror."

Maddie's eyes widen and at first, I think its fear I see there, hearing me talk so violently and seeing how unrepentant I am to have killed someone but she walks to me, pauses, then throws her arms around my waist and sobs 'thank you' repeatedly. It wasn't fear in her eyes, it was shock and relief. Katie and Maddie no longer have to live in the shadow that creep created.

"I promised you she'd be safe with me and I only half delivered. You have nothing to thank me for," I whisper dejectedly. I vowed to keep Katie safe and I failed. Watching her battered body on life support is proof of that.

Maddie tightens her arms around me, "She's alive, Asher, because of you."

"No, she's in here because of me. I wasn't with her when she was attacked. Had I been, that asshole wouldn't have managed to even breathe on her, let alone lay a finger on her. I left her in the care of someone else and they got hurt too."

"Shut up," Max interrupts. "Wallowing in self-pity isn't attractive, man. You don't deserve to do that to yourself. The police had a lead, they'd set up extra patrols, she was in the care of a more than capable man. It was just bad luck David got the drop on Bill. You can't anticipate every eventuality but you can do your damnedest to fight when shit hits the fan and that's what you did. You gunned that mother fucker down and you saved the woman you love. It looks a long road right now but Katie is alive and fighting. She already looks much better than she did a few hours ago. Before you know it, she's gonna be up and about and she's not gonna want to see you lookin' guilty and beatin' yourself up for saving her life. You did good, brother."

He's right. She does look better than she did; it gives me enough comfort to stop my pity-party for one. The next few days are going to be tough enough on us all and I don't need to throw my own self-doubt into the mix.

After a few hours, Dix drives Maddie and Max to a motel so they can get some sleep. I refuse to leave and they know better than to try and make me. Besides, Dix had his hands full with Maddie after he put his foot down and told her she was sharing a room with him. Yeah, definitely somethin' up there.

The next day passes in a strange blur of fragmented time. Katie's vitals improve and her skin looks less grey and lifeless with every passing hour. Detective Jones and his forensic specialist arrive. I have to leave the room while the specialist collects her samples, including a rape kit. The very notion has me spitting with rage. I understand why they have to take the samples, but it kills me to let them while Katie can't consent to it. It's like violating her all over again. The air in my lungs freezes when I think about how David raped her while they were together. I know she was unconscious during the assault and I'm thankful she doesn't have to live with those memories but it still happened to her and she knows it. Not sure if that's worse? Knowing it happened to you but not being able to remember it. Now here she lays, unconscious once more while someone touches her most intimate places without her knowledge.

Sensing my difficulty, Maddie gave consent for the collection of the samples. Katie always spoke highly of how Maddie could take a step back from a situation and apply the logic it required to solve a problem. Maddie shouldn't have had to make that call but I'm more grateful than she'll ever know that she did.

I use the time away from Katie's side to give my statement

to Detective Jones, who confirmed the DA won't be bringing charges against me as I acted in defense of another on my property.

Lucy arrives a little while after to offer sympathy and collect Max; Maddie was intent on staying and Dix was insistent on staying with Maddie. That left Max without a ride. Thankfully, he has the love of a good woman who didn't bat an eye at making a six-hour round trip to collect her man.

While Lucy and Maddie are acquainted from the club, Katie and Lucy hadn't had the opportunity to meet in person and that realization twists the knife in my gut. In my mind's eye, I can see how well Katie, Maddie, and Lucy will get along and I hope it's an opportunity Katie gets to have. There are so many things I wish for Katie – I just need her to pull through. I'll give her the goddam world so long as she wakes up.

Bill and Moira also make the drive to Denver, though I told them not to. I feel guilty for putting them in harm's way and Bill needs to rest his concussion. But there's no stopping that pair when they get an idea lodged in their heads.

They look as exhausted as I feel and it's obvious, they both feel no small amount of guilt over Katie's condition. No matter how much I tell them otherwise, they feel responsible. I love that they've taken Katie under their protective wing as they did me; it makes it feel like Katie is family. I mean, she already is as far as I'm concerned, but to have the other people in my life love her like family too – that squeezes my chest in all the right ways.

Not loving Bill's guilt burden though. David was a big guy who got the drop on him and there's no shame in that. It happens. Especially as the working theory is that David was already lurking inside the house, so they effectively locked themselves inside with him. I don't know how he got in but I've arranged for a security firm to overhaul all the security at the lodge and ranch house. I'm considering gated access where the long drive meets the main road. I even thought about knocking my house down and rebuilding so Katie doesn't have any permanent reminders of the bad shit that happened to her. I'm not ruling it out but I think that's a call I need to make with Katie when she wakes up.

She's been making good progress and they are keen to take her off life support, as long as she continues to improve throughout the night. My hope comes with trepidation; there are so many variables at play and I don't want to get excited for a milestone that could be delayed if her recovery stalls for whatever reason. The team of medical staff is cautiously optimistic, saying things like 'no longer in critical condition' and 'over the worst' but until those big blue eyes are open and looking at me, I'm not getting carried away.

By morning, Katie has made enough progress for them to remove life support. I swear my heartbeat shudders to a stop while the whole room tensely anticipates her first breath without the ventilator. Doctors and nurses hover closely in case she doesn't breathe on her own. Seconds tick by, my anxiety is damn near stratospheric and the atmosphere in the room begins to waver. I feel like a statue; clenched so tightly my white knuckles ache and my teeth grind together, but I'm terrified to move. This moment is balancing precariously on a knife-edge that is teetering the wrong way.

Just when I fear they will need to reconnect the ventilator, Katie draws a ragged little breath and her chest begins to rise and fall rhythmically on its own.

My body sags with relief and I slump into the nearest chair, hiding my face in my hands while my eyes moisten. This woman makes me *feel* so damn much – I've never been the guy who cried…until I met her.

"What happens now?" I ask, my throat thick from fighting back tears.

"We wait for her to regain consciousness," replies an older doctor.

"How long does that normally take?"

"It's different for every person. It could be minutes, hours or days. In very rare cases, months or years." My head snaps up at this. *Years?* "Comas are unpredictable and I would be remiss not to make you aware that some people never wake up. Having said that, I'm optimistic that Katie will wake sooner rather than later. Her scans and vitals are very promising. Continue talking to her and holding her hand – let her know you're here."

So, that's how the next few hours pass; me and Maddie holding Katie's hand, Dix sat by the door and all of us silently praying she doesn't make us wait too long. But Katie's not one for takin' anythin' slowly – you only have to look at how quickly our relationship started to see that – and true to form, a couple of hours after coming off the ventilator, the long lashes framing her delicate eyelids begin to flutter.

Slowly, she focuses on her surroundings, taking us all in and gently flexing the muscles in her body and flinching when she finds something that hurts.

Dix returns to the room with a doctor and nurse in tow – I didn't even notice him leave – and they start checking Katie over and asking her questions. Her eyes zero in on me, wide and relieved while her tiny hand squeezes mine as if she's afraid to let go. It doesn't help the assessment as it forces the nurse to work around our connection.

I don't care if it's awkward; if Katie wants to hold my hand for every second of the rest of her life, then that's what she'll get.

The doctor asks what she remembers and explains her injuries to her. Despite the fear, adrenaline, and beating she took, her memories are in remarkably good shape. Again, not sure if that's a good thing.

Her voice is a hoarse whisper and she winces when she tries to speak.

"There is swelling to your vocal cords. It's going to be sore to speak for a few days so try not to talk too much. The laceration to your foot is healing nicely but I'd like you to keep from bearing weight on it for a few more days. It's your ribs however, that will be the most bothersome for you. You have a fracture to five of them: three on your left, two on your right. They're going to take around six to eight weeks to repair and they're going to be quite sore for the first few. Breathing may be uncomfortable and we'll give you pain meds to take home with you when you're discharged, but I will need you to take things easy so as not to hinder your recovery. Don't lift heavy objects, no exercise or exertion and try not to twist or bend suddenly; it will hurt if you do."

"It's okay baby, I'll take care of you," I try to soothe the panic in her dilated eyes.

"Would you like a drink Katie?" Maddie asks. She nods and Maddie walks out of the room with the doctor, leaving us alone. I can't hold back anymore and lean in to kiss her lips as gently as I can, avoiding the bruises to her face. She groans and I pull back immediately, worried that I've hurt her, only to see a flash of fire in her electric eyes. There's pleasure mixed amongst the pain and it would be too easy to lose myself in her, but I need to restrain myself – I'm not gonna knock her recovery backward just because I can't control my eager dick.

"You killed him?" her whisper is barely audible and I'd much rather she not waste her precious words on David but this conversation is inevitable. I just have to hope my actions don't scare her out of my life. The last thing I want her thinking is that she's replaced one violent man with another. I am nothing like David Marks.

"I did, Sunshine, and I'd do it again," I answer solemnly.

Her pale lips quirk into a small smile. "You could've shot him in the shoulder."

"Could've, but didn't. I chose to remove him from our lives. Permanently."

Katie reaches for me with the hand I'm not holding, grabs my shirt by the collar, balls it in her tiny fist and pulls me towards her. "Thank you," she breathes before pulling my lips to hers and kissing me tenderly. "You'll never know how much that means to me."

"So, you're not scared of me?"

"Why would I be?"

"I ended a man's life…by choice. He deserved it, but I didn't give him the chance to be tried in court. I took the law into my own hands and made him pay for his crimes."

"And I love you for it, Ash. I'm not afraid of your capacity to harm bad people; I've always known you're not a man to mess with but I also know I'm safe with you. I detest David for everything he's done to Elsie, her family and me. It's a burning hatred so fierce that I took satisfaction from seeing his head explode and the light leave his eyes. I'm not a macabre person, but I could happily watch him die on a loop and not get sick of seeing it. I'm ecstatic he's dead and filled with so much love for you for taking on that burden and ending a life for me."

"You're my family Katie, and no one gets to mess with that and walk away breathin'. He was always going to be a menacing specter haunting our lives from the shadows. No way am I letting you live like that. No fuckin' way. I want a safe and happy life for us, a home we can bring children into without fear that some psycho could destroy it."

"Children?" she asks, her scratchy voice breathless.

"I told you, Sunshine, I want it all and I want it forever. I don't have a ring and a hospital bed is far from romantic but I can't spend another minute not knowing if you'll be my wife. Katie, will you marry me?"

Chapter Seventeen

Katie

My knuckles are white and my fingertips numb from clinging to him. This man saved my life. *My* man gave me a future, gave us a future. A future free from David's darkness. A future where he wants me to be his wife.

"Of course I'll be your wife," I croak. "Yes! A thousand times yes!" Ash crashes his lips to mine, no longer being gentle and it causes me to wince a little – I don't think there's a bit of me that isn't sore – but I'll take Ash's pleasure however he gives it. He quickly rights himself though, kissing the tip of my nose and apologizing.

Maddie returns with a drink at that point and promptly drops it while screaming her excitement and approval for our out-of-the-blue engagement.

"I knew it," she squeals, clearly delighted.

"Knew what?" Dix asks. I don't know where he's been for the last ten minutes but I'm grateful he left the room and gave Ash and me our privacy.

"They're engaged!" Maddie singsongs.

"'Bout time," Dix grunts as he wraps Ash in a backslapping bro hug.

Huh.

Guess it's not that out-of-the-blue if everyone was expecting it. Did Ash talk about his plans while I was unconscious? Not necessarily I suppose; Ash and I have been pretty intense from the get-go, getting married is just the next natural step for us. We do everything quickly and getting engaged after only a few months is no exception.

My eyes feel suddenly heavy and exhaustion catches up with me. I have a lot to process, not least, being Asher Scott's fiancée.

* * *

When I wake from my nap, I'm alone in my hospital room with Maddie; Ash and Dix are nowhere in sight.

"They've gone out, probably to pick you an engagement ring. Ash was desperate to ask you but I think he's a little frustrated at himself for not having a ring all ready for you when he asked. But honestly, the poor guy wouldn't leave your side while you were unconscious, so I'm not sure how he thought he'd get one."

"He never left?"

"Only to use the bathroom. He slept in that uncomfortable looking chair" – she nods at the chair next to me – "and we brought food and drinks to him. It would have taken a natural disaster to move that man from your side."

"The doctor said I was unconscious for two days?"

"Yeah. Asher says you were conscious when he reached you but you slipped under just after that. The hospital then kept you in an induced coma and ventilated you to help you breathe through your swollen airway."

213

"I remember seeing him before I passed out...I remember it all."

"How are you feeling about it?" She gently presses her index finger to my forehead to emphasize that she's not talking about my body.

I've been trying to process my jumbled thoughts since I woke up and all I can come up with is relief. Bone deep relief that makes your whole body feel lighter than air because the anchor that kept you shackled and weighed down is gone.

"I think I'm okay. Part of the fear I lived with was knowing David was out there, free to hurt others and free to find me. Now he's not. I no longer blame myself for his actions, they're on him and he paid the price for it. Before he killed Elsie, I thought that maybe some of it was my fault. That maybe I had made things worse and pushed him to behave that way. Stupid, I know. My therapist was always telling me otherwise, but it took hearing what he did to another innocent woman for it to finally ring true. Elsie didn't deserve what happened to her and neither did I; David was the only person accountable for his actions. He chose to inflict pain and suffering. I don't choose to be a victim. Not anymore.

"Now he can't hurt me. I don't have to worry about him being on the run or released on bail because he's nothing more than worm food. A man I never saw coming, a man brave enough to take on my baggage and break down my barriers, stepped up and took on the burden of ending David's life. He killed for me, Mads. Ash made the ultimate call, one that could've ruined his life and he did it for me. Is it weird that I find that hot?"

"You always were kinky, Katie," she chuckles. "Ash only did what he's been doing from day one – putting you first. Gotta say I'm pretty jealous he got to shoot that motherfucker. You know how much I was itching to do that myself."

"You and me both."

"You really are okay, aren't you? I keep waiting for you to retreat back into your shell, build up those walls and be justifiably scared."

"It's surprising even me, but yeah, I really am okay. Twice he tried to end me and twice he failed. I win. He's the corpse, not me. I get to live my life the way I want, free from him and free from fear. I just wish that Elsie Cade had the same opportunity."

"Nothing will bring her back but maybe her family can find some small amount of peace from the heads that will roll because David wasn't convicted after his assault on you."

"Here's hoping. Now tell me about you and Dix – the looks he's giving you aren't the ones of a man ignoring you." It's true, I'm intrigued by his behavior but I'm also desperate for a change in conversation topic. Other than getting engaged, the only conversations have been ones that contain David and they need to be as dead as he is.

"Nothing to tell croaky-pants. You need to rest your voice; it's getting scratchier and harder to hear by the word."

Hmm.

My voice is suffering from all the talking but I'm not oblivious to the fact that Maddie just used it as an excuse to shut the conversation down. I'll let it go…for now. She can bet her life that I'm bringing it up again later though, as it's not like her to keep man-talk on the down-low from me and it makes me worry when she's too afraid to share. Dix has always seemed a decent guy to me and I appreciate all he's done for Maddie while I've been in hospital, but I'm not above kicking his overly muscular ass if he's hurting my girl.

* * *

The next morning sees me developing a serious case of cabin fever. Yes, I still hurt, but I'm bored of these dreary four walls and tiny window overlooking the parking lot. I want to go home – with all the pain meds I can get my hands on.

Dix and Maddie left an hour ago, which doesn't help my mood. They're on the road in the sunshine and I'm purple and blue and constantly reminded of what happened to me every time a new nurse comes on shift, reads my notes, balks and then gives me a sympathetic yet pitying look. And if they're not looking at me like I'm some broken puppy, they're making eyes at my fiancé. I get it, the man is beyond handsome with all his beautiful bulk and sensual lips but the man is *mine*. Surely that much is obvious? Those smoldering eyes barely give them a second glance because he's occupied with looking at me…in all my pulpy glory.

I look down at my still naked ring finger; I half expected him to put a ring on it yesterday when he got back from wherever he went with Dix. Apparently not. Unless he did get something and it needs re-sizing? But he didn't mention anything…in fact, he's been uncomfortably quiet on the whole being engaged thing. I'm not doubting his feelings – the man killed for me, for Christ's sake – I'm just surprised. When you couple that with how *friendly* the nursing staff is with Ash and I've just about had enough and want to recuperate at home. Alone. With Ash.

I look up when Ash enters my room but I'm not quick enough at smoothing out my scowl.

He's immediately at my side, compassion in his eyes and a calloused thumb smoothing out the little 'v' wrinkle I get between my eyebrows when I'm annoyed. I lean my cheek into the palm of his hand and it hurts less than it did yesterday.

"I want to go home," I grumble, catching sight of a sexy red-headed nurse slowing to walk past my room and casting Ash a longing glance. "Do you mind?" I snap at her. She blushes deeply and looks guiltily at me as the scowl Ash just smoothed out deepens.

"Baby," he chuckles, so I turn my scowl on him. He throws up his hands in surrender but still looks far too pleased with my display of possessiveness.

"I almost died and all these pretty little nurses can do is ogle my boyfriend," I'm practically growling at this point. I may not be looking my best but that's no justification for my fellow females to be making eyes at my man.

"I'm not your boyfriend, Sunshine. I'm your fiancé," he whispers lovingly in my ear. The deep gravel of his voice soothing me.

"Maybe you should tell them that so they show some fucking decency." I'm so goddam frustrated. I'm uncomfortable, broken, trapped in a bed and sexually frustrated. Ash and I have pretty demanding libidos and this is the longest we've ever gone without making love. Because of my injuries, Ash handles me like delicate glassware – I know he's trying not to hurt me but feather-light kisses and barely-there touches just aren't cutting it.

I'm a battered pulp of a woman with a high sex drive, watching attractive flirty females zero in on my husband-to-be right in front of me...this makes me feel less than stellar about myself.

"You know, the only reason I'm so well looked after by the nursing staff is that they all want to check you out. They actually use me as an excuse to be in the same room as *you*. I swear to god, if I have to hear one more stupid, breathy, little girl laugh, I'm going to scratch their fucking eyes out past their hyper-fluttering lashes."

Ash is the one man on the planet who truly knows me and how to handle the emotions I feel, so he's smart enough to stop smiling at the situation. He can sense that it's just another stressor I don't need at the moment.

Cupping my face in both of his hands, he lowers his lips to mine, pressing a little more firmly against them than he has previously. "You know I only have eyes for you. Once you're recovered, I'm going to fuck you so hard until you never forget that you belong to me and I belong to you. Flirtatious nurses won't change that."

"No, but they're wearing on my last nerve. How would you feel if you were laid up and looking like a battered piece of fruit with all the attractive men in the near vicinity trying to flirt with me and they were being less than discreet about it?" Ash's face immediately sours. *Yeah.* I didn't think he'd like that.

As if on cue, the guilty redhead from earlier waltzes into the room asking if Ash needs anything.

Unrepentant bitch.

I'm the goddam patient; surely, she should be addressing me first. I look pointedly at them both.

"Get out," Ash barks at her. Startled, she makes a hasty retreat. "And close the door behind you."

I quirk an I-told-you-so eyebrow at him as the door clicks shut. "Point taken baby, but I have some good news that

I'm hopin' will make you feel better. They're talkin' about discharging you tomorrow. You've made amazing progress, I'm so proud of you, Sunshine"

I know I'm just having a bad day but I don't feel proud. All I've done is lay here and slip into a grumpy rut. The thought of being discharged does lift my spirits mind you. Continuing my recovery somewhere I'm comfortable and surrounded by people who care about me sounds like the best course of action as far as I'm concerned.

* * *

Despite Ash now scowling at every nurse who enters my room, my day doesn't improve. Medication has managed the pain to a throbbing ache but that ache is fucking irritating, constant and *everywhere*.

Don't get me wrong, I'm grateful to be alive and feel liberated from my demons but I'm fed up with hurting and being trapped in the hospital. I've never been a good patient; you'd have thought the number of visits I've made to the ER over the years would have taught me tolerance…it didn't.

I HATE being in pain.

Ash has nothing but patience and compassion for me, despite my mood. His bedside manner is the stuff doctor's dream of. He's busy chatting quietly about planning a night for us at the Rock Hard Club once I'm recovered – not sure whether this makes me aroused or angry considering the length of my recovery time…probably both – when a dark shadow appears unwelcome at my bedroom doorway.

I recognize him the instant he crosses the threshold; his is a face I will never be able to forget. My body tenses, a sharp rock sits heavy in the pit of my stomach and I can feel the blood draining from my face, making me lightheaded. Beads of cold sweat form on my mottled skin as Ash, seeing my reaction, jumps to his feet and turns quickly in the direction of our intruder. He comes face to face with Peter Marks…David's father.

The resemblance isn't lost on Ash who stands tall and firm, chest puffed out to make the most of his imposing size and block Peter from advancing any closer to me. The corded muscles of his forearms flex and bulge, skin drawn tight with raised veins as he clenches his fists but holds himself back. Angry Ash is an intimidating specimen and I'm glad I don't have to stare him down.

For the life of me, I cannot think of one good reason why Peter Marks would find himself visiting my hospital bed. The man loathes me. He's always looked down on me as some sort of gold-digger he was forced to tolerate. He has a high opinion of himself and his family's status and, given that I was an orphan with a small inheritance, I wasn't worthy of his son or of being considered as anything other than a scrounger. He took every opportunity to tell me how *lucky* I was to have a man like David.

Lucky was not the word I would use.

If Peter Marks is here, he's here to cause trouble. And that alone makes me want to vomit all over my over-starched bedsheets.

He looks at me quickly before staring Ash straight in the eyes, his face a neutral mask as he sizes up the man in front of him. Ash has height and muscle on this guy and Ash is also no one's fool, but Peter Marks has a fiercely sharp and cutting intellect that he wields mercilessly and that makes him fearsome in his own right. It gives him a god complex and he performs mental acrobatics designed to maneuver himself into advantageous positions and his foes into trouble they can't get out.

Peter Marks is not a man you want as an enemy.

He makes my skin prickle with unease and has no right to be in my hospital room. My fingers creep towards the nurse call button, ready to call for help and have him escorted out by security.

"You're the one," he speaks directly to Ash, his mask finally slipping, revealing a flash of hurt in the eyes that are too like his son's. "The one who killed my son."

Oh. God.

Ash doesn't bat an eye and replies evenly, "Damn straight. And I'd do it again in a heartbeat."

Panic grips me to my core. Peter Marks isn't a man you should admit things to.

"Ash. Don't say any more. That's *Judge* Peter Marks." I'm close to tears at this point. Ash just admitted to murdering his son; Judge Marks is going to bury him. He'll ruin him and our life together. After everything we've been through, Judge Marks will destroy our future and do it with a smile on his goddam face.

Ash still faces away from me but I see the steel muscles of his back tense.

Just as I think he's comprehended the danger Judge Marks presents, he takes two menacing steps and closes the distance between himself and Peter. Towering over him, he jabs a finger at Peter's chest and speaks with a cold fury. "So, you're the reason David was never charged after assaulting Katie; you helped him get away with abusing women. Well, I wasn't about to let him get away with murder. You have a lot to feel guilty over; I have nothing."

Ash snatches my hospital notes from the container at the foot of my bed and thrusts it at Judge Marks. "Here are the consequences of your actions. Take a look at your son's handiwork. You're an educated man, I'm sure you can make sense of Katie's patient notes and x-rays."

Peter opens the file and his stern and intimidating façade cracks. The man who always made me feel two feet tall breaks down before me. His eyes flit between the medical notes and my injured body.

"Be sure to look at the notes from the assault you helped him get away with; I'm sure you're familiar with them but best to refresh your memory. They're further back in the file," Ash has reached a level of menacing sarcasm I've not heard from him before. Moments ago, I was worried about what Peter Marks was going to do to us, now I'm worried about what Ash is going to do to him. He deserves it all and more for standing idly by and enabling David to hurt Elsie and me. Ash is in control of this situation and his strength gives me courage in the face of someone I spent years cowering from.

Ash pulls his phone from his pocket, scrolls through a news website and pulls up an article on Elsie's murder. "You're the reason my future wife had to fight for her life – again – and the reason your son was able to murder this young woman. Look at her. Look at the face of the woman who will never get to see her family again and try to work out how many lives your son irrevocably destroyed with his actions. Yeah, I killed him and he fuckin' deserved it," Ash spits venom and the mighty Peter Marks breaks down and sobs.

"I'm so sorry," he whispers as his shoulders shake and tears stain his cheeks.

"Sorry is just a word," I croak. "A word created to help ease the conscience of the guilty. A word that begs forgiveness and absolution from victims when the guilty have no right to ask for it. 'Sorry' doesn't change the past or make the hurt go away. 'Sorry' doesn't bring Elsie Cade back from the dead. You always preach that actions have consequences...well, now you're living with *your* consequences."

"He was my son and I loved him more than life. I would've done anything to protect him. I didn't want to believe he was capable of what you accused him of. To me, you were an aggrieved ex out to destroy his future and I wasn't about to stand by and watch that happen."

"You are a judge. You're supposed to stand as a beacon of justice, not distort it. There's a due process for a reason. If you had let David face the consequences of *his* actions, both he and Elsie would be alive today. David would be alive in jail, Elsie would never have met him and I wouldn't be lying here, barely able to talk with broken ribs. This is me getting off lightly."

"I know." His response is simple but pained. His interference started the chain reaction that led to his son lying downstairs in the morgue...and he knows it. "I won't live a second of my life without knowing what I caused...and what I lost."

"Welcome to my world," I don't say it with hate, I say it with genuine sadness because I know the pain he's going to live with. The memories he doesn't want but has no choice but to live with. I wouldn't wish it on my worst enemy, which Peter Marks qualifies. I may not like him, but I still feel his pain. Before me stands a broken man, a father mourning the loss of a son he loved dearly. A parent with the primal instinct to protect their offspring at all costs, no matter the consequences. A deep bond and fierce love that should never be broken by the loss of a child.

Suddenly, he grabs for my hand before Ash can stop him and before I can snatch it away. I can feel something crumpled up being forced into my palm just as Ash clamps hold of him by the shoulder and shoves him away. Peter throws his hands up in a show of surrender while I unravel the clump of paper in my hand. It feels like thick, heavy stocked paper, is rectangular in shape and when I turn it over, I see that it's a cheque for a considerable sum of money.

I drop it immediately, "I don't want your money; you can't buy my silence."

"It's not a bribe…there's no keeping what David did quiet. This can't undo what you've suffered but it can compensate you for your medical bills, the cost of moving and help set you up with a future you deserve –"

"And help ease your conscience. I won't be beholden to you for anything or bribed to not testify."

"The money is none of those things," he pleads. "The case against my son and the investigation into my involvement will steamroll ahead with or without your testimony. At the very least, I will lose my job and be charged with obstruction. There aren't many wrongs in this situation that I can fix, but the financial penalties you've suffered are something I can help with. There's a life and career you would've had if you'd never met David. Instead, your path deviated and it cost you emotionally and financially. You aren't where you thought you'd be career-wise, you've had medical bills, therapy bills, the cost of relocating to a different city…it all adds up and I want to help alleviate the burden you've suffered. I know it falls so far short but it's all I have to offer."

"I'm perfectly capable of providing a more than comfortable future for my fiancée," snaps Asher.

"I wasn't making an assumption on your ability or financial stability. I just want to help."

Ash seethes, breathing heavily through his nose but I'm starting to get it. Peter Marks was never intentionally a bad man; by the very nature of him becoming a judge it's clear he wanted to do good in the world, but that desire got tangled and fucked so far sideways that this is all he can offer to make amends. I don't want the money – my future is mine, free from the Marks' family – but I'm not going to throw it in his face. It must've taken a lot for him to come here, to face the reality he helped create and I'm determined to be the bigger person. I want to move on from all of this.

My future is mine…and it's free.

"Thank you, Peter," my words are quiet and hoarse, my throat scratchy but it cuts through the tension of the room clearly enough. "I'm not sure I'll have a need for your offer but I appreciate the gesture. What's happened isn't something that I can forget easily but I can choose to forgive and that's what I want to try and do. You don't need my hatred, you have enough of your own to live with. One thing I will say, my forgiveness isn't going to make you feel much better because it's not *my* forgiveness you need. It's the Cades you need to reach out to – if they'll let you. If they don't, you need to try and make some sort of peace with what's happened on your own."

He bows his head, whispers 'thank you' and with slumped shoulders, quietly leaves my room.

"You don't need his money, baby. We're more than fine

financially without his blood money. That man has done nothing but try and ruin you." Ash is barely restraining his anger but he reaches for my hand and strokes gentle circles with the rough pad of his thumb.

"I know that. I've had very little choice over the things that have happened to me but forgiveness is something I can *choose*. I wasn't lying; he doesn't need my grudge because he hates himself enough already. He lost the one thing he loved more than himself. Surely you can empathize with that? You've chosen to love me and love me so fiercely that you killed for me. We don't have children –"

"Yet," he interrupts.

"Yet," I agree. "Imagine how protective of them you'll be when they get here. That instinctual love eclipses everything we've ever felt so far in our lives and our love is already crazy intense. I know I'll do anything it takes to keep them safe. Peter went about it all wrong, but that's what he tried to do for his son. I don't agree with his methods but I can understand."

"I love hearing you talk about our children, makes me seriously impatient to put a baby in that beautiful belly of yours. So, yeah, I suppose I can *understand* what he did, but I'm not as magnanimous as you, Sunshine, I can't forgive him so easily."

"And you don't have to. I'm not doing it for his benefit, I'm doing it for mine. When we leave this hospital, that chapter of my life is over. All of it. Including my resentment for Peter Marks. Now, about those babies…"

"We can start makin' them anytime you want, Sunshine. I'd fuck one into you right this second, but I'd hurt you and I'm not prepared to damage your ribs further and set back your recovery. Once those bad boys are healed though, all bets are off. Your womb is mine to put as many babies in you as I can."

"I'd prefer it if we were married first," but only just. The thought of carrying his baby is doing deliciously strange things to me and I don't think I can wait the eight or so weeks my ribs need to heal. I want him now. I wish we were married yesterday so I could take him as many times as it needs to make our baby.

"Done. You get yourself better and then we'll get married."

Chapter Eighteen

Katie

My injuries take longer to heal than we'd hoped and I'm discharged, finally, after a few more tortuously slow days. Shuffling out of the hospital towards Ash's big ass, black truck in the glorious Colorado summer sunshine has me grinning instead of wincing at my still aching body.

Ash gently hoists me up into the cab of his Ford F-150; it's not a convenient car for the injured but I'm pretty comfortable once seated. I used to joke that men with large vehicles were overcompensating – the bigger the car, the smaller the dick. But Ash buries that notion without trying. Big man, big truck, *huge* dick. He's almost too much man for the truck to handle.

We drive in companionable silence until we pass Denver's city limits, the fingers of Ash's right hand laced with those of my left. Like a planet with my own gravitational pull, Ash has barely left my side in days. He refuses to be too far from me and where possible, he touches me at all times. I only just managed to stop him short of following me to the bathroom once my catheter was removed. Although, given how badly it ached to sit there and wait for my bladder and bowel to start working again, I nearly caved and called him in. I'm not sure if it's romantic or disturbing that he'd happily sit there supporting my ribs while I shit. It's almost like the night of my attack flipped a switch in him and things that would be distasteful for people who haven't suffered a traumatic experience, don't even make him bat an eye. In his mind, he'd rather wipe my ass clean because it's too painful for me to twist and reach it myself because the alternative very nearly saw me in the morgue.

"I had a phone call this morning while you were in the bathroom," he says in a deep but quiet tone. I give him my attention and smile for him to continue. While my voice is no longer husky or sore, I still feel like I'm swallowing past a large lump when I speak. It's fading a little more day by day but until it's gone, I only speak when I have to.

"From Elsie's father," he continues. "Poor guy could barely speak a sentence and I could hear crying in the background. He sounded uncomfortable to be callin' but he wanted to speak to the man that ended David Marks'." A dark shadow settles in Ash's eyes. For the most part, he's made his peace with his actions but his expression is turbulent. He's not haunted by it because to him, the alternative was unthinkable, unliveable. However, Ash was never a soldier; he was never trained to deal out death, despite how efficiently he did it, and there's always a dark blip when he remembers that he now wears the title of 'murderer', no matter how justified.

"What did he say?"

"Thank you," he answers simply. "The Cade's wanted justice but they didn't know how they'd cope with facing David day in, day out during a trial. Killing him saved them the torture of facing their daughter's murderer. I don't know how anyone does that. I know for a fact; I wouldn't be able to share the same room as someone who stole someone I loved. Watching them draw breath in the place of someone who deserved life more doesn't sit right with me. Doesn't sit right with the Cade's either."

"Do they want to talk to me?" I ask uneasily, not sure how I feel about it.

"No, baby, they don't. You're the woman who lived and while they aren't the sort of folk to wish harm on an innocent woman, they can't help but wonder why the world took their daughter but spared you. Then they feel guilty for thinking that way. They know it's more complicated than the universe or karma or whatever bullshit they want to believe in. You and Elsie both fought hard but you survived while they buried their daughter yesterday. They don't wish it were you instead, but life doesn't feel particularly fair to them at the moment."

I nod in agreement.

"They did pass on an apology though," he continues. "Turns out Elsie told them about the time you called her and tried to persuade her to leave David. As you can imagine, they trash-talked you. Sayin' you were the crazed ex out to ruin David's life. Hindsight is always twenty/twenty though, and now they wish more than anythin' that they had listened to you. Heeding your warnings would have saved their daughter and Mr. Cade is takin' that pretty hard because deep down, he had his reservations about David. Gotta say it took a lot of teeth grittin' to listen to them say what they said about you before they knew the truth. They wanted me to pass on their apologies for not believing in you when it could've made a difference."

"They don't need to apologize to me for that. They need to work out how to forgive themselves. Life is going to be hard enough for them without burdening themselves with shoulda woulda coulda's."

"That family are never gonna forgive themselves. You and I both know it." He squeezes my hand and I look back out the windscreen at the dramatic, jagged peaks casting shadows across rolling hills of wildflowers in the morning sun. Snatching glimpses of Ash's powerful profile while he drives one-handed, easily mastering his beast of a vehicle, I can't tell which view I love more.

About an hour from the ranch, Ash's phone rings through the truck's speakers followed by the sounds of Josh's voice.

"Hey, Boss. Just lettin' you know that the fence is mended and the last of the cattle rounded up. All's goin' to plan."

Plan?

None of what Josh said makes any sense but the last bit stands out oddly. Ash doesn't react to it but it's almost forcefully deliberate. A subtle tick in the corner of his eye that tells me he's straining at nonchalance.

Hmm.

"Thanks, man. We're 'bout an hour away," he answers before ending the call.

"Cattle got outta their pasture," Ash says to me in answer to my curious stare. Ash owns so much land that I barely see the cattle and frequently forget he even has a small herd. He keeps them far away from the hotel guests due to the fact that not everyone appreciates the country-farmyard-manure stench of cow shit. Ash has big plans to expand the hotel pool area into a full spa and then market the lodge as a wedding venue and I quote, 'no one wants a scented side order of cow shit with their spa day or wedding cake'. He's so good at keeping the cows away that I can't remember the last time I saw one.

"How'd the cows escape?"

"David cut the wire fence. That's how he evaded capture – he went cross country. Cut his way through a wire fence and got onto the property the back way. Took a while for the cattle to meander through the damage he made and for us to find it, but the guys have it fixed now."

I take a moment to enjoy the fact that the sound of David's name no longer affects me in any way. There's no fear, no anger, no resentment...nothing but beautiful ambivalence.

It's almost starting to feel like it all happened to someone else, like a nightmare I've finally woken from and never have to dwell on again.

I shift in my seat, trying to keep myself comfortable and give up because nothing is comfortable currently, and instead decide to try and nap for the rest of the journey.

* * *

The truck going over a bump as it passes from the main road and onto the ranch drive wakes me with a start.

"Hey there sleepy, finished snorin' for the day?" I shoot my fiancé a withering look and notice that his joke hasn't reached his eyes. The deep, molten browns don't sparkle with mischief like they usually do when he jokes at my expense...he's nervous.

Is he worried about bringing me back to where my attack happened? We've spoken about how I feel about the ranch and our home now and I can honestly say that, given David's current state of decomposition, I'm not afraid to come back here. I rule my memories, not the other way around. My vehemence was only just enough to stop him bulldozing the ranch house, mind you.

We ride the last ten minutes in awkward silence. Him worrying and me worrying about his worrying. All quite pointless really if we dared to talk to one another but Ash seems so absorbed by his thoughts and I'm starting to seize up from sitting in the same position for too long.

Thirty seconds later and everything suddenly makes sense: Josh's comment about 'all going to plan' and Ash's distract-edness…it all clicks into place when our ranch house comes into view and I see that the entire front porch has been decked out with fairy lights and flowers. Hundreds and hundreds of vibrantly colored flowers in all varieties adorn nearly every inch of the rustic wood porch while a homemade 'welcome home' sign hangs above the front door. The fairy lights twinkle lightly but most of the light is lost to the early afternoon sunshine.

Even if I wanted to scan the surrounding hillside for signs of what happened, I'd never be able to tear my gaze away from the beautifully romantic and thoughtful display in front of me, complete with everyone I know. Seriously, everyone I know is stood in front of our house, smiling and waiting for us. Josh, Mike, Jack, Moira and Bill, sporting stitches above his right eye. Even Carly is there with a broad smile. She's stood next to Max and an attractive woman I assume is his girlfriend, Lucy. In front of them all, and hopping impatiently from foot to foot, is Maddie with Dix hovering not far behind her left shoulder.

I can't believe they're all here to welcome me home. I'm overwhelmed by how good it is to see all their faces and how, despite everything, this place, these people, it all feels like home.

"Welcome home, Sunshine," Ash murmurs in my ear as he eases me out of the truck and gently lowers my feet to the ground. He keeps an arm around my waist as we walk, shouldering some of my weight while my seized muscles loosen with each step.

My adopted family clap and cheer, hug me gently but allow Ash to half carry me past them and up the porch steps. I thought I'd get longer to talk to everyone unless he means for them to follow us inside but no one makes a move towards the porch steps.

Confused, I turn my attention back to Ash but I'm not staring at his chest like I expect when I'm stood this close to him and my eye level only reaches the hard planes of his pecs. Instead, I see the top of his head and that's when I notice he's down on one knee with a little black, velvet box tied with a small red, satin ribbon – *Oh* – in his hand.

"I thought we already did this," I half squeak, half choke.

"We did. I was desperate to ask you. So desperate that I didn't have a ring or a clue about how to do it properly. It means the world to me that you love me enough to say yes to what was essentially the world's crappiest proposal but I want to do it properly. Down on one knee, ring in hand, in front of all the people we hold dear and free from the past. You said it yourself, when we leave the hospital, we're starting a new chapter of our life. So, I'm making sure we start it properly. With a ring on my beautiful fiancée's finger. Where it should be. I'm hoping your answer hasn't changed and that you still want to take me as your husband and be my wife, be mine. I love you. Katie, will you marry me?"

Asher Scott had not gone uncomfortably silent on the marriage front as I was starting to fear, he'd gone into proposal planning overdrive. His thoughtfulness, his words, the love smoldering in his molten eyes and the hopeful smile tugging at his full lips…all of it overwhelms me. I've never felt so happy, so safe, so loved. This man is the greatest gift of my life.

With tears moistening my eyes I simply answer 'yes'. His hulking frame stands and swoops me into his arms and takes my mouth in the lushest of kisses before I can say another word. His tongue massages mine with long languid strokes while our friends whoop and holler around us. Ash parts just long enough to slip a beautifully simple solitaire diamond ring onto my finger before cupping my face in his hands and kissing me tenderly.

* * *

Our engagement party lasts long into the afternoon until I'm almost too tired to stand and our nearest and dearest start to take the hint and vacate. While I love seeing them, by the time I can barely get my ass up off the sofa, it's time for them to disappear and let me sleep.

One thing I have spotted this afternoon is that there is definitely some tension between Dix and Maddie…and I mean the good kind of tension. The kind that speaks to hours in bed and lots of orgasms. Lucy, who's adorable and hilarious by the way, noticed too. We're joining forces to get to the bottom of what's going on; she's going to press Max and possibly even Dix himself for information while I beat it out of Maddie. But that's a plan for another day, right now I'm working on how to walk up the stairs without it a) hurting too much and b) looking like I need a zimmer frame to move.

While I ponder this conundrum on the bottom step, a pair

of large, warm arms wrap around me and sweep gently under my knees, pulling me up so that I'm cradled against the steel strength of the pec-tacular chest I've come to love almost as much as the man himself. Being tiny in stature can sometimes drive a person to act more independent than they need to be – a sort of defense mechanism to make up for literal short-comings. *Look, see, I am capable of reaching the top shelf in the supermarket, or replacing a lightbulb way above my head without your help.* Being tiny doesn't mean you're helpless and sometimes I push that point a little too far – especially given how helpless I ended up in my last relationship.

Ash doesn't make me feel helpless though. When he picks me up or grabs things that are out of reach for me, I don't feel patronized; I feel precious, loved and cared for. I don't feel my size; I just feel protected. Being cradled in his arms is one of my favorite places to exist…next to his warm skin…his beating heart…the musky man scent that drives me wild. A little sandalwood type aftershave, a little sweat and a lot of all-man smell that literally makes my mouth water.

Yeah, I'm not tired anymore.

I wiggle closer in his massive arms and bury my face in the crook between his neck and shoulder, running my nose delicately along the gently throbbing vein that pops to the surface whenever he gets aroused. Good to know I still affect him even in my state.

He chuckles deeply as my breath tickles the smooth skin of his throat.

"I thought you were tired, Sunshine."

I shake my head, "not in the slightest, Cowboy." I know what I want but his heavy sigh as we enter our bedroom tells me that I'm going to have to fight hard for it. My body might still hurt enough for prescribed painkillers, but there's another part of me that aches for the feel of him and that pain is getting harder and harder to ignore. It's as hard as Ash's impressive erection that I have the pleasure of sliding down as I'm placed on the floor, face to face with my man and his strained expression.

I know what he's going to say; I'm still too injured for us to have sex and he'd rather we both suffer a case of blue balls – *blue ovaries?* – then do me any more damage. I can't cope with that rationale though. As previously mentioned, we both have ravenous sex drives and mine is goddam thirsty for a drink only Ash can provide. It's not optional, I need this man inside me and I need it now.

Ash, on the other hand, is perfectly capable of being a martyr. He's worried that, given how physical our lovemaking is, we'll crack one of my broken ribs further. His concern gives him enough willpower to take a step back from me, creating an ungodly distance that has no right existing between us. With space comes the ability to think and speak and I don't want that, I want to smother his senses until he's consumed by me and loses control and gives me what we both want.

The problem is; Ash *is* dominant. Even when I think I'm in control, it's because he's letting me – he controls me having control. And in the bedroom, that works for us. It's the one area of life that thrills me to submit. But submitting comes with its drawbacks...namely, not being able to make my fiancé fuck me when he's made his mind up not to. Ash is dominant and stubborn and that combination means it's unlikely that pushing him will yield positive results. It's never been a problem before because the man is an insatiable sex beast who's always ready to go. The lightest kiss has his cock engorged and making a break from his jeans. He tells me that's just the effect I have on him, so he must be some sort of tantric master to be ignoring the beast in his pants begging for release. I can see the strain on his face, the tiny tense lines crinkling around his eyes, the tick of his locked jaw, the throbbing neck vein and his quickened, shallow breaths. He wants me, but he has the clarity and control to ignore it, which just fires up my determination all the more.

"Please," I whisper beg.

"I can't hurt you," comes his gruff reply.

"You won't."

"Really?" he quirks an unbelieving brow. "You're telling me that when I touch your delicious little body, you can keep from thrashing around?"

Lie. "Yes," I squeak and I'm not even convincing to my own ears.

Ash chuckles darkly, takes a step towards me and lightly traces his fingers up both sides of my torso. Flames ignite in my skin as he touches my curves before cupping my breasts through my shirt. He takes their full weight in his hands and like the torturous devil he is, grazes his thumbs across the pointed nubs of my sensitive nipples. I buckle at the touch and wince at the sharp pinch and then bone-deep, dull ache of my damaged ribs.

"Didn't think so," the comment could almost be smug if not for the genuine disappointment in his chocolate eyes.

"There must be something we can do?" I'm outright begging/whining like a needy teenager.

"You mean a way to restrain you so that you can't move? Sure, there is. But it's whether or not you want that baby."

I know instinctively what he's getting at and I'm so on board with it. Nearly dying has flipped a switch in me also. No more half-living or being afraid of what I desire. To keep me still, Ash is going to need to restrain both my wrists and my ankles; a level of submission we'd not managed to reach before my attack. I'm changing that now because I want nothing more than for him to take total control of me. I was willing to submit totally the night of our fight when I ran off to Maddie after he dropped the 'L' bombshell for the first time and Maddie sent me back after giving me a verbal kick up the ass. But we didn't do it and then David showed up and treated me to a stint on life support, so now I'm desperate to be Ash's wholly and completely.

I've never been surer of anything.

"Yes. I want it."

"You sure?" he stays unmoving.

"Yes, goddamit. Just take me already. Make me yours."

Ash takes my face in his hands and kisses me like he did when he proposed: softly, deeply and lush enough that it curls my toes and makes my knees weak. His fingers drift south, unbuttoning my blouse while his lips work magic against mine.

He undresses us both deftly and pulls a pillow into the center of the bed before laying me delicately down so that the pillow sits in my lower back, tilting my hips upward and opening me up for him. Dragging his lips across my skin, lighting a fiery trail, he places my right arm above my head and to the side and kisses his way to the tips of my fingers. Holding his weight above me, he reaches underneath the mattress for the restraints we had attached to our bed frame. I feel him buckle the soft cuff around my wrist before tightening the strap so that my arm is taut. He then kisses his way back down, across my chest, laving each nipple as he passes before kissing and nipping his way up my left arm. He repeats the process until both arms are stretched and secured, leaving my upper body useless and at his mercy, while he kisses his way back down to my chest. This time he swallows my nipples, sucking them between the sharp bite of his teeth and rolling them with the wet heat of his tongue.

As I still have too much leeway to wriggle, the assault on my breasts is short, sharp and sweet before he moves south, gently caressing my now yellowish-green bruises and nibbling the sensitive skin of my hips. He avoids my pussy completely, knowing that I'd never be able to be still enough during that level of pleasure until my legs are tied. Ash kisses down my thigh, the crook of my knee, my calf, ankle, instep and finally my toes. He flashes me a devastating smile that makes my heart thump heavily in my chest and gives me a moment to stop him before he cuffs my ankle.

As if.

Before he tightens the strap, he reaches both hands up to my hips and pulls me higher onto the pillow, angling me perfectly for him and ensuring there's no give what-so-ever in my arms. Kissing his way up my leg, he skirts around my core once again before ensuring my other leg receives the same loving attention.

Once all four cuffs are attached to my spread-eagled body and the straps tightened, he takes me by surprise and dives his tongue straight into the wet folds of my pussy, licking greedily up to my needy clit where he sucks hard and then detaches with a wet popping sound.

I cry out at the devastating pleasure, my nerve endings desperate from so many days without his intimate touch

"Just checkin'," he chuckles.

"I'm not going anywhere, Cowboy," I answer breathlessly. It's true, I couldn't flinch away from his touch or thrust towards him if I tried, which is the whole point. I can't move to hurt myself in the throes of our passion.

"So beautiful, baby," he gazes adoringly at my restrained, bruised body but I can see it in his eyes that he's not just saying it. He means it; to him, I am beautiful. "I'm not going to blindfold you, baby, because I need to see your face, the pleasure and any pain you try to hide. If things start to hurt, you need to tell me. If you don't, then I can't trust that we can do this safely and it'll be a long fuckin' eight weeks until you get the all-clear from the doc. I mean it, Sunshine; I won't make love to you during that time at all if you try to conceal any pain that you feel. Do you understand me?"

Oh, I love authoritative Ash.

"Yes *Sir*," I purr in needy desperation.

He chuckles as he reaches for something from the nightstand. "There's no need to be callin' me 'Sir'. God-of-sex or Master-of-orgasms will suffice." The humor in his eyes warms me from the inside out. Were my hands-free, I'd still swat him for his sass, mind you.

"Those titles need to be earned, *Master*. So far, I'm orgasm-less. My sex god is slacking."

"Is that so?" he quirks that sexy eyebrow at me again and produces our favorite red, satin ribbon from the palm of his hand, dangling it between his thumb and forefinger.

Color me intrigued.

What follows is nothing short of the most exquisite torture as he trails that silken ribbon across every inch of my body with feather-like finesse. The flower orgasm scene in *40 Days and 40 Nights*…that's totally me right now. I never understood that scene and used to think it was just exaggerated Hollywood bull, but being restrained heightens other senses. It forces you to *feel* everything. You can't escape the pleasure; you're literally at the mercy of sensation and the sensation of satin tickling skin? It's fucking epic. Sometimes, Ash just trails it along every secret sensual spot I have and other times, he pulls it tight between his hands and whips it gently, flogger style, on my nipples and a few times on my clit. I'm not too much into pleasure/pain but the tiny bite of the ribbon hitting me intimately has me pulling on my restraints, gasping his name and rolling my eyes in sheer bliss. I'm balancing so close to the edge that when Ash whips the ribbon on my nipples and flicks my clit with his tongue at the same time, I fall over it and splinter into a thousand brightly lit pieces.

I scream my pleasure and fight to keep my muscles relaxed – I don't want him stopping because he thinks I'm pulling too hard on the restraints. Relaxing my core muscles has the added bonus of prolonging my orgasm…a fact I'm immeasurably thankful for.

With a devilish smirk, Ash crawls up my body, kisses me and bites my bottom lip as he sits upon his knees and lines his magnificent cock up with my now sopping wet pussy.

He winks before inserting only his tip inside me and I realize that the torture is going to a whole new level…and there's fuck all I can do about it. I can't thrust my hips forward to drive him deeper. I just have to lay there, begging for more of his steel shaft. And that's what drives me wild about submitting. Surrendering yourself to a man who gives a shit about your pleasure and no longer having to chase your own climax because your partner has you and can drive you towards the peak you're desperate for. To me, that's fucking ecstasy.

I claw at the cuffs, frantic with need and Ash just pulls out. He. Pulls. Out.

I cry with frustration and he takes pity, lining himself up again. His muscles tense and I brace myself for the punishing nine-inch onslaught of his thick cock. I'm ready for it, eager for it, even in my broken state I'm desperate for it. What I'm not prepared for is the slow, gentle, heart-wrenching lovemaking he gives me when he slides inside with painstaking care and slowness. Once he's seated fully inside me, I expect him to move. He doesn't. He just holds himself there, hips flexing minutely, molten chocolate eyes locked with mine. Reading me for any signs of distress or pain. This is anything but the hard, fast and dirty sex that Ash and I like so much, yet it's more. More because he touches me deeply, physically and emotionally, while taking care of my body in every way it needs. He's seated so far inside me that the gentlest rock of his hips nudges me in all the right places. I can feel him everywhere; feel how much of him impales me, radiating white-hot pleasure like an uncontrollable wildfire. The overwhelming nature of the man I love and his mammoth cock rubbing my G-spot over and over pushes me back into the throes of euphoria. I'm blinded by it and shuddering around his throbbing cock.

My body still shakes when I open my mouth to speak with a trembling voice.

"I've stopped taking my pill," his eyes go wide in recognition of what I'm saying. I've not taken my daily contraceptive since the day before my attack. I forgot that morning because of the argument we had and then David put me in the hospital where no one thought to administer something while I was on life support – probably wasn't a priority for the medical team trying to save my life – and then Ash mentioned having kids so I just didn't bother taking any more. If anything can make him lose his carefully constructed cool, it will be the knowledge that he could be impregnating me at this very moment.

"Fill me up, make a baby with me," I gasp.

"Holy fuck," he grunts, his eyes laser-focused on mine. "That's so fuckin' hot. Skin on skin, no barriers or protection against my cum fillin' your sweet cunt, markin' you as mine and makin' our baby."

"Yes! Oh, God…yes," his dirty talking mouth has me poised on the edge, quivering and needy as he loses control and spills himself inside me. Thick ropes of white-hot cum jet into me, coating me deeply as he roars his release. The feeling of his pulsing cock spurting deep inside sends me spiraling into the abyss of pleasure once more.

Once our orgasms subside, Ash unties my shaking body, massages the blood back into my taut limbs and pulls me into his chest, little spoon style with my back to the broad expanse of his chest.

"I love you, Katie Morgan," he murmurs, his breath tickling my ear.

"Katie Scott," I correct, trying his name on for size.

At that, he rolls me to face him, the swirling chocolate of his eyes searing themselves into my soul. "Sounds fuckin' perfect, Sunshine."

He swallows my *I love you* with his lips and tongue and a thoroughly indecent kiss, which may or may not lead to being restrained and at the mercy of his insatiable cock for several more hours…not that I'm complaining. The future Mrs. Scott is one satisfied lady.

Epilogue

Katie

It takes longer than it should for my body to recover from David Marks' attack, thanks in large part to the insatiable sexual appetites of myself and my fiancé – I love saying that – Asher Scott.

Try as we might to be gentle, it was never going to last for the eight or so weeks it takes for bones to heal. Inevitably, we got carried away, but that's half the fun of being newly engaged.

A few folks around town assumed that Ash and I would have a long engagement considering how quickly we got engaged…those people obviously don't know us very well. Taking things slow isn't our M.O. I'm not sure we'd know how to.

However, we're not swift and stupid people. We're sure in our decisions and then we execute them, as we are both far too aware that life may not be there tomorrow, so why on earth would we put off what we desire when there are no guarantees in life? David Marks was very nearly successful in stealing our future and we're not waiting around for an arbitrary amount of time that society thinks is acceptable, before we take our vows and become Mr. and Mrs. Scott.

Life has been full throttle since I came home from the hospital; I'm responsible for the wedding plans while Ash is project managing the spa expansion of the Lodge. It's amazing how quickly things come together when you throw money at contractors...and they're being project managed by a formidable cowboy with a dominant streak.

Once the spa is complete, we'll be marketing the Lodge as an exclusive wedding venue and we've already hired full-time spa therapists and are interviewing for an event manager in the next few weeks. Our wedding is the first on the books and we're going to use the professional photos from our big day as promotional material for our new venture.

We've taken a massive risk by doing this as the contractors have barely any wiggle room to blow through their deadline. If they do, they destroy our wedding and will have to deal with what I imagine will be, a very hormonal bridezilla. There's no option of delaying our nuptials because I refuse to be a fat bride...yes, you heard right...Ash was my greatest gift and now I have one for him – not that he knows yet...

Ash has been pulling out all the stops to fuck a baby into me ever since we came home from the hospital and I announced that I was no longer protected by my pill. Not that I'm complaining, I just didn't think it was possible for us to make love any more than we already did. It's a wonder that anything – besides me – gets done around here. It's a good thing I'm so hot for him that I never get sore; otherwise, I'd be walking around like a cowboy too.

With how busy life has been, even with Maddie being my maid of honor and taking on a fair share of wedding planning duties, I'd not been keeping a close tab on my monthly cycles.

Ash wasn't concerned about fertile days of the month, he was happy to take me all the time, so I hadn't been paying attention to them either. Our usual routine was at least once a day (excessive for some, but I really wasn't joking when I said we both had high sex drives) so why change it up just because we were trying to get pregnant. No such thing as too much sex when a beautiful little baby is the end goal. But, because I'd been too busy to pay attention, I didn't notice that I'd missed my period until something really inconsequential sent me into a rage and my boobs ached. Thank God I don't wear bras is all I can say because I'd have burned the fuckers. Those were my clues that Ash and his vigorous and insistent lovemaking had been successful and I just had it confirmed by the doctor.

Today was my last appointment to check the progress of my injuries; I've felt fine for a good few weeks now, so this appointment was just to confirm that I was indeed fixed. While I was there, I got the doctor to confirm my baby suspicions – one awkward pee in a sample cup and a pregnancy test later and I had the news I was dying to tell Ash.

Excitement bubbled to the surface like a little kid on their birthday as I drove the route from town to the ranch. As desperate as I was to tell Ash his baby daddy news, I needed to hold off. There was something I wanted to do now that I had the official 'all clear' from the doc. Ash and I may not have been engaging in the gentlest of sex but it was still well below our usual explosive, animalistic standard. We like it all-consuming, crazy powerful and intense but we've not unleashed that side completely since before my attack. I've no illusion that once Ash finds out our precious baby is growing inside the sanctuary of my womb, he's going to keep going easy on me – not that he medically needs to, he just will because he's a gigantic softy under his alpha layers. He's going to be more terrified during this pregnancy than I will until our baby is safely delivered. Therefore, I want it hard and rough just once more before I tell him.

I walk into our bedroom and hear Ash in the shower and this gives me the opportunity to ensure I get what I want.

Over time, Ash's kinky leftover toys and our new ones found their way to our bedroom – the walk-in closet has an assortment of very fun things hidden away, including a few drawers of seductively sexy underwear. I pull out a new lingerie set I've been dying to try – it's one of the few times I'll actually wear a bra – and quickly change before Ash finishes his shower. It's a simple, sheer black lace set comprising a peek-a-boo bra and side tie crotchless thong…perfect easy access to my nipples, ass, and pussy. Ash slowly reintroduced anal play and today I want it all. I have an uncontrollable urge to be utterly consumed by him. Just wearing the lingerie ignites my skin in a way that has me clawing at the all-over-body-itch for him. I feel sexy, beautiful and oh-so-desperate to have him throw caution to the wind and take me with wild abandon.

Knowing that time is of the essence, I slip my feet into a pair of teetering, black stilettos and reach up to one of the high shelves and retrieve the spreader bar Ash hid up there. Following our argument over the sex toy in question, Ash hid it – poorly – high up on a shelf he thought I couldn't reach…with stilettos and a chair, I can. I guess he thought it was a case of 'out of sight, out of mind' and although I was happy to play with the spreader bar after our row, Ash was too afraid that with David's attack, the spreader bar would push me over the edge again. That and he's been trying to be gentle with me…thank god that ends today.

Somehow, I climb down from the shelf without breaking an ankle, retrieve the assortment of toys I want us to play with and lay them out on the bed just as Ash turns the shower off. On the bed, I've placed a length of softer nylon rope, nipple clamps, and an anal plug. I smile down at my selection, pleased with how far I've come in the seven months I've been with Ash. I'm back to being the sexually adventurous and confident woman I was before I met David.

In the corner of our master suite, the remnants of an open-flame fire flicker in the fireplace, the heat enough to keep me warm in my skimpy underwear considering it's November and the first snow of the season fell a few days ago. Despite the early snow, the contractors are still on target to complete our renovations in the next few weeks, just in time for our winter wedding.

The door to the bathroom opens and out walks Ash in a billow of steam, moisture glistening on his sculpted body and a towel wrapped low on his hips, revealing his delectable 'v' that arrows down to the dick of dreams. He stops short when he sees my scantily clad body before him, blindfold in one hand, spreader bar in the other. He glances at the bed and heat floods his eyes.

"You've been busy, Sunshine. I take it you got good news from the doctor?"

"Very." *If only he knew.*

"And now you'd like to play," it's a statement, not a question.

"Damn straight. I'm done with gentle and as my fiancé, you have a duty to oblige," I wink.

Ash flashes me a devilish smirk while his, suddenly very erect, cock tents his towel, causing it to fall to the floor in a heap around his feet. He stands there handsome and proud, deliciously naked, thick cock jutting skyward and I can't help my tongue darting out to lick my parched lips in anticipation.

Ash takes two predatory steps towards me, bringing his body flush with mine, toe-to-toe, hip-to-hip and chest-to-chest. "Your fiancé is *more* than happy to oblige," he growls before crashing his delectable full lips down on mine. I suck and bite at them before he plunges his tongue to dance deeply with my own. No man has ever kissed me as masterfully as Asher Scott does; he makes me want to make out for hours. I cling to the hard planes of his chest to stabilize myself from being weak-kneed in sky-high stilettos. His skin burns hotly beneath my hands and his fingers trail down my body with devastating pressure, over the lace of my panties until he finds the deliberate gap in the material and my glistening folds. He parts my labia and sinks two thick fingers into the depths of my hot, wet cunt. My knees buckle out from under me at the raw power of his touch deep inside me, right where I need it and the only reason I stay upright is because of Ash's massively corded arm muscles wrapped around my waist.

All too soon, he withdraws his fingers, leaving me whimpering against his chest at the loss of him where I need him most. Ash chuckles, brings his fingers glazed with my desire, to his sensual lips and licks them with the tip of his tongue. Showing me what that talented muscle could do if it were between my legs; my own private show as he performs oral acrobatics on his fingers before finally sucking them clean of my essence.

I groan with need.

Ash threads his fingers through my hair and holds me so close to him that we are sharing the same breath. He trails his nose and lips up the column of my neck, across my cheek to the shell of my ear, making me shiver.

"What's your safe word," he purrs.

"S – Sunshine," I stammer with want.

"Use it if you need it, baby," he whispers, his hot breath tickling my over-sensitized skin as he takes my hands – that have been creeping further south, seeking out his cock – in one of his and leads me to the bed. He grabs the rope with his free hand and tightly binds my wrists. I would love to say I'd paid attention and know exactly what sort of knot he used but truth is that normally by the time he's tied me up, I'm already sex mad and have lost my mind. The same is true today. I'm melting into a puddle of desperation, the evidence slick between my thighs.

Once he's satisfied I'm secure, he sits down and pulls me over his lap using the tail of the rope. I gently fall into position, his cock hot against my abdomen, bound hands scrabbling uselessly for purchase while my ass is high in the air. Ash holds me in this position as if he were going to spank me but inflicting pain isn't really our thing and given the bruises he's seen on my body, he doesn't have much of a desire to mark me.

With my weight evenly distributed, Ash returns his fingers to my aching pussy. One large hand spreads my ass cheeks while the other maintains his sensual massage of my G-spot, pumping languidly, driving me to the edge of sanity with the feel of him and the wet sounds of my cunt dripping around him. Being restrained always made me blisteringly hot and intensely wet and this is no exception. I'd be ashamed of the loud slurping sounds if it wasn't such a fucking turn on for us both. I moan loudly and roll my hips in sync with his touch, climbing higher and higher; I'm about to crest the wave of pleasure when he withdraws his digits and trails them back to the tight rosette of my anus, slicking the path with my juices and lubricating the puckered ring of muscle. I'm a mix of emotions: frustrated at being denied my orgasm but loving the feel of his exploration. Ash isn't usually one for delayed gratification – he's more of a *give-her-as-many-orgasms-as-possible* instead of the *deny-her-till-she's-begging* type of guy. The fact that he denied me means he's really out to play with me.

Bring it on.

Ash puts firm pressure behind his finger until the tip pops through the tight muscle, the sensation dark and dirty. Again, he retreats. His hand leaves me completely to grab hold of the anal plug that he then runs through my wet folds, probing my pussy and coating it with my juices so that it's lubricated enough to penetrate my ass. I fidget and rock on his lap, eager to be filled and oh-so-slowly, he gives me what I want. Pushing the plug and stretching me as I relax around the flared head until it's almost too much, too wide, too overwhelming and then it pops through my stretched ring completely and it's seated fully within me. A stuffed back passage is a bizarre sensation – oddly conflicting, yet sinfully erotic.

Ash helps me to my feet, hands bound, ass full and guides me on shaky legs to a wall where a discreet hook has been placed. Every step heightens the anal intrusion, making me clamp around it, causing sparks of the sweetest torture to lick through my body. Ash turns me so that my body faces him, lifts the tail of rope and ties it to the hook so that my arms are taut above my head. Elongated and on display for him, I whimper for more. My body is combusting and I've no way to give it what it needs, the release it craves. I'm at

Ash's mercy and I thrive on it. Unconsciously, my thighs rub together, giving my aching clit the tiniest bit of friction in the vain attempt to ease its beautiful discomfort.

Ash's deep voice tsks, "We can't have that, Sunshine."

I groan at my thwarted efforts to placate my need while Ash stalks me with the spread bar in hand. He stands flush with my body, forces his thigh between mine and rubs my core, allowing me to grind down on the solid stone muscle, the coarse hair of his leg tickling my clit for a moment before he kicks my legs wide and breaks contact. The evidence of my arousal leaves a gleaming wet patch on his clean skin. Ash takes in the sight, his nostrils flaring, eyes burning with barely restrained lust. Like an animal in heat, I've marked him with my scent, with the very essence of me.

"Damn baby, I can smell your arousal from here," he growls hungrily.

"It's entirely your fault."

He chuckles at my breathless reply, "I'll take that."

Trailing his fingers down one leg, he affixes my left ankle into the supple leather cuff before moving my right leg into a wider stance and doing the same. He grins up at me before adjusting the bar and forcing my legs wider still. I'm teetering on the edge of balance, forcing me to pull more of my weight up through the rope. If I don't, I'll topple and end up hanging by my arms. I'm in no danger of hurting myself – Ash won't let me come to harm – so being positioned on the brink like this is hot as hell. I'm so open and exposed to him, the wide position forcing my ass to clench harder around the plug. My hips couldn't go wider if he tried and the warm breath of his sharp exhales hits me right where I want him as he continues to kneel in front of me, eyes level with my needy, dripping cunt, bared for his perusal.

"It this what you want?"

"Yes, please."

"Maybe later," he teases before standing. "Time to kick it up a gear, baby. Are you ready?" I nod enthusiastically. "Answer with words, I need to hear you."

"Yes," I bite out, a mixture of frustration and excitement.

Ash lifts the blindfold from the bed and gently places it over my eyes, tying it firmly so I can't peak. As soon as the darkness engulfs me, my other senses soar into the stratosphere. Everything intensifies; the fullness of my clenching ass, the exposure of my wet, open pussy, the pull of the rope around the delicate skin of my wrists and the burning of my skin that's becoming too hot for my poor, needy body to handle. I don't know where the next touch or caress is coming from and that has me panting in delirious anticipation.

I'm not waiting long before a sharp pinching engulfs my right nipple. He's attaching the nipples clamps to my exposed, tender peaks through my peek-a-boo bra and I nearly explode on the spot. Ash adjusts the tightness of the clamps to the right side of barely manageable before giving each clamp a firm tug. The sensation spears its way to my clit and Ash massages the pain away with the lapping of his tongue against each bursting bud. Nipple clamping is the one form of erotic pain that I don't mind...in fact I downright love it.

"It makes me so fuckin' hard to see you like this – strung out and coming apart from my touch. It's beautiful. You're beautiful." He then takes my lips and swallows my moans with a kiss so deep I feel it in my toes. Being the master of tease that he is, the kiss doesn't last anywhere near as long as it should. My lips are left bereft and tingling while I blindly wonder what he'll do next.

I thought the level of trust needed to play like this was forever out of my reach; I guess the universe was looking out for me when they gifted me Ash.

My pulse roars in my ears, pounding in time to my heaving breaths, my skin shivering with the ghosts of his touch.

He draws the moment out, building unbearable anticipation, the room silent but for the sounds of my gasps and the crackle of the waning fire. My ears strain for the slightest sound of him, any clue as to his next action but the man moves on silent ninja feet – seriously impressive given the size and bulk he carries.

Suddenly, his hot mouth is on my clit, his wet tongue spreading and devouring me with decadent licks, lapping at my dripping desire. I can't contain the scream that claws free from my parched lips. I mewl constantly at his onslaught: the feel of his fingers gripping my hips in place and his mouth buried between my legs magnified sublimely by my inability to see.

I feel like I climb the peak to orgasmic bliss in seconds but time is an abstract construct when you're blinded physically and with pleasure. My body coils and then snaps with euphoric bliss, my climax shuddering through my bound body, tendrils of fire licking across my sizzling skin from the white-hot knot in my core. He doesn't relent, causing the pleasure to crest over and over like waves slamming onto the shore. Moments later his lips find mine and I taste the tang of my arousal mingled with the taste of him. Ash demands everything from me and I give it all, willingly, desperately. He runs his fingers down my side until he settles them firmly on the curve of my hips, tilting, and angling and then thrusting into my still quivering cunt with his thick cock in one debilitating thrust. I lose the ability to speak, to think…to almost breathe.

There's almost not enough room for him inside me with the anal plug still occupying my ass. It's taking up vital Asher-dick space, forcing his meaty girth and penis-envy length into a much tighter channel and it feels mind-blowing.

If Ash's grunts and growls are any indication, it's not just beautifully intense for me either. He pounds me like a machine until I'm forced over the edge of ecstasy yet again, free-falling without a safety net, my body falling apart, my muscles shredded with the constant tense and release of soul-shattering climaxes.

This one might just have gone too far though; my poor pregnancy hormone boobs can't take the pinch of the clamps anymore. The pain has notched too far in the wrong direction and I need the clamps off my tender, swollen nubs.

"Ash! My breasts…the clamps…get them off. Please!" There's an edge of alarm in my voice – I'm not panicking but the pain crept up quickly and has consumed my poor nipples.

Suddenly the blindfold is whipped away from my eyes, causing me to blink and squint in the bright light of the morning sun streaming in from the panoramic windows. Ash's handsome face fills my vision, concern etching his features and he must see the pain in the depths of my baby blues because he swiftly loosens and gently removes the clamps. He massages the tender peaks against the first sting of blood rushing back into them and the throbbing ache that follows. Normally I like this sensation, the reminder that we've played and that the sensitive aftershocks continue well after we've spent ourselves but today it's different. My pregnancy has changed how my body processes pleasure, our tiny baby making itself known and that thought, the early physical reminder that I'm carrying our child brings a beautiful happy tear to my eye.

Ash mistakes my display of emotion as distress and rushes to release me from my bondage. He's on his knees in seconds, unbuckling and gently rubbing each ankle free from the spreader bar and removing my teetering stilettos. Gingerly, he places my feet on the floor and stands to untie my wrists. His hands firmly trace the curves of my body, ready to catch me if I become too unsteady.

"I've got you, baby," he murmurs against my lips, his hands continuing to travel up until he unhooks the rope. My body slumps forwards into his and Ash picks me up, legs around his waist, chest sagging against his, and carries me over to the fire. He sits down on a soft rug with me in his lap, my shoulders shaking as the blood returns to the stretched muscles. With deft fingers, he unties the rope from my wrists and then massages my arms from my shoulders to my fingertips, only pausing to unhook my bra and discard it.

Once my breathing calms and the ache in my muscles relax, Ash moves his fingers to the ties of my panties and, holding the black ribbon between his thumb and forefinger, undoes the bow with teasing slowness.

My soaked panties fall away, leaving me naked in Ash's arms while he whispers seductively in my ear. "Talk to me baby, what happened?"

Asher

The adrenaline rush of what we'd just done still pounds through my veins. My cock is still engorged with a burning need for my woman, but not even that was enough to stop me hearing the pain in her voice when she begged for the clamps to be removed.

We've played with all of today's sexual elements before but this is the first time we put everything together in such an overwhelming capacity. The first time we've played with the spreader bar, the first time I've clamped her nipples and blindfolded her at the same time. And, the first time I've strung her up and filled both her ass and cunt in such a restrained position.

Maybe we should've taken our time combining so many filthy kinks in one go, but walking out of the shower and seeing a scantily clad Katie and an assortment of toys destroyed any resolve I may have had…especially when she gave me the all-clear from the doctor.

Katie is my queen of tease; those perky rosebud nipples peeking out from the slits in her lacy bra, the fact that her thong had a similar peek-a-boo slit right across her beautiful, blushing pussy, all complemented by the killer black stilettos…yeah, I was a fuckin' goner. My dick was hard in seconds and when I eyed that she wanted to be blindfolded, spread, tied, clamped and double penetrated, I nearly came on the fucking spot.

The most beautiful thing about her sexual submission is that it's not just for me; Katie is so fucking hot for our games that I can visibly see her arousal dripping down her thighs. I could smell the thick scent of her the moment I walked out the bathroom and all she'd done to herself was dress in a seriously sexy lingerie set and eagerly await my response, which was instant and all-consuming.

It was so *hard* refraining from slamming my cock home in

her welcoming heat the second I saw her but the sounds of her screaming my name in sheer, undiluted ecstasy made it worth the ache in my balls. I almost couldn't lick that greedy cunt fast enough; I wanted to savor every drop of her sticky honey but Katie gets so wet for me, it's almost impossible.

Her climax saw her pussy gush with desire and I was all too happy to drink from my woman while she came hard on my face, her desire running down my chin and her thighs, coating us both. It made the first thrust into her eager channel as smooth as butter, even with a plug filling her ass.

So perfect.

So tight.

I could feel it seated inside her as I began my thrusts, rubbing me through the thin internal wall between her ass and pussy. God, it felt like heaven. Barely enough room for both me and the toy, her cunt clenching like a vice – again, I nearly lost control and shot my load. Especially when her pussy convulsed with her second orgasm; it almost hurt it was so powerful.

But then the moaning stopped and her little alarmed voice begged for me to remove the clamps.

We play and sexually explore – *a lot* – so I know she can take more pressure from nipple clamps than I gave her, and for a lot longer.

At that moment, her trembling words made my heart pound for a whole different reason; I couldn't untie her fast enough, quietly panicking on the inside that I'd crossed the line and hurt her. The only saving grace for my poor, adrenaline battered heart was that she didn't safe-word. She wasn't approaching a limit that she needed me to pull back from; it's almost as if the pleasure from her climax was too much and made her nipples too sensitive.

Now I have her cradled naked in my arms, the flickering flames from the fire warming our skin – not that we aren't already hot enough – and me begging her to talk to me, to explain what happened so that I can avoid it happening again. We make love and fuck intensely, but I've never caused her pain before and I never want to again. I *need* to know where I went wrong.

Katie's breathing begins to even out, even though her hips undulate gently against my still-erect dick that's sandwiched between us. Yeah, I'm worried about her but my cock didn't get the memo. Or maybe that's just how we are around each other when we're naked? Her unconsciously rocking her pussy along my length and me as eager as a rocket to launch myself inside her, no matter what.

"Talk to me baby," I soothe, my hands caressing the hollow of her spine. She shudders at the touch. "I didn't mean to hurt you, Sunshine."

"You didn't," she affirms, bringing her gaze up to sear with mine, her fingers trailing patterns along the tendons of my arms.

"It sounded like it," I bring my lips to gently kiss each flushed and pebbled nipple.

"The sensation became too much," she sighs at the caress of my tongue on her punished peaks, "and it became painful but *you* didn't hurt me."

Her gentle inflection of the word 'you' sparks my curiosity.

At a loss for what she means, Katie trails her fingers to circle my wrists and pulls my arms from around her, placing my hands on the curve of her hips, my thumbs circling the smooth, supple skin.

"What do you mean, Sunshine?"

"They're just extra sensitive at the moment…and probably will be for the next 34 weeks or so," her lips quirk in the cutest of grins as she waits for the penny to drop.

But it doesn't. There's the sense of something dawning on me but I'm obviously not getting it fast enough because she moves my hands to settle low on her abdomen.

A frisson of excitement builds beneath the surface.

Is she sayin' what I think she's sayin'?

I cock my head to one side, questioning but unable to speak due to the sudden Sahara-like dryness of my mouth.

"It takes about 40 weeks to grow a baby but the hormones are kicking in already," she beams at me.

"You're pregnant? We're having a baby?" I ask, dumb-founded and beyond hopeful. I know she just said it but I'm so excited to start a family with her that I really need her to spell it out for me, just so I don't get my hopes up. I want to father her children so bad. I'd never even thought about it before I met Katie but now, other than marrying her, having a baby with her is the only thing I want. Fuck the ranch, the renovations…fuck everything. All that matters are my woman and our baby she's growing.

"Yes!" She squeals excitedly. "About six weeks along, which means the pregnancy hormones are about to hand my ass to me in the form of morning sickness, most probably. The doctor confirmed it this morning; it was almost impossible keeping quiet until now."

"Did you suspect before today?" I'm grinning like a Cheshire cat at this point and the notion of Katie – *'can't-lie-for-shit-Katie'* – trying to keep a secret as big as this, cracks me up.

"I realized a few days ago that I'd blown past my period due date by a number of weeks and then my boobs just fucking ached for no reason. So, yeah, I suspected you'd knocked me up but I wanted to be sure so waited for my appointment this morning to have it confirmed."

"And how many times did you nearly crack and tell me?" I chuckle.

"Oh, god, like so many times you wouldn't believe," she laughs.

"How come you didn't mention it when I got out of the shower?" I'm not upset, just curious as to her reasoning.

"Because I wanted one last hard fuck before I told you. I knew you'd go easy on me if I told you, you were a daddy."

"Baby, I'm not one of those dumb guys who thinks he's going to damage our baby when we make love. I know it's safe to have sex while pregnant and I also know that I'm not actually fucking your womb when we have sex. I paid attention during sex ed." I smirk.

"So, we'll –"

"Still have mind-blowing, dirty rough sex. I'll always give it to you as hard as you can take, Sunshine."

"Thank fuck for that. Don't get me wrong, I'm ecstatic to be pregnant but I was a bit worried I'd have to mourn our sex life."

"Not a chance, my naughty little temptress."

"You love me and my tempting ways," she teases.

"Damn fuckin' straight I do. I love you Katie, and our baby so much," and with that, I push her gently onto her back on the soft, plush rug and kiss her tenderly on her abdomen, right above her womb. There is a time and place for crazy, hard fucks; this moment isn't one of them.

I kiss Katie deeply as I line my cock up with her slick opening, holding my weight above her as I push through her drenched folds, both of us groaning at the exquisite feel; I'd almost forgot she still has the anal plug buried deep inside.

We make love passionately on the floor, rocking and bucking into one another. Our sweat-soaked skin sliding against each other, lips locking, tongues exploring, teeth grazing until we drive each other higher and higher and finally, we freefall into the sweetest, soul-shattering climax I've ever experienced. We cling to each other, calling out the other's name, staring deeply into eyes that mirror the same intense love back.

We've found our happiness and we made a beautiful baby to share it with.

The End

Thank you for reading and I sincerely hope you enjoyed Ash and Katie's story as much as I enjoyed writing it! In every book I share a little something of myself with one of my characters and in Her Cowboy both Katie and I share a dislike for bras (only she is braver than I am and has ditched them)! I think there was an element of wishful thinking when I wrote that detail into the story!

So, if you enjoyed Her Cowboy and can spare a moment, it would be amazing if you could leave a review on Amazon. Reviews are so important for independent authors as it helps our books reach new and amazing readers, which means I get to keep writing all the stories floating around in my head! And if you are hungry for more Flirty, Dirty Romance from the All For Her Series, check out the link for my FREE book Her Firefighter and a sneak preview of Her Boss.

Subscribe to my newsletter for an exclusive free book!

Get your exclusive copy of Her Firefighter, an 'All For Her Series' prequel featuring Aspen's hottest firefighter, Max Cooper, when you subscribe to my mailing list.

Subscribers get all the juicy gossip, sexy sneak peaks and hot giveaways first.
No Spam. Happy Endings Guaranteed.

Click Here for your FREE book or type the link into your browser: BookHip.com/KVJDJR

Her Boss Preview

Prologue

Dix

There are certain things only people in couples should know about one another and I know a bunch of these intimate little factoids about Maddie Wilson, who is most certainly *not* my girlfriend.

She's my employee, but all the same, I know them. And what's worse? I can't forget them.

Fact number one: bra size. Maddie is a perfectly proportioned, 34B handful. Not that I've had my hands on them, but I've seen and held enough tits in my time to know they'd sit in my palm real nice. Perky but not in a fake way; Maddie's tits are real and the giveaway – instead of gravity defying cleavage, Maddie's breasts are fuller on the bottom curve, giving her the most spectacular under-boob in some of her costumes. She also has no scarring on her creamy under-boobs, which, you know, sorta gives it away that they haven't been tampered with.

You see what I mean? I'm not her boyfriend; I shouldn't know this shit about her tits but the damn costumes leave little to the fucking imagination.

Speaking of costumes: fact number two…Maddie always

267

rehearses in one of her spare costumes. She's an aerial dancer so when it comes to pole acrobatics – the pole being made of chrome – the grip comes from her *bare* skin. This means she'll never not be strutting around my club in skimpy fucking lingerie.

As if my poor dick needed any more encouragement – it barely gets a break to go soft as it is. But I digress, none of this is fact numero dos. Oh no, no; fact number two is that I know her favorite lingerie set is a strappy, red one-piece that crisscrosses her body dangerously and has such little in the way of material, that it looks like a two-piece. I also happen to know that her second favorite set is a white, lacy bra and thong set…I honestly can't tell you which one gets me harder but they both garner the same response from my cock, so I guess that's all that matters. I'm a difficult man to please, even harder to attract, so if I get a boner over you then you best believe my clients are fucking cumming in their pants, which is good business for me.

What other inappropriate shit do I know about the delectable Maddie Wilson?

She rehearses on the pole *a lot.* And despite the club music she has to perform too, which is all slow, erotic, grinding beats, Maddie practices her routines to soft rock and pop music. The other day she was throwing her lithe limbs around to 'Hey Look Ma, I Made It' by Panic! At the Disco.

I also know that, because she rehearses in next-to-nothing when the club lights are up, she has a dark, slightly raised, blue/black mole on her right ass cheek. I've dubbed this cute little mark 'Bo'…as in 'Bo-Peep' because it peeps out from under her lingerie and drives me up the fucking wall. Calling it 'Bo' also drives Maddie up the wall, so fairs fair.

She's tall with legs that go on forever, long chestnut-colored hair that I want to wrap around my fist and stormy grey eyes that I want to see melt for me.

Don't.

I *don't* want them melting for me. Melting is bad. Very fucking bad.

I don't care that her eyes are disturbingly penetrating or that her smile lights up the whole fucking room – just ask my salivating clientele.

I do not care about any of these charming characteristics that conspire to eat away at my carefully constructed resolve, which in turn, pisses me off. And being the emotionally shut down guy that I am behind closed doors, this makes me want to chip away at *her* until she's as pissed off as I am…or I just ignore her…that works too.

You see, Maddie makes me want her and I'm not okay with that. She doesn't do it on purpose, but she does it all the same and as I said, my interest is very rarely piqued so I'm fuming that it's been piqued for her.

An employee.

A woman who couldn't possibly handle all that I am without breaking.

My buddy Ash might be happy to fall for an employee but I'm not, because I don't shit where I eat and make no mistake, relationships for me, are nothing but shit. Ash may have got lucky with Katie, his fiancée, but Maddie and I aren't them and we ain't fucking happening.

'Her Boss' Coming Soon...

About the Author

Kat Catesby is a lover of headstrong heroines with sass, sexiness and formidable inner strength. You won't get the better of these ladies! Strong, beautiful women in all shapes and sizes deserve alpha men who know how to handle themselves and their lady. These book boyfriends don't shy away from what they desire and hunt down what they want with fierce determination and a lot of passion. Join them on their deliciously dirty journeys with steam so hot you'll be panting for more.

Kat Catesby lives in Plymouth, UK with Mr. Catesby, the Mini Catesby's and their assortment of tropical fish (they're low maintenance, what can I say)!

When not writing sinfully hot contemporary romances, Kat Catesby can be found running around after the Mini Catesby's with Mr. Catesby. When the Mini Catesby's allow it, she spends her time binge reading her favourite authors, singing and dancing with her local theatre group and dreaming of vacations, cocktails, and chocolate.

Kat Catesby loves to hear from her fans so follow her on social media using the stalker-friendly links below…

You can connect with me on:

🌐 https://www.katcatesby.co.uk

📘 https://www.facebook.com/katcatesby

Subscribe to my newsletter:

✉ https://dl.bookfunnel.com/vhfpepr8bb

Lightning Source UK Ltd.
Milton Keynes UK
UKHW011157251019
352293UK00002B/602/P